Conquistador
of the Night Lands

ROBIN WYATT DUNN

By the same author:

Books

CITY, PSYCHONAUT (forthcoming)

POEMS FROM THE WAR

JULIA, SKYDAUGHTER

LAST FREEDOM

A MAP OF KEX'S FACE

FIGHTING DOWN INTO THE KINGDOM OF DREAMS

LINE TO NIGHT ISLAND

MY NAME IS DEE

LOS ANGELES, OR AMERICAN PHARAOHS

Films

AMERICAN MESSENGER

PARTY GAMES

A WILDERNESS IN YOUR HEART

Conquistador of the Night Lands © 2015 Robin Wyatt Dunn
Published by John Ott
San Diego, California

ISBN: 978-1-940830-10-0
Library of Congress Control Number: 2015912908

www.robindunn.com

To Andy Robertson,
a brave man with a big heart.

It's now:

Though I hold the Night Lands like a bauble spinning in my hand, it too spins about me . . .

(Please let this message reach the past I need—

PROLOGUE:
IN NEXTSPACE

Nextspace was whiter than death.

"What is it?"

"Planets."

"Here?"

Captain Maug held his wife's hand, watching the dark visage of the star fill up the viewport.

They were all still sane—which was itself already cause for celebration. They were Unity Six, a crew of sixty-eight. What had become of Unity Five, they did not know. You could not transmit from Nextspace to real space.

"Go below and get them ready," said Maug.

"All right," Madeleine said.

They had been married five years.

Outside the ship, the crackling electric spirals of the dark star coursed across its shadowed penumbra. There orbited what appeared to be small planets. Satellites of this first dark sun in Nextspace.

They had crossed in six weeks ago, and had moved through the endless white, coursing towards the small black spot on the horizon. Like sailors of old, the infinite sameness tended to bring on hallucinations, and the crew had been having movie marathons the last two weeks, with nearly all the portholes shut. Maug had done his best to infuse a kind of holiday spirit, though he was not by nature a partygoer.

His wife was his first officer, Madeleine. His love and his honor. She gave him a small wave as she turned into the stairwell to the decks below.

* * *

Nextspace was named by Unity One, the only Unity craft to enter Nextspace and return, and remain sane for an appreciable period. Every crewman and officer aboard said the same: they knew what the infinite white space was called because the same idea had all come into their minds more or less at the same time: it was called Nextspace. It could

1

have no other name. It was what was next.

In part because of the queer uniformity of these reports, the psychic shielding for Unity Two had been ten times stronger. And it was the first craft to go completely mad.

Maug remembered the face of captain Spinoza, his long nose and sensual brown eyes, filled with horror on his video report.

"I am the sacrifice! I must be the sacrifice!"

Upon returning to Earth, Spinoza had been on suicide watch for three months because he'd tried to brain himself with a portable entertainment consul after his debriefing. In what afterwards appeared to be a carefully orchestrated performance, Spinoza gradually improved, and at his urging the 24-hour watch was reduced to 18. Then he had made his final video recording, and hanged himself with his own socks, knotted together.

*   *   *

"What transmissions are we getting from these planets?" asked the captain.

"They're trying to get through our shields," said the navigator, Barnett.

"I know." They could both feel it in their skulls. "What else?"

Seen through the porthole, the planets burned with a fascinating sheen, silvery where the sun was ominous black and the "interstellar" regions were a deep, blank white. They drew the eye, hovering above the dark mass of the star. There were five of them, all in close orbit, an orbit close enough that if the star were Earth's sun, they would be burned hotter than Mercury.

"I've copied the other signal we're getting down to the crypto team, Captain. It seems to be based on color."

*   *   *

Madeleine smiled carefully at the crew, as she spiraled down the stairs, and moved down from the bridge through decks one through four. She was a careful politician.

Marcus drew her aside, with his dark face, thick beard, and glowing eyes.

"What do you think they are?" he said in a low voice.

"Planets. Worlds. Here in Nextspace."

"Do you think this could be what drove the others mad?"

"I don't know," Madeleine said, touching his shoulder, and moving past him, to chat, and to nod, and listen. Although she was a trained intermediary and shaman, she had learned over the years to do as little as possible. The lightest touch could move large weights. Like the human heart.

*   *   *

They drew closer in, the orb of the dark sun thrilling to behold, viscous and rich with shades of black and grey and streaks of unnamed colors twisted in, thrillingly alive, and chilling.

Down in crypto, Red and Lucy watched the patterns in the colors.

"What does the computer say?" demanded Lucy.

"Fuck the computer. Don't you see what I'm saying. Look at the first sequence again."

On their work screen a blue shape twisted, like a rag in a wind, and then gave birth to red circles, which spun fast, adjacent to the blue.

"You see the fourth red circle?" said Red, named for his flaming eyebrows.

"Yeah . . ."

"It's moving."

"They're all moving."

"The rest are all moving in place. It moves closer to the blue, and then back again. You see that?"

"Yeah. I see it. What does the computer say?"

"A million things. We don't have enough yet."

"How much do we have?"

"Umm, maybe five hours worth? It's highly compressed."

"How do you know that?"

"Because if you slow it down and play it back, it unfolds like an umbrella."

*   *   *

Scouts had found the white hole beyond Betelgeuse. It radiated exclusively one way, and the way was away from Earth—hence, it had never been seen by telescope. It wasn't until a scout had first entered Betelgeuse system and sailed half a light year beyond it, that they'd passed its peculiar horizon—now you don't see it, now you do. A gate into Nextspace.

*   *   *

On the bridge, Maug watched in horror as, from one of the four planets, there stretched a thin and silvery fiber, moving towards them.

"What the hell is that?"

"Shields are up," said Barnett.

"It's coming right at us."

"What are your orders, captain?"

"Wait. See what it does."

It seemed to writhe, shaking like a wounded worm, and Maug felt part of his mind writhe with it.

"Shut off the viewscreen. Close all portholes. We are at a full sequester."

Maug touched the intercom button.

"Unity. Everyone to your psychic shield stations, please. This is a big one."

*   *   *

Over the centuries of psychic study, humankind had developed a rudimentary understanding of some of the basic physics of mental and emotional penumbras.

An appreciation for its range and its tactical uses. An appreciation for the fluidity of the mind—not only the human mind.

Have you ever had a recurring nightmare? What you're supposed to do to avoid them is positive visualization before you go to bed. With practice, you can encourage yourself to dream certain things, or not dream others.

Even as a cross country running team, after a meal of pasta to prepare their bodies for the next day's race, will prepare their minds with that same kind of visualization, imagining their bodies flowing, faster, seeing each turn in the course, seeing their feet first over the finish line, so Unity earned their name and knelt at their stations to commune.

Outside, the silver thread moved across the coursing dark orb of the star and spoke, vibrating on the Nextspace white.

WELCOME, it said.

And Maug wept. And Madeleine stifled a laugh, a thick and rich laugh without logic.

The screen leapt back into life.

BOOK ONE:
WORLD AND WORLD

The Earth is Dying. But in fact it is already dead. We are alive now on its corpse, which is made of metal. One astronomical unit distant from the black dwarf of Sol, who was and is no more, circles our second earth, dark and cold. There is no moon.

Tell me, do you know the difference between life and death? What is the animating force? We still have not discovered this, even now as the boundary becomes ever blurrier.

The Earth is dying but it is alive! And though we live in the Night Lands our Day is brighter than it ever was, horrifyingly bright, the light of knowledge and the light of ecstasy, in our Redoubt, inside the human soul, unconquerable, divine, we humans if we are still human shall fight to the last . . .

But that is not what I wanted to say.

Rather: welcome to the Night Lands. I know this reaches you as history. Reader, I am honored by your attention. Know this: everything we have recorded is also in the hands of our many enemies. If you imagine that this message is yours alone, you are mistaken.

Did we make it out? I want to know. I want to know more! Can you tell me, brother of my future? O tell me, brother, send me a message as I send this to you!

*　　*　　*

I live in the Redoubt. This is my testament, to last the ages, depending on the encryption. What transpired here is a human story, though by most definitions we are human no longer. It is strange to me that I am the one to tell this tale; there are far better men.

These are the ends of the Earth.

*   *   *

"Daddy!"

She climbs into my lap, to look at the screen.

"Who's on today?" she asks.

On the screen, a Gorbit holds its mutant head within the range of the camera. It is blue and green, with enormous eyes; it is a friend of ours, though this is forbidden.

"Kantu!" my daughter cries. The live translation is almost immediate. The mutant answers:

"Elizabeth."

"How's your home?" she asks.

"It is fine."

"I want to come visit!"

"You can't, Elizabeth. Not yet."

"But I want to!"

"You'll die."

*   *   *

I feel these are our last nights. But there are so many of them, a billion, a trillion last nights, always the last night here on Earth, after the sun has died, but when, when it will be the last of the last? Always we say it is the last: every night, is the last.

From the darkness came new life. New life that is not our own, abhuman, strange and corrupt, lovely, some would say—those who are adapting—and perhaps I would too.

My title is Philosopher and Mark-of-Pain, for I bear the scar within my brain, that allows me to communicate to you, and to the abhuman. Communication is painful. Messengers are so often killed; for they bear this message: *they too, think.* They too, want to live, and they too, love, whatever their shape. Any honest translator and diplomat must first communicate this message. That the enemy is just like us.

*   *   *

I do not want to die. The Earth may be dead, but why must I go with it?

Come with me, reader, if reader you are, and not some translation program in a vault with no eyes, if you are there, you, perhaps a biped of long ago, who, though I find it difficult to believe that you will read each "word," one, after the other—know that I love you because you remember me, in your dreams.

I am no romantic. You see, I do not believe that greatness is lost. I do not believe that we are fallen, or that you are. I believe in change. And in argument.

Would you argue with me, the Mark-of-Pain? Follow me with Soad, into the spaces beyond our Earth:

Soad's Story:
A Journey Into the Sky

I am Soad and this is my story. What I experience here is the record of my journey into the wormhole. Our Visitors, like the gods of the ancients, arrange for us poor humans various tests. This test of mine is one of escape; one I have undertaken for my people. For my family of Level Seventeen. To see if we can escape this dead Earth . . .

As an experiment to understand the metaphors and vestigial "terrestrialness" that makes up the human mind, my ordeal was arranged by our Benefactors. Within their simulation I was to take my journey into the sky, a simulation designed to control a satellite into the wormhole, even as I climbed into a wide blue vista as our ancestors saw, with my sister . . .

At first the blue sky took getting used to. But I no longer have time for adjustments.

I am walking into the sky, up the stairs. Like an old-fashioned journey into heaven, which in so many ancient languages is the same word as sky, going up, going up, going up, going up.

The clouds are broken by the sun and it shines through and I smile, wondrous thing the sun. I want to die here, today, under this sunlight.

"It's pretty," says my sister, but I say nothing, because I do not want to speak, only enjoy the view as I climb the stairs. Up the stairs and to the gate, so far above. I have brought my oxygen.

We are engaged together in this great task, me and my sister who I never cared for very much. Younger than me, but smarter. Always the negotiator, my sister, always playing the Devil's Advocate, and now that we are beset with devils, I cannot abide my own blood being their damned lawyer but so it is, she defends them all the time, all the time, as though they are what she wants to be . . .

We are linked inside the immersal nutrient bath of the simulation, hallucinating our way towards the Great Gate. Each experience here a metaphor, from *meta pherein*, the bearing across, the signal through the noise.

I and my sister are dreaming in the Redoubt, my body inside the tank filled with fluid the consistency of phlegm and I am climbing stairs into the sky.

As we climb, our decisions correspond to the movement of a telepathic and remote-recording probe, negotiating its way towards the LaGrange, where the wormhole is kept in relative position to this metal earth, the dead sun, and the largest craft of our Visitors, larger than our old gone moon, but more distant, colored like the darkness of space.

But I am able to forget that now, forget all I have ever known. The stairs are stone and metal and they extend upwards, as though forever.

As I said, the Visitors are like gods, and like the gods of old, they have set us with tasks. The only problem with this metaphor is that in the old histories of the divines the buck stops somewhere: Mama Goddess and Daddy God are at the top, manipulating everyone, and their mommy and daddy is long dead and no trouble to anyone.

But like K. knew inside the Castle, it goes *ad infinitum*, it is turtles all the way down, all the way up too, and we cannot see that far and so we need a way station, you see, we need the receiver for the metaphoric signal, something to encapsulate our awareness and give it the right edges, give it the force of logic, give it the womb it needs to grow.

For our minds are growing. Growing to the stars, but too slow, some say, too slow! Citizens, I burn too slowly! I burn too slowly, citizens! Please throw another faggot on the fire! For I am a heretic, it's true. My gods are not congenial or quotidian, they are neither anthropomorphic nor ingenious, they are like the forces of science, gravity and electromagnetism, deeply impersonal and personal all at once. My gods are life and death, and they are coming closer together, here at the End, here at the Beginning.

But I digress. Suffice to say that, we're all taking orders from someone. The Visitors take their orders from their higher ups, both known and unknown, and I take mine from the Redoubt. And the beauty of freedom is that while you can acknowledge your orders, you don't always have to follow them, and when you follow them or when you don't each decision to act and in what fashion is like the translation of a signal across time, moving through the aether, moving towards your brain into your heart.

This my transmission reaches you and you decide what it shall mean and so I who must go beyond, into the sky or down into hell, I am always selected for the job no one else wants to do, but more joyful for that, more joyful in my lonely fate (except for my damned sister . . .) —

"It's time to eat, brother."

"Alright."

We eat. The stairs curve a bit here and there is a dimple in the curve of carved stone where we can rest our backs comfortably and open our backpacks. I eat the fish sandwich and it is delicious. I have never eaten fish before. Our Earth has no oceans.

My sister is crying.

Orwell was right, unfortunately. Ignorance is strength. For a very long time. On the longer time horizon, knowledge is stronger, but that horizon must be long enough to cross the generations, you see. For knowledge and pain are almost indistinguishable from each other; I believe they are in fact the same thing. Although pain makes you stronger, in your will, it damages your body and your mind, and in this sense you grow weaker, more sensitive, for so often pain does not inure your body to that suffering, but only makes you even more sensitive to it, more "appreciative" of its gradations. Knowledge is this way too: with everything we know, we grow more in pain.

And so Orwell knew that so many choose to stop knowing, and try to be. They let others learn the hard things, and wait, like the follower for the shaman, for the evil poison to be translated by his body into urine which will be palatable for all.

It is the same thing, you see? Somebody's got to go first. Up the stairs. Into the vein.

My name is Arthur and I am a dragon.

I sing! I sing a music you must hear! I am the dragon that you need! My breath is fire . . .

I live inside the sky. I am powerful, it's true, but my mind is weak: it is so far, you see, it is so far ahead, it is so far ahead . . .

O Adventurer, O Gilgamesh! O Beowulf! O Man With Your Stick! O Ape With Your Rock! Come to me across your savannah and feast on my beauty!

For I am wide. I live inside the sky.

Here is what I say to heroes, some of them, the ones who never paid attention in school:

"Hero! Bold warrior! I shall destroy you!"

Here is what I say to the heroes who did pay attention in school: nothing at all.

Is Every Dragon the same? Was Jesus Mithras? Was Z, Y? Was Sheol Abaddon, or Hell Hades?

When I say nothing I have time to look this wise hero in the face, and see them. What sort of man or woman is this hero? Why do they come to me? Will this be the time that I die?

Another thing about your legends: have you never thought what we are doing when we're not inside the cave atop our gold, breathing smoke out of our nose?

We're alive too. We have children, and dreams. Some of you are learning this. Some of you will, perhaps, never understand it.

Come to me and show me your blade! How was it made? See my teeth? They grew inside my mouth.

I am Arthur! I love you! Ignorant or fool, bold wise broken or berserk, my lover with your wild eyes, come into my nest inside the sky. I salute you!

For we are commingled like love and violence, knowledge and pain.

Move over me. Shape me with fervor and with your eyes. Hold me with the forever on your tongue, I am changed, I am burning whirling exegetic curve, the words you heard:

*   *   *

The dragon is sitting on the step and my sister has stopped crying.

Its voice is like twisting metal.

"I am Arthur. Are you a King's Man?"

"My name is Soad."

I toss the dragon the rest of my fish sandwich and he gulps it down, steam curling out of its nostrils as it swallows.

"Thank you," the dragon says, and I feel a humming in the stone, and we all look up, up into the sky.

"I come from the Redoubt. I am headed for the gate above. This is my sister, Weel."

"Well, I am a gatekeeper, and a dragon. Thank you for telling me your names. And thank you for the sandwich."

And he leaped off of the stairs into the air.

*   *   *

All the while the robot curves its way into the atmosphere, negotiating the tentacles and curves of the flesh that hover over Earth . . .

*   *   *

Soon after we entered a realm of light and fire.

My sister and I stumbled on a crevice in the stairs, leading to a passage out into the air, over which the dust was scattered, and as we walked out, over the airy abyss, dragons flying in the distance overhead, great and small, we saw a city.

(I suspect now that this was a faction within our Neighbors. Within their vast hive mind, there is much room for crevices that harbor heresy).

From the rooftops fires burned, and dancers with their lizard skin threw their torches into the air in spirals, as though for our approach.

"We should ask them for food," said my sister.

One of the lizard men approached then. I wished I had a weapon of some kind, but I knew this desire was foolish. Even a nuke would do no good; my mission was to break through the wormhole alive, not kill and then be killed along the way.

"Have you brought any words?" the lizard asked. Its eyes were burning.

"What words?" I asked.

"Clever words. We enjoy them," it rasped.

"Our names are Weel and Soad," my sister said then.

"If you don't have words then I will take this," and faster than I could see the lizard had snatched my pack from off my shoulder, and was making off with it.

"That's my pack!" I shouted like a fool, and started to run after him, but my sister held me back.

I didn't know what to do. Ahead I saw the lizard disappear into what seemed a warehouse.

"What should we do?" my sister asked.

"Ask for food, like you said. There wasn't much in my pack anyway."

"There wasn't?" Her eyes always know more than she says.

"Mainly my lucky charm."

"We should get it back."

The lizards whose fire had danced through the air now were nowhere to be seen, and darkness was coming on us fast; it felt like coming home.

I heard a voice in my head then, as we approached the warehouse:

We cannot go in the wormhole, you see. We built your planet. But some dimensions do not welcome us, while they will welcome you.

"Who are you?" I said aloud, without thinking.

"Soad?" said my sister, worried.

"Nothing."

There was no door, only an opening in the side of the building. I stepped to the threshold and looked within.

Suddenly the place filled with the light and fire again and I felt tears in my eyes. They danced before us, and quite without our volition my sister and I fell to our knees and watched their dancing, the red orange yellow and silvered violet in the dusty air. The dusk came over and then real night was there and this light, it was different from the abhuman phosphorescence, different from our hearth fires, it was brighter somehow, and purer, a color and a feeling that I know I will be unable to describe adequately except to say that it marked me. Then they began to sing, in a language I could not understand but which I will invent here anyway, to approximate the moment that was then:

Cold, cold our hearts fire!
Will you teach the old ones to abjure?
Will you teach the children to resist?
We listen for the prayer that is your step,
And we succumb to all your breaths,
Which we will take full out of you,
To redeem you in your death—

We slept. I dreamt of a city by an ocean, and a woman.

When we awoke there was hot food on plates, and one of the lizard children smiled at us by the entrance to the warehouse, if that's what it was, perhaps a temple too, and then the child slipped around the corner and was gone.

We ate. It tasted of earth, mushrooms and garlic. Light and rich.

I touched my sister's hair. "It tastes good," I said. She nodded, chewing, watching me.

I went outside. We did not have as much time as I would have liked. The longer we spent submerged in the unit the harder it would be to return. After a week, I knew, we might suffer brain damage, or worse, the kind of nightmares that would not leave.

I knew I already loved it here, within the simulation.

*　　*　　*

I was drawn into the city along avenues that shimmered with that strange fire, a luminescence that seemed to stick to the skin. My sister I quickly forgot, or rather, the city and its denizens soothed thought of her away from me, and like a child I wandered into their maze quite unawares. A mother lizard spoke to me from a window:

"Go back, Soad. Go back. We don't want you here any longer."

"But I must be here," I said automatically.

"No. You must be only who you are. Go, go!"

But I would not. I knew that the woman lizard was lying; that she concealed something vital from me, something I needed. My pack? No, that was almost forgotten now, no, I needed a sign. A sigil or a word. Yes, a word . . . a password?

I smiled and I know it was a lunatic's smile but lunatics have wisdom too. The focus of lunatics brings others to the light (of the moon . . . gone so many millions of years now . . .)

"Soad!" my sister was calling me. Didn't she understand the secret? It was right here! It was so close to me, like the heat of a fire on my cheeks . . .

"Soad!" I turned. The whole city seemed to move, swirling around her, and I saw my sister's eyes, afraid, and I went to her. I realized we were ordinal coordinates. The compass. More than just the command structure for the robot going towards the wormhole's meniscus, yes, we were also like pointing dogs, being primed to our task. Hunting a target.

Yes, Soad.

Yes. I held my sister's hand. "It's okay."

"Did you find food?" she said.

"They're leaving more for us at the building where we slept. We must leave."

On our way out everything seemed haunted, not with life as before but with death, and those near to death. I felt the woman lizard's touch along my neck as we departed, and I saw my sister shiver.

We had forgotten the food entirely. Once back at the stair, the crevice was no longer there.

"Come on," I said. "Up, up!"

We climbed.

*　*　*

I know some things are perhaps best left unrecorded. Adventure is by its nature compressed, and in its urgency the fate and gospel of the generations is recorded and co-opted to our purposes of exploration, we conquistadors of the night. Still I believe that a true narrative carries with it those gaps which are so often left out, which demand explanation and which can have none.

This is one of them:

I know that on that climb I lost my sister. She became . . . someone else. And you know, so often we encounter our friends and family changed and we adjust because we must, and quite often we insist that the change is less than might be supposed, because we can only bear so much.

And this is it, you see? Because I do not know how my sister was changed. Even she does not know. Was I willing to make that sacrifice when we left? And is this truly the nature of companionship? The hellish logic that if not you, then I, and if not I, then you, will make it cross the gap?

The gap into knowledge. But is survival ever really logical?

I must not write more about this.

*　*　*

We are a pointer. We signal for the Earth-Builders. We show the way towards the fox. The sly fox. The red fox. The sneaky fox. The quick brown fox that jumped over the lazy dog, we smell it and we point, we site the arms and hands and set the sequence towards its hidden lair: we are climbing.

"Are you all right, Weel?" I ask her, but she says nothing, a dozen stairs above me, climbing steadily. We are as high as a small mountain now, and I marvel when we stop to drink from sister's diminishing bottle at the luxury of plant growth down below. This must be the Earth of my ancestors. It is too beautiful for words. And yet, it lacks the dark beauty of our home. In shadow, the faintest detail and color comes to hold so much, and so we at the Ends of Earth worship subtlety. Fine gradations.

I saw a lance of fire shoot across the stair and I shouted: "Down!"

We both crouched by the lip of the stair, my sister ten steps above me.

"What is it?" she whispered down to me, her eyes wide.

"WHO IS IT?" I called out, my voice huge. I have a good voice when I want to use it.

Another shot.

Though my sister and I had of course memorized what information we had on the various aerial abhuman factions, the truth is that the Redoubt's intelligence is very limited. In addition to the fact that the skies are forbidden to us by the abhumans, the religious cults within the Great Pyramid that is our bastion and home often succeed in stopping our gathering of new knowledge altogether. It is a danger in any inbred and inward-looking community, of course, that the final gates would shut. In a sense, my sister and I are some of our vast city's final messengers. Our message being: *let us out!*

Eschatology, the study of "final things," has always seemed to me only a form of psychology. In our imagination of The End, we see who the narrator wishes to be his murderer. A bug eyed alien? An angry punitive God? An Enlightened Race from a higher dimension?

Would you have the universe end in fire or in ice, brother? And why would you have it end at all? Aristotle saw no end. Aristotle said it went on forever.

And how long that is, eh?

"WHO ARE YOU?" I shouted.

"STOP IT!" my sister shouted too. "STOP IT, PLEASE!"

And then there was music in the air, a thick and thunderous drum. The stair shook

"I think it's the goddamned Redoubt," I shouted.

My sister's mouth dropped open.

Soad, in the Redoubt:
A Little Civil War

▌▌▌▌▌▌▌▌▌ Inside the Pyramid we are fighting. We fight to hold the Eye.

*   *   *

In the Level above security measures were being taken. Not all seals and firewalls worked and so the boys were wheeling the pumps like mad to suck the air out of the stairwells, hoping the invaders would suffocate.

In the city of the night, all harbingers speak of light. There is nothing else. Nothing else but the voices, that is. For who have you sworn allegiance to?

I am Fell and I speak blood, says one.

Or perhaps you worship *Klow,* whose motto is:

I Eat It.

They have a lot of names and faces but they're all much the same: power is their game and hunger is their modus operandi and while metal Pyramidal walls do well at holding out the aliens themselves, they don't hold out their *minds* very well, now do they . . .

"I can't get it, Shell!" shouted the boy to his friend, his hands clenched around the pump wheel. Below them they heard the battle screams of the attackers echoing as they climbed the thousand stairs to this entrance.

"I'm coming, Kol!" shouted Shell back, he was bigger and stronger, not by much but by enough, and he sealed his entrance and ran to his friend's.

*   *   *

I watch the sky blink out.

"Oh God!" I shout. "They're rebooting us!"

"What!"

The world departs, and I am vomiting phlegm. Mixed with blood.

Above our metal Earth, our probe veers towards the mouth of an Eater, its spirit, us, having prematurely exited . . .

My eyes feel blind. My handlers, cursing, help me out of the disgusting liquid and thrust a rifle into my sticky hands.

"We're under attack!"

My sister and I, naked, hurry into the citadel, from where we can fire down below.

"The probe will die!" I shout. I see that I am crying. But then all thought goes away as our own god comes into our minds, and I see the eye of each approaching man and woman, though they are of our blood, our cousins from a Level below, I see them as the worst kind of abhuman, as monsters unspeakable, and I wait to see the whites of their eyes and then I fire, splattering brains all over the grey metal stairs, and my sister and Ontul and Max do the same, we fire and we fire and we fire. From the right, Kol and Shell, our apprentices, run in. They've sealed the last gates.

"What door is still open?"

"I think they cut through the wall!" shouts Ontul.

The god lives inside our heads.

"Come on," I say. Somehow calm. "In five minutes this will be all be over anyway, one way or another. We can't make it through another reboot."

And I leap over the barrier, and fire down the steps, curving, curving, here where the architecture was built to honor our ancestors its filigree and symmetry is marred now by the burns of lasers and demolitions. My face insane, my family cuts through the enemy and we are at the hole.

Looking through it, another four dozen or so are on their way, having climbed the thousand-foot ladders in the access passages.

"We blow it," my sis says.

This is our last thermal explosive. The apprentices open their thighs and take out the pieces, you need at least two to be combined. We set them, and say a quick prayer, and run. The only way out now is through.

The Redoubt is Falling, brothers.

Some part of my brain notices my sister's naked beauty, and I find myself wondering if her husband is still alive, down below.

We are the Eye, still sighted! We will see through the sky!

*　　*　　*

I close my eyes as I sink back into the oxygen-rich mucus bath.

Why do these great powers care so for us? If we are only their tool, surely there are more efficient ones. How long before the next group of suicide-ready fighters storms our barricades, drills another hole into our Eye of the Great Pyramid? I believe we will find help past the wormhole. Surely these great powers intend to save us, as we are saving them!

I feel the bath warm as they engage the electricity. Part of my mind feels the probe re-engage, in orbit.

I dream waking:

*　　*　　*

My sister looks ill.

"What is it?" I say.

We are sitting on road markers, squat, flat obelisks. The light is warm, mid-afternoon. My sister hunches over, sitting, her arms wrapped across her stomach.

"The transition," she says.

We are at an intersection, the obelisks marking paths along the grey stone and white marble lanes, anchored by some magic in the sky.

"Something is happening," I say, watching the sky change color, fluttering like lightning but in color, and part of the sky seems to bend, and I feel an energy there, one that is not our masters.

Arthur lands on an adjacent obelisk, regarding my sister and I with cool eyes.

"Back for more? Of course, of course you are. Well, what do you think? Do you like the show?"

The small dragon turns and watches the sky, and my sister and I do the same. It was indeed like a show, fireworks on some unimaginable scale.

"Who do you think you're working for, human?"

"I don't know, Arthur. You seem bent on telling me, though. Why don't you?"

"You've been here a long time, I know. Under their watchful eyes. Slaves. Slaves learn to love their masters, yes? You know that. Do you love your overlords? Do you wish them well? Do you want them happy? Do you want to make sure they have enough food?"

"Who are you?" I said.

"My name is Arthur and I am a dragon. This is the truth. Where do you think we are, hmm? Do you think this is only a "simulation"?"

"We need to go, brother," my sister said.

I followed my sister down the west marble road, wide enough for five men standing abreast. Arthur flew alongside, his blue-grey skin mottled and shining. His eyes reflected my own unease.

"Where do you think we are, hmm?" said Arthur.

"A simulation, as you said. We work to bring the probe to the wormhole."

"And what happens then? Magic? Poof? Humanity is saved? The war ends? All ends happily? Is it not just as likely that that penetration will be the final straw, allowing all of you to be eaten at last? The last of your free will, tasty food?"

"Our protectors look out for us. They built us our world. They built us our Redoubt, to face down the abhuman menace."

"You don't believe that!" snarled Arthur. Still my sister said nothing, walking ahead.

Arthur continued, his voice harsh and rattling: "This is what I believe will happen, Soad. I believe you are imperfectly awake. I believe your intentions are honorable and that your mind is slow. If you truly wish a free Earth, a free humanity, you must help me. We dragons are being enslaved as well. And our enemies are like yours; huge, vast. Their appetites are unquenchable. And they live long. Do you believe me?"

"I don't know. Why should I?"

"A fair question! What if I said I could help you back on Earth? What if I said that?"

I watched him close, as he hovered at the level of my eye. "And can you? Will you?"

"I will. If you help me first."

"What do you want?"

Arthur smiled. It was not a pleasant smile

"Will that dragon not shut up!" my sister said. But Arthur only laughed, a sound like a sea gull, echoing through the air. He flew off.

We walked for a time, saying nothing. The air smelled wonderful.

"What happened in the battle, brother?" Weel said.

"Don't you remember, sis?"

"No."

"We killed a lot. But we used our last explosive. We won't be able to stop another attack."

"What happened to me?"

"You fought bravely. You don't remember?"

"No."

"I'll keep you safe," I said, and put my hand on her shoulder.

"Will you?" she said, looking at me.

"Yes. Yes, I will."

*　*　*

We slept next to one another, huddled on the stones. I looked up at the stars. So many of them it makes me wish I had been young, when the Earth was made . . .

*　*　*

Escape. This old planet. Escape, this old body. Escape, this wondering evil beautiful world—I do not know how I can take this, yet I must, it is my duty, it is how I was born, it is a mission and I am missionary, I am the wanderer, I am the diary, I am the diarist, I write myself into this future—

"Soad!"
I am turning—
"Soad!"
I am turning—
"Soad!"
My sister is falling!
She is falling into the clouds!
"Weel!"
She is gone.

*　*　*

Shall I throw myself off too?
I need to reboot.
I need to reboot! Reboot me, dark gods! Make me new! Take me from this terrible world! Make me yours as something new! I need the fever and the fervor of your terrible mad joy, I need to feel it in my veins, I need to feel that it is something I can use, that it is something I can be, that it is a fathomable thing, a container, a prison, a dark and unending joy servitude and last lives, take me away —
The clouds are all around. I can hear a distant bird, and it is cold, my feet upon the marble, only stairs and up—
"Reboot me!" I shout into the air.
But I will not be. Wherever my sister has gone, she is either dead or still here, on another level of the world. I must find her.
O, into the castle! Into this the staired and scary castle! My sword and my joy! My life and my tragedy! My course—

*　*　*

A castle in the sky. Castle in the clouds. So delicate that it just barely exists at all—it is spare, mighty but spare, a ligament or a span of spider silk—
I am climbing.
Can you help me?

*　*　*

Let me hold you; let me, please.
Sister, and the rest of you here.
I am afraid.
For you, and me.

Soad:
Saint Michael

▊▊▊▎▎▎▎▊▊▎ I have been working for three weeks now. The advocates stay in their offices, largely, picking their nits, watching their fish in the tank. The castle is not known to me. Only this small part.

"Come look at the fish, Soad!"

They are blue damsels, and they swim about inside the tank, adjusting to their new prison. I know they are not happy about it. But am I? Ferreira seems so, gazing at their small blue bodies.

"The last ones escaped! Threw themselves to their deaths! I don't want to talk about it."

I copy the orders and the correspondence and file the copies in the cabinets. I am a secretary here, recommended by forces I do not understand. My sister is lodged inside my cranium like shrapnel, an infection waiting for the right moment to spread and dominate me.

"Soad!" It is the other adjutant, lither and darker of skin, with a better smile, friendlier, and with more dishonest eyes. His office is larger, for his clients tend to the wealthier. "Please, come to my office!"

I obey the summons, touching the spring-loaded happy Clown for luck as I move down the hallway, listening to its whispered laugh atop the file cabinets—

"How long have you been here, Soad?"

"Three weeks, sir."

"You were recommended to us."

"Yes, sir."

"The usual firm?"

"I believe so, yes sir."

His eyes have grown large, and he picks at his nits with one spare finger, curled into his cat-leather chair with strange grace. His fish circle near his head, their eyes hungry behind the glass.

"In fact I know it was not the usual firm. Your recommendation was peculiar, Soad. Because it came from a washerwoman."

How long have I been here? I feel as though new memories are infecting my brain . . . I must concentrate. The word "washerwoman" is not said with contempt by the brown-skinned advocate, no, but with a queer kind of horror—

"Your cleaning staff, sir?"

"No. No. One in the street. She whispered in my ear, and then you arrived. I have learned to trust my instincts. But now, I want an answer. What is it you have brought, Soad? What are your aims, here?"

"Only to serve, sir."

He laughed.

"I almost believe you! Go, we'll talk later!"
I work at my desk. The daylight does not seem real.

*   *   *

The city is increasing in size. Not in area or volume but in a geometry of the mind, its actuaries and tunnels the avenues of a vast brain, not alien but profoundly human. Sometimes I think I sense that our Benefactors who gave us the Metal Earth are actually a future we, us after an Age, us come again, and I know that I am slipping in, ever deeper—

*   *   *

This region of the castle is filled with sunlight, it is a kind of medicine, a shield. I do not see the sun; it is hidden somewhere, like the people's eyes, slanted away into a dimension I cannot perceive. It is not a region where there are many workers, most are noblemen and women, practicing their graces, the artful cruelty of court in every step and lance, the working rule of so many men from so many times, I am drinking stimulants outside beneath umbrellas the women in their purple hair and long shoes ignore me but for the occasional glance, I am unseen, a secretary in the piles of paper hidden behind their many oceanfront walls, I am unseen and I force myself to remember, day after day after day after day: *Weel is not dead.*

One of the purple-hairs sits down next to me; she is young, I see, and I recognize her now, she mans the coffee machines. But she does not have the working eyes like me, the eyes I feel inside; she is a noblewoman slumming.

*   *   *

What happened to my sister?

Soad, in Saint Michael:
Earth and Earth and Earth

The purple-hair says, "We call the homeless 'creekers' where I come from, the canyon, they live down by the creek. Not as bad as here, I don't have to scare them away from anything, they keep to themselves. They're nice."

Suddenly I find myself thrusting my chin into her face: "What do you think they think of you, woman?"

A serious error.

"I beg your pardon?"

"Nothing. I . . . I have a nervous disorder." I flee in confusion back to the advocates', climbing the spiral stairs past the guards, into my room where I stair at my glowing indices of light . . .

*　　*　　*

The world is not enough nearby—it keeps moving away. I must find it, the world. I must find it...

*　　*　　*

Is the city a castle? Or is the castle a city? Work has ended. I wait my turn for the elephants, climbing onto their backs, bourn eastwards through the aching slums, across the avenues and plazas, under the palm trees. The light is the most powerful soporific I have ever known, it could defeat invaders on its own, and it does. The yellow is so piercing it is a needle so sharp you cannot feel it enter your heart. Its injection the dream you will always feel across your face, limning dusk resonating hope, squeezing your gonads tighter into its horrors—

I am caught.

*　　*　　*

The city whispers to me; the castle. The castle is inside my head; inside all our heads. We dream in its energy in birth, we die to make it live, it is our ossuary, it is our lifeline to the stars, the gods beneath below at sand and wine we'll dine to keep the key we know is ours, inside our palm inside our heads, the city and the castle dream us and we dream them, knowing things are ours but not knowing when they'll stop—

"Boy."

"Arthur."

The dragon hovers by the tired elephant train. We're climbing towards the park, towards the apartment building where I have found my room.

"Boy!"

"Dragon!"

I am tired.

"What are you doing!"

'Tell me!' I shout back. The other passengers ignore us.

"You're changing!"

I am. Gods help me. May I be aided. *M'aidez m'aidez*—

* * *

Dusk in the alley. The purple hair is there, no, it is another purple hair.

I walk carefully towards my gate.

She smiles at me I take her inside this is the moment and the dream I am inside her she inside me there is a city inside her mind I must find the key I must find the way inside her brain—this is the city that I dreamt of as a boy, each avenue an aspect of a woman's face, each corridor the throughput of my energy but she is crying—

"What's wrong?"

"Don't leave . . . don't leave me . . ."

Each moment underneath each moment of her skin against my own, each second is something I must now mistrust, I must now misremember, I must disguise myself from who I am, I have become what the city wanted, I know this, I am this tool, I am this tool and I am free!

She is washing in the shower and I am waiting for the meaning to come, waiting for a download...

"Honey?"

She is not in the shower, she is running, naked, back out through the gate, onto a motorcycle, climbing on behind a man, who turns as he drives off, his helmet flashing, raising a pistol at me which he fires, shot over my head. I must go to sleep.

* * *

No one will remember me now.

* * *

Saint Michael is free. The Saint of the Old. My city. How long have I lived here?

This is the city: the low manicured lawns, and the fragrant asphalt, the music of the dawn the birds and firetrucks screaming I am crying but the dawn is beautiful I must not stop, I must not stop dreaming—

"What'll you have today?"

"Coffee"

"What brand?"

"Syrup."

"Syrup brand, coming up!"

The people are slaves like me, happy and free, we celebrate the meaning of our burden and our truth with civilization, we await the coming of another disaster, one happens every day, they are our truth, the instantiation of our gods, the alphabet of a new language, the murdering world abroad and into this hated sky, this beautiful world, I am dancing in the café—

"He's dancing again," a customer says, and I am, me in the Laundromat that doubles as a café, me the Freemason, me the lover, me the feared, me the horrendous mistake—

Saint Michael. Where did you grow from?

I must get to work. I step onto the stairs to await the elephant train, the whips cracking in the air. The paving stones are worn and look like an old woman's face.

Do you know? Can you tell me? Where is my escape? Have you found the password primeval in my bone, buried in your world?

I remember the barista now, with her purple hair, she is crying my name, I am cumming inside her, I am atop the elephant with the thousand colors of people heading west to the ocean, to the beach cities, to the loved world, to the oligarchy's center, to my office and my duties.

It takes two hours, hurtling through the mazed world of buildings streets plazas cemeteries gardens pits libraries ossuaries temples courthouses and forested parks, to the sea—

The sea air surrounds us now, and the guard bows at me as I disembark from the elephant and I bow back and inquire after his week's winnings.

"The lizards were good to me this week!" They race faster than anything you've ever seen, tails lightning in the sand. I smile and nod and he keys me in to the elevator and I rise like my ancestors from the ocean towards the fifth floor, the ocean below, and the filing cabinets awaiting my gloved hand.

*   *   *

I dream of my sister that afternoon; I nap in the shower room, the other office workers scrubbing their bodes in the heated water, I curled in the corner on my towel, the heat and the steam help me relax, I remember her worn face, her worried eyes— is she still falling?—

We must escape, I know. The Earth is metal because it is temporary. It is not Earth but it is Metal and it is only a Figure in our generational story, the story our Benefactors gave to us so wisely and so generously, I must make this escape our last, why did we return to our Old Dying Sun?

I am afraid, so afraid. What will happen?

"Time to go back to work," the guard tells me. I dress. I file papers. I copy papers. I watch my face reflected in the glass. I still feel young.

*   *   *

This Earth the number Three. How many have there been? I must remember. I am a cipher but also an avatar. My name is Soad. I seek my sister Weel. I seek my life before me; we are in the Redoubt but we shall not die; I salute you my memory—

*   *   *

"Soad!" She's outside the window.

"Weel!" I can see her eyes. She is the violet haired woman but her eyes look like my sister's.

"Go away!"

"Soad!" Is she a window wiper?

She's banging. I unlatch the glass.

"Let me in."

She steps inside. The bosses are out at lunch. Only an assistant advocate huddles in the far office, hacking away at a document. He does not hear anything but the sound of his machine.

"What are you doing here?"

"I came to get you."

"We can't talk here." But she grabs my arm.

"I'm leaving. Didn't I tell you? I did tell you."

"Not here!"

I open the office door and step into the corridor, filled with bad paintings and artificial air. She follows me.

"Will you come with me?"

"Yes, I'll come," I find myself saying.

*   *   *

She is pushing a little rowboat into the water.

"Don't you trust me?" she says.

I nod, but I do not. But I get into the boat.

Refinery towers levitate above our tiny vessel, their cables snaking through the air and down into the water. We push oceanwards, taking turns rowing. My skin feels electric, partly from the magnets of the refinery towers, partly from sheer wonder, the joy of surrender to a strangening fate.

We strangen, we grow strange, to each other. Like a separate evolution, not of the body but of the mind.

"This is the Third Earth," I say to her, the violet hair, but she says nothing, only rows, watching me and watching the darkening sky.

'Do you love me?" I ask.

She nods, slowly, but says nothing.

It is growing dark.

*   *   *

"You knew me as a girl," she says, in the moonlit darkness. We're still rowing.

"When?"

"You were three years older than me. I was seven. You were ten."

"Where?"

"Right here, Soad."

I shiver.

"Do you remember?"

"No."

"You do remember."

"No . . ."

"What do you remember."

"I remember your face. I remember it."

"I remember yours too," she whispers, and she lights a fire in her hand, and lights her pipe. She smokes in the dark under the moon.

"Where are we going?"

Her eyes are unreadable.

"Tell me," I say.

But she just puffs the smoke from out her pipe.

"Tell me, please," I whisper.

"Down into the sea."

*   *   *

Full stop. Full stop, friend. Whatever I have said before I must forswear. I am not sure where this is leading. Tell me, do you know?

Can you tell me?

I am so afraid. I am so afraid! Tell me the ending! Tell me!

Tell me how it ends! I need to know! I need to know, brother! Can't you tell me! Tel me! Oh gods---

We're going under—

*   *   *

Conquistador in the night.

Soad and Maug:
Ocean

The vessel curves beneath the waves, fragrant and divine, its spurs and lightning elements filling the marine water with whitening fire.

Captain Maug holds onto the wheel of the metal craft, floating inside the white fire sea.

A dragon swims by the ship and Soad and his woman Weel wheel under waves, their eyes white and burning, their mouths drinking the sea, fluid and air, alive and near death, waiting for the airlock to open.

Arthur smiled. The airlock opened, and Maug's wife Madeleine took the pair in, stripping off their wet clothes and holding their hair back as they puked seawater, then blow drying their nude bodies, to remove infection. She handed them overalls and shirts, and ship shoes.

They cycled through the lock into the ship.

Bubbles swam past the portholes and the blue white light of the ship's corridors made Madeleine seem like a fairy in the woods, her hair glinting.

Under Nextspace a fire, under the world a world.

Under every breast, the heaving heart describes a palpable maturing fervor for this world under world inside world beneath the world we are standing on and reading.

Under Soad's arm, Weel felt at peace. They stepped onto the bridge.

"You're here," said Captain Maug.

* * *

We're firing rockets. They heave through the water towards the surface, tipped with fire.

We rise underneath them.

A celebration is at hand. Paper hats and papier mache boats and masks, the fever dream excites everyone as the submarine surfaces and Maug laughs, like Dionysus himself, come to join with his dolphins.

I am mad, I know. But I do not know how mad.

The sky is on fire with rockets.

Weel's hair is violet and I hold her hand and watch the sky on fire and the boats, the parade boats with their finery and bunting shining beneath the refineries' glow.

"I wasn't here before," said Maug to me.

"Nor was I, Captain."

* * *

"I'm your sister," Weel whispers to me, later, as I kiss her in our room.

"I don't believe you," I say.

"It's true," she says, but she kisses me.

We hold each other urgently, her skin fire her eyes timeless. I forget everything—

I lie beside her, after. She is not my sister. She looks like my sister. Perhaps I made her my sister. I adopted her. It is not incest. Surely not. She is too beautiful for incest.

"Soad."

"Yes."

"I didn't tell you."

"What."

"Why I brought you."

"Yes?"

"You won't like it."

"Okay."

"We need your eye."

"My eye?"

"Just to borrow it."

"Who?"

"Me. And Madeleine."

"What do you mean?"

"You're smarter than me. In this way. Your eyes: they're better. You see more. Or different. I don't know. You could go back, maybe. Are you sorry you came?"

"What do you need?"

"We need to borrow your eye."

"Right."

*　*　*

Right as rain. Right as the rain mainly on the plan. This network is a sibilance of stars, I think, I'm being connected—

They take the eyeball out several inches, injecting it, but the optic nerve remains connected and I see the map inside my brain, like the floaties in the aqueous humor, galaxies.

"Do you see it?" Madeleine asks my sister. My almost sister.

"What am I looking for?" she shouts back, head bent over the machines.

"You'll know it when you see it." The captain's wife watches calmly. I can fear Maug laughing in an adjacent cabin.

30

"Are we under way?"

"Yes," says Madeleine. "Twenty knots. A red sky tonight." She smiles, and I see how beautiful she is.

* * *

I go to sleep. The map still sloshes around in my brain, and my eyeball aches, slowly more and more, as the drug wear off.

* * *

Storms Coming

▌▌▌▌▌▌▌▌▌ We say we know the way. We say we have a lot to say, about what is what.

But the child knows so much more than you, never forget that. Never forget the richest of information in their heads, the base programming, the assembly language of the gods and all their servants, *instinct*, more powerful than any epic tragedy, and *instinct* is so beautiful I don't even know how to begin to describe it.

It may even be that Vonnegut was wrong, our beloved Hoosier himself, and that instinct is the instruction manual he longed for (granted to infants at birth to explain what to expect from this life). Of course, he wanted a kinder, gentler manual and so in this respect he was like Reagan . . . but at any rate . . . instinct builds us better like widgets, it throws us against the world, the ultimate empiricist. Empiricism only means *experienced*, like Jimmy Hendrix knew, God bless him, and so empiricism really is just instinct, walking its terrifying music of the soul down the tracks of the earth and stars, for Soad is breaking his old bones upon the wax of life, and making his voice heard over the storm—

"Aiiiiiiiiiiiiiiiiiiiiiiiiiiiiiiiiii!" He screams and promptly inhales a batch of saltwater and the sailors punch him in the ribs to lower his center of gravity and as he bellows over they swoop him off of the poop deck.

In the glory of the storm, like in the rich and mellifluous flutter in the eye of an insane animal, we celebrate the violent murderous glory of the earth and its hallucinatory treasures: always trying to kill you off, it demonstrates its love.

(But was the Founders' metal Earth equally as loving?)

We say we know why. We say we know how it started. Did a bear shit in the woods? Did Madagascar ope wide its mouth and hum a tragedy to fill a world? Did the bearded white man on his throne intone a Latin singsong to ream the day right up its own asshole and start the engine of Time running?

Well we're not sure, to be honest. And as we work on that one, Soad is hustled into his cabin and taken prisoner in effect; he has proven, for all his supposed battle-readiness, decidedly unseaworthy.

Crouching and shivering on his bed, Arthur the Dragon creeps out from the ceiling to regard his prey, his companion, his charge, his onus and his muse, Soad. A more worthless hero Arthur has rarely seen, he longs for the wings of Galahad, in his sea-green glory like the coming of a hurricane . . .

"Soad," says Arthur.

"Arthur," says Soad.

"Take a detour?" says Arthur.

"Yes," says Soad, and spits more salt out of his mouth.

"Soad," says Arthur.

And Soad looked into the eyes of the dragon, perhaps the most ancient eyes he'd ever seen.

"Where did you come from, Arthur?"

"My brothers are coming, Soad. Tell me, how can I save you?"

"What?"

"My brother dragons are angry. They say you are an inferior champion. They say that you are easy prey; that you are meat and we are hungry. They say that they have divined that it was you, or perhaps a recent ancestor of yours, that defiled our sacred ways by dismantling our Great Heart in the forest."

"What?"

"Don't just say what, it makes you look like an idiot. You can die here as well as anywhere, Soad. You're a sniveling boy!"

Suddenly the dragon's roar was louder than the storm.

"I'm working hard for you! *Do you understand that?*" Arthur's scaled face was beautiful and enraged.

"Yes," said Soad, with wide eyes. "Yes, I understand. What can I do?"

"Work, you idiot! Work, you goddamned human! Because my brothers are jealous! And there are more of them than there are of me!"

Arthur flew out into the storm, his wings shining from a light that could not be seen, and the boy-man Soad, made young again in the long afterlife of our Earth, shoved his head out of the porthole to drink in his prize: *life.*

Arthur flew south over the Green Bow Dragon Sea, which is not made of water but of air, the finest air you've ever seen, for it comes from a refinery, made in space and sent to land, by the Newcomers, by the Settlers, abhumans all, he permuted all equations and he roared out his name which was not Arthur amidst his people but was—

O a star!

And his name was

I am coming!

And Arthur the Dragon's name was: *I sing! I sing a star city!*

For what is a name but a mark on a map that changes? And who is a dragon but a sword of the many gods in these many worlds? And I ask you, which is more powerful, more useful? If you had to choose between the map and the sword, which would you have?

And so: uttering his name to guard his dragon body shifting in the half light between universes, Arthur roared and changed, and made it through the Green Bow Dragon Sea.

We who live in simpler times sometimes still imagine that a journey into the sky is a simple business of gravity, and maintenance, jet engines, propulsion, mathematics and strong engineering. But remember: engine and genesis share the same root, *beginning*, and while it's true the beginning was a word, a word is itself a sound, and it may be said that the kick-starter of a jet is itself this genesis: *the sound of the engine itself* is part of its deeper beginning . . .

But I go on. Suffice to say that the sky, the one we know, is still a mystery. Is now was then and shall be again, and so it was for Arthur on his journey from world to world, from dimension to dimension, a being with many names, a journeyman with many passcodes, a wanderer without map but with a cartographer's brain, shimmering:

Arthur landed in the vale and his brothers squawked their strange music.

Dragons know so many things but they are ornery.

"*Arthur,*" she said, and Arthur knew he was in trouble.

The small white dragon Cecilly curled up against the grass to gaze into Arthur's aged face, his lithe metallic limbs.

"*Arthur.* How are you?"

Often the light of tragedy is born in a woman's voice.

*   *   *

Madeleine held the wheel. She shouted out orders and the sailors bent the ship to her words, its ropes singing under the storm. The light was horrid but enticing, and they seemed to exist in no space at all, the sea a white disaster and the air filled with strange color.

Rickmorad had secured the mainsail and they listed now, held in abeyance between the winds and the rain and the light, and Madeleine could feel the tension coming to a snap.

A furious sailor dragged Soad out of the porthole and slammed it shut, and dragged him back onto the deck.

"Bail!" he shouted and the two men set to it with buckets as the ship continued its eerie angle along a great wave, threatening to tip everything into the sea into the hurtful light, but not yet. Not quite yet.

*   *   *

The chart is slow but it is kind; we hold it all inside our mind, the story. The music rises and the chart survives, trickling images and trailing after-images, the winded and the ghostly, hovering in the dark spaces of the mind, the wind and the door, the fragrance divine, we need it more than anything, our guide:

The chart is slow but it is kind and its courses and its edges we are coursed between a dream and a memory, we write the way we want to be:

In this chart:

A broken sail like a lacy curtain wafts in the no-breeze of space, the infinite stars behind.

The sail is alive.

We are accustomed to maps, charts, with names, with lines, with colors and with shapes susceptible to easy handling, but there are other maps too, with compasses built into them, maps that are in their own way *guides*, because the best map changes with the territory . . .

*   *   *

Eklaihah! The dead city. Perhaps a universe all its own, one pernicious and promiscuous, to insinuate its shadow into so many other universes just as a reminder, that *it's still there* . . .

Ruin! Oh great gods the ruin! Oh the gods the ruin! Oh the ruin burns! Oh the ruin burns inside! Oh the ruin burns inside our heart!

Eklaihah, I am coming, I promise. I come to you to bring you the gifts we bring you always, food and a little shelter from the sun, though it is dying red.

Oh my god the ruin it is here and we are it, and it is beautiful, like cemeteries are beautiful, their memory and their ornery a shade of truth so painful, their houses and their ventures a great and verdant music that cannot know an end.

But each ruin is a mystery, even as each archaeological dig reveals a whole world, each distinct, each filled with life.

Eklaihah I am coming and I bring you water, I bring you stones. I bring you stories, Eklaihah, beautiful! Don't you want them? I bring you stories and I bring you bones to make your tragedy unfold again, so we may know its shape. So we may know again your fatal mistake, so we may know again the way it was and the way we are now . . .

O the ruin! Inside its mind we're tied.

*　　*　　*

"Bail, you bastard!" shouted the sailor. Soad did. And the ship groaned through the fire white sea.

*　　*　　*

I bear across to you brother, meta my phor, hold my hand.

I bear across not news, you see, it is not news, for it does not take any time, we are outlasting everything, we are connected in this moment as we bear across and as you hold my hand. In this signal, all is true and nothing is despised. In this signal, the music of the world is stars, and we can see the music like the gods may do, written out across the sky, where we too will die, the dust of the thousand dust mobs of galaxies unwritten and never dreamt of.

Will you come with me? There, I've let go your hand. You've come this far.

You must decide for yourself. It is okay to turn away! All messages are free, as you are free! I can promise only that I will be faithful to you. You will likely betray me! But I shall be loyal to you even in your betrayal, for I am come to you as a brother and I must remain so, for that is my task, and that is how I go on. I do hope that you will come, you see—

Already, sooner than I had thought, we have come back to the map, the stirring fragment of a space ship, its sail tattered, its mast alive, it is a being and it is a map and it is a guide, you understand? Treat it holy if you wish, that is a reasonable approximation.

Near its eye we can stand here, in the space near to it, and listen to whisper:

"I was a man who was a god. And my name was Eklaihah."

That is what the sail says.

Yes, hubris. Yes, it is hubris again. Hubris again, and again. It is hubris, again, again, and again. Tell me, is it wrong to know an answer? Is hubris the mistake of knowing? Must knowledge always be destruction?

And the sail says,

"I stormed a night. And I stormed it in the dawn. And for my troubles, a castle was given to me. A Redoubt. A fortress from the storms that raged and worried at my tribe. "In Saint Michael I was made holy, I was given robes of finest linen, and a diadem of fire, and anointed in oil. My children were destined for worlds unknown . . .

"But it was worlds unknown we found, worlds unknown inside. I tell you, the sun died even as Eklaihah did, and it did not happen slowly, it

happened in an instant, in an instant all was gone, all was rearranged, and in our tragedy we lied, you see, we lied and was that hubris? It was only human. Is human hubris? How can I know? Was I a god first or first a man? I have gone insane.

"Inside the castle I taught my children to fight the aliens. And slowly, we grew strange . . .

* * *

Eklaihah! Eklaihah, I am coming! Though I despise you.

* * *

Inside the storm the energies rock and roll. Each wave competing with each other, fighting for control, mirroring each other, copying and diminuetting, ad infinitum, the roaring hoard, the mob of angry children, thrilled to be in the midst of summer—

Soad was a boy who was a man but the storm changed him. Lightning life and light miraculous lethal soared through his being an ecstasy uncountable and without words, and so his eyes deepened and his flesh aged, and he grew, he grew the way a tree grows, bending with the storm.

The way the mast carries with it the wind! The way the ship moors its old root into the curve of the Earth, changing history with every swing of its jib.

"Land! Land! Land!" But it is too soon. They are coming up on rocks.

Inside Soad inside his heart his beating force was beaten back, he shook like a leaf in a growing wind, clinging to the mast like Odysseus, fearing the angels, the muses, the voices of the deep, the women who watch to see if you will be their next surrender, their next diminuet into the Change, a sufferer over the deeps. Heroes are made for it. We like to believe that these heroic acts enfold the hero in grace, enliven the hero with force and richness, but the truth is that so often, even if the hero is not broken, he is shaken, he takes that darkness within, for he must have accepted some of it, to come so close to the disaster. Like the mast of the ship in the storm, he had to bend so he would not break, and in that bending, in that diminution, in that curving to the will of the world, like the curve of the earth, he let himself be marked within like planets and comets and suns are marked, and galaxies entire. With that curve, that limning light and strange lingering dawn, the truth is marked—for rulers know only straight lines, but heroes always follow the curve.

The ship sailed into the rocks and was broken on them. Many drowned in despair.

The captain Maug watched his wife drown. And though he tried to swim to her to save her he could not, and she was swept beneath the waves, along with most of his crew.

How did Odysseus return? How can Man ever, ever return to Woman?

*   *   *

Beyond the rocks the hurtling darkness whirled, for like the light it is alive, and its thunder was a voice, and its steam was like a dragon, sailing in the spirited night, and it spoke in many tongues.

Soad. Where is your sister?

Maug. Where is your wife?

The men screamed in the dark on the beach, tossed there by the angry storm, each in their madness they grieved and raged in a noise so vast it was like silence.

Weel was taken by the naiads underneath the coral reef, into their secret corridor inside the heart of the island.

*   *   *

When he awoke, Maug could not speak. He stalked the beach, an angry living ghost. He saw Soad crouched in the sand, staring at the horizon. Its beauty both men found horrible.

Soad would not look at Maug but Maug looked at Soad, staring in silence. The waves rolled in, slow and foamed, slipping in splinters of their broken ship.

In the Night Lands:
The Abhumans

"They're coming in!" screams the Adjutant.

We need what you have: memory. Ours is slower than yours, and the way you pick up stuff; it's incredible.

The Night Lands are Longing. They Long for you, Sufferer, and we long for your flesh even as you long for ours. Will you not come to us and make amends?

*   *   *

Soad

I am not sure that I am awake. I've felt this way before, on the edge of sleep, or woken from a dream, my body heavy, my mind heavy, my dream not faded, but the world crept up on me anyway, asking if I'm ready to come back, to return—

I lie in the tank and I am thinking. My body is hungry. I have no wife. I have no children. My sister, she is dying of cancer. Me, I feel as though I have no meaning. I feel as though this end would be as good as another.

Can Arthur save me?

"Arthur . . ." Bubbles in the tank.

Soad.

"Arthur. What happened?"

Soad. Come back.

"No. I like it here. It's dreamy."

Soad. What kind of man are you.

"A bloody annoyed one. Kill me off already, I'm tired."

They always say that. Men are always whining. No matter what the Geoffrey of Monmouths and the Thomas Mallories write later. It's kvetching all the live long day.

"Arthur."

Don't sweet talk me. Just go back to sleep already. We have work to do.

"What work?"

You have to save the world.

"Arthur. That's silly. The world goes on. It doesn't need saving."

I am only a dragon. What can I tell you?

"Do I need to save *you*, Arthur?"

Yes, man. You need to save me. Won't you?

Yes.

*   *   *

I know this narrative may not be what you expected, but what of that? Have you ever been to these places? To render the ineffable in language is a fraught adventure even with the most sympathetic of audiences. And if you doubt everything, then all I have hoped for is lost. Believe with me. That is all I ask.

Interlude: Childhood

▌▌▌▌▌▌▌▌▌▌▌ Soad and Weel play the waygog in the minaret, watching the tides of radiation sweep over the metal Earth. They are five years old, and the radiation, colored by the computers' interpretation through the viewing portals, looks immensely beautiful.

The waygog is a two person instrument, blown with the lips and held with three hands, like bagpipes mixed with the didgeridoo. Its sound is holy, and it's hours of fun. The two siblings taught themselves to play from the archives. What is not recorded within them?

Soad stops playing and Weel stops because he has, and they look out over the blasted landscape in its terrible beauty. The End of the World is gorgeous.

The Island: Soad

▌▌▌▌▌▌▌▌▌ I'm awake. The light has fallen and it's dark. I'm on an island. I can see the city of Saint Michael glowing over the water, its Ferris Wheel spinning.

Maug watches the lights.

"What is it?" asks Maug.

"A city," I say.

"What city?"

"Saint Michael."

"Is it a good city?"

"No."

"Beautiful though."

"Yes."

A distant light of Saint Michael plays over Maug's face for an instant, a lost spotlight.

"Are you all right, captain?"

But Maug is crying.

*　　*　　*

Saint Michael, Saint Michael, the divinity of things is watched and starred, it waves goodbye in order to slip the dirk into your back . . .

Well appointed nobles hover over the stimulant bar, preening musically like heavy birds, their voices braying over the synthetic pumped-in music, gravely refined and sad, captains of industry corpulent and cheerful days before their fatal heart attacks . . .

Raking in her curls the girl sheening with sweat and a smile moves fluidly between the nobles, dressing their drinks and swishing her long dress and her bare arms. Her sad mouth and hopeful eyes and lithe body, chestnut hair. Saint Michael is spreading like a blood stain, an algae bloom.

This Saint Michael, horrid and alone, beautiful and growing tired, the fleshy ripe orb of the last fruit of the season, begging to be eaten, waiting for the fall to Earth, Versailles again, Versailles forever—Versailles which means "to turn over and over" to spin in the dark of the deadliest dream you ever had—are you going to wake up?

We're here alone with you. All our people. Are you going to make it? Will this be the moment? What can you do for us? What can you do for me?

I am Soad! I'm dying! On the sandbar off Saint Michael in Pacific, by the roving doom and dying light, in the rich frequency of the last sadness of an empire unimaginable, I hold Maug's hand—oh take me away!

*   *   *

What makes a capital? A crossroads town, more or less by accident become the center, for a time, of the world? A charismatic leader who simply announces that here shall be his treasure horde?

Saint Michael is a capital. Its limbs and roads and doors and, most of all, its dreams, draw many from the stretches of the imagination, over this galaxy and others, intertwined and space and time into this little bubble.

And this great and terrible privilege means that things that happen in Saint Michael happen elsewhere as well.

Beneath the level of intention, at, perhaps, the logic of fate, the events within Saint Michael's small community extend far outward . . . like suns dancing with their invisible dark matter partners . . .

So it was that, to celebrate a simple holiday, the beginning of spring in Saint Michael, they launched fireworks into the air.

And as the first exploded into color over the beaches and condos of Saint Michael, in the Night Lands a new world was born:

(language is a sun.

Dear God, my love—

Ö!

O!

O! the sun!

O the sun is born inside the sky!

Shimming inside the yellow white course of the nexus of the event, the stunning frozen moment of the re-ignition of Earth's star, burns our Heartache Longing for the Life We Left behind—

Fusion radiation storms over the surface of the Night Lands, bringing unknowable unbelievable fear hope madness desire and death—still this fury of the light, this horrifying amazing light, this light does not destroy the Metal Earth. It courses over it, it makes it glow, but the Earth is there.

The Night Lands creatures first smile and then begin to howl, their billion teeth a Grand Canyon of Truth and Desire, a modernist painting of indescribable dimension but with a fractal form that we can recognize: the self-similarity within, the cell and then the galaxy, their smiles the fusion reaction that drives the center of the universe—

BOOK TWO:
THE BEGINNING

I took my son out into the wasteland and we removed our space suits in the horrid light of dawn, the indescribable atavistic joy and love that comes with standing right beneath a star.

Our brothers and sisters were dying. The Night was coming to an end.

Crepuscular creatures, those who hunt in dawn and dusk, these shadow dwellers appreciate these interregnums of the light, the magic hours. Magic exists, you know? Not only is it technology sufficiently advanced we can't tell the difference, but simply the woof and weave of the universe itself, the beautiful beckoning of the cutting hurting truth, the brutal truth that we are here, and watch your water, and eat at Joes, eat at Joes, if you can, because TANSTAAFL, motherfucker, you gotta fight for it.

Crepuscular creatures are who we are. We insist that there be a border so that we can stand within it, neither post nor ante meridian, but meridial, we burn inside the border. We burn inside the border like hydrogen inside the sun, making musics that ache, and fuel the death we need. We need it so bad—

"Aakkghghhhcgh!" says the Waelred, its eyes exploding in the light and its many arms lurching across the blasted plains towards my son and me, under the shadow of the Shining Redoubt. The Last Stand of Humanity, improbably victorious.

The Alamo won.

But where are our heroes? Where are Soad and Weel? Their genetic message primed the pump and this glorious engine is on the move, and the celebration demands them, the triumph demands the generals for our shining arch, but where are they?

I have never seen such things. How can we bear this beauty?

"Dad?"

"Yeah, son?"

"I want to go inside."

"Yeah. Okay."

We walk through the orange and the red, the glow and the mutant yellows burning in the air, this landscape from nightmare lodged now into the quality of religious experience, the birth canal—

The Redoubt is opening its doors. The abhuman and the human stare into each other's faces—ancestors and cousins—to ponder their meaning.

* * *

All that rises must converge, in love—but what is the fuel that launches all our spirits from out of the gravity well?

The word miracle comes from an ancient word, *smeiros*, which meant to smile, or laugh.

What is a smile and a laugh? Equally miraculous as the rebirth of a sun, the smile with all its strange dark glory can contain a will all of its own, transmitted cross the ether to enact its portents . . .

The sun can smile too. And its portents are our future:

Arthur the Dragon

Laugh, cookaberra, laugh—
Arthur the dragon sleeps inside a fire, cooked in ash, meditating.
"Cecilly!"
His wife has awakened him.
The laugh is the wondrous work of God, the belly laugh of Buddha,
whirling inside the dragon's mind; he smiles:
"Cecilly!"
He shakes off some of the ash.
"What the hell is going on!"
And takes into the sky.

Asmodeus

||||||||||| My name is Asmodeus and I am screaming; I do not know how long I have been doing it. What memories I had are changing; I remember only my children. Where are Weel and Soad?

My name is Azzy and I cannot wake up.

*   *   *

Light and Dark, Day and Night, these worlds hint at the grey behind them, the half-light:

For the half light is dream, and in dream we are still novices, still unprepared for the enormity of what we are to encounter.

Down with the dichotomies! For if we can map the half-asleep, if we can make sense of the edge of consciousness itself, we will be freer and more solid than we have ever been: we will be at last, in some strange far way, adults.

For the dream is like music: and if you an understand music you can understand our identity.

Identity comes from Latin roots for "sameness," "over and over," *idem et idem,* and so identity, like music, is about a beat, a pulse, a rhythm to the pulse of generations, reiterating their forms, 25 years, 23 years, a little syncopation--

Identity as a word is related to "id" as well — *it* — for there is an it-ness to the self, a thing that will not die, even when it dies, it is not dead, for there are others, other yous, other partial copies, beating at the drums of life.

Music derives its pleasure from this structure: any simple rhythm provides an architecture within which the improvisation and personality of the drummer has room to play, to mark his time as music-maker in the room, and to lose himself in the pulse of our human community.

Dream, music, and identity are closer than is commonly believed. Indeed, the Old English word "dream" meant "joy, mirth, noisy merriment, and music" it did not mean sleeping sensations and visions at all. Perhaps our ancestors, like the American Indians, did not make serious distinctions between dream and waking life, and it is for this reason that their language has survived. The identity of English is the identity of dream, its traumatic fervor skipping over the stretched sheepskin pummeling our beating heart to remember this word, this feeling, the symbiotic reverence we bear the Earth, and the under-Earths, our shared awareness and our parsing souls—

In dream, with every dream, we see again our connection to a huge world, a logical and changing, moving place, written and rewritten, writing us as we write it, compressed or condensed or illogical as you like it. In dream we remember who we are and where we may be going.

If this waking life is but the glimpse of the surfacing whale, the tip of the iceberg, the 1% visible matter skimming over the surface of the huge dark beneath, then be a strong whale. Your breath will take you deep when you are ready to dive—

Crepuscular creatures, rich inside the magic hour, dragonfolk, ab-human monsters and questing heroes wailing and willing and working to make the day their own—they are only one beat or two! Tap the drum at the right time, *senor*, and make it count, and make it your own, *idem et idem*, the sun is coming up!

* * *

I do not know what I've become. For how can I conquer a dream? I am conquistador, yes, I represent my nation and the spoils of these lands shall be made our own as is our right but this land, this land is foul with tricks and madness streaks over its skies as it shakes inside my mind—

I am a benefactor. This is what I tell myself. History and its monuments will remember my name; I am a god, a small one, but divine! Why must I suffer these doubts, then, if my divinity is assured?

Idem et idem, come round again, *Fortuna*, in your sunny and toothed surprise, my life for you! My life for you, Fortune! A billion *reales*, a quintessence of dust and my name, my name unforgotten.

Can I say that I came, I saw, I conquered? What is it to conquer? First, you must amaze the natives.

* * *

My name is Asmodeus. I proclaim Saint Michael my own; all its boulevards and way stations, all its muted glories. This is something that I say inside my mind; and it only later, only once this certainty becomes a glow I feel behind my eyes that I may use it! That I may spread my seed of words into the minds of the people of this strange, rich city—

(if only it were easier)

Soad, where are you?

Soad

I move into the street. The elephants and the jitneys scream and shout, swerving; I raise my arm. Above me is the streaming sky, purple and red, in the crepuscular light the commuters move, and the animals groan, I must look a mad homeless prophet but I wear my Spanish metal helmet in my mind, I shout:

"Saint Michaelans! In the name of the Redoubt I salute you and declare you mine! Bow to the Redoubt!"

(You have to call to your nation, sometimes, you know? Why not wear it on your sleeve, sister? My love is falling—)

Can you understand me, interlocutor? I tell you:

I am inside my body and you are inside your body.

And I am inside your body and you are inside my body.

And these bodies melt, inside the sea.

Inside the sea of dream! I blaspheme to say I conquer this our dreaming ocean but it is good to do so! So I blaspheme! So in this way I conquer! In this way I render your saints ash and your homilies the belches of gnomes, meaningless disaster farce and rent blooded bupkiss is yours, traveler, without a name, without a following. So follow me!

Follow me into this Kingdom of Dreams! Into the Dagger in My Mind—

(And I know I will go further, further than perhaps I ought, but this is in the nature of the explorer: from ex and *plorare*, to cry out! I cry a sea, sister! I cry a sea, my own, oh let it be our own for if it shall not be I am already wrecked in a thousand realities, my children never to be, I salute you sea, and I name you:

Oh, I name you—

Kaen! I name you the sea Kaen! And into its disaster I bid you follow!

The Sea of Dream
(an accounting)

So let us fill the ocean then. Inside this ocean is dream and it must be filled, the fluid of the mind is made, so here my bean counters and we have:

One (1) Quintessence of reality
Two (2) Whale Roads
Three (3) Blank Memories
Four (4) Troubadours

Mix them up inside your wizard's bowl, enfold the envelopes of their syrupy liquids within one another, and smell . . . smell the dream as it is made.

(Why do you think the Sandman carries sand? It's made by waves...)

On the ingredients

—A quintessence is like a Big Bang, you need it to get some visible matter going, to stimulate the eye, to suck some gravity onto the board. A little stardust and you're ready to go ...

—Whale Roads are the known sea, a category of the vast dream ocean delimited simply by the memory of the whales. (They have long memories).

—Blank Memories are rather dangerous. Remember anything you want to ...

—Troubadours!

Oh the troubadours, inside the portent I mean inside the cable, I mean inside the balm, no, the temple, no, the rod, no, the birth, no, inside the chapel, no, inside the rend, no, inside the world, inside the court—

The court of many things, of many colors, many waves, licking at the edges of glass, at the edges of the mind—

For if we would understand dream then we must understand madness; if we would understand dream we must understand waking; if we would understand dream we must understand our consciousness, and I am only a man.

And must I understand it to conquer it? Can I not amaze the sea? And figure it all out later?

Surely I will be damned. But have we not been damned a thousand times over? We keep going. The sun is born again, born again inside our darkening sky—

*   *   *

I must wax and wane like a moon. I will be what you need. Please:

tell me what you need. Overhead, and on mast, furious, and warm.

I will be gentle, and loving. I will be cruel, and forever. I will be forever for you, if you need me to.

Can you imagine what was intended, what was meant, what was imagined when we set out to course uncharted waters?

The enormity of it all; this already is a kind of madness, to throw yourself into the void, and trust in God or yourself, or both, or your crew, or all of the above, or none of it, and do it anyway, launch, close your eyes, dream:

I tell you, these words haunt us for they are our prison and our key, the Gnostic rhythm of these memes and phonemes is to circumvent the end; all language is call and response, in this way, an Aristotelian eternity of world building.

They build our world. In more ways than we can know, though we can sense it, and we have, and we are acting on those senses to divine a message and to construct a path out, and through--

You see these dangers. The same as Columbus' sailors feared: the edge of the world.

Close your eyes.

Close your eyes, sister.

And the ocean courses over our bodies, lifting us up, and sucking us under—

*   *   *

The Quintessence we can call the Sandman; and this is an envelope too, or, more precisely, a Mobius envelope, the sand from the ocean that made the ocean, the stardust, though it is the ocean that made the sand—but the stars and the spaces between them are another kind of ocean, after all, even as the darker matters that course over our visible bodystuffs are waves and eddies of reality, tidal pools of their own, and so we wind the clock, and so we cast the dust, and whisper a magic word—

(one we mustn't write down)

And we are born, born again, born again, born again, eternal recurrence and the identity, *idem et idem*, over and over and over and over, my face is yours, on the opposite platform brother, but this one is hard—*hold on, hold on, hold on*

—you are still you!— even as the ship is still the ship!—though it becomes part of the sea ...

And so let us become a whale. If we would follow the road of dream we must understand our cousins in the sea, mammals just like us! Only grown older! Only grown winded in the sturm and drang, the storm and the drive, that wails and whirls and wills our weapons and our dreamstuffs down beneath the waves, the urge the demiurgos!

I am a whale! My name is Woad! I cry beneath the sea!

My sister! Where are you!

(I am here, Soad. I am Weel. Why did you change your name?)

I am become a whale!

(Soad, we're losing it— this gate— we are going through the gate! Can't you see it?)

Sister!

(Hold on, Woad, Soad, my brother, you ass, you fucked it all up—)

I am diving.

Woad

║║║║║║║║║║║ I turn and smile. The color of light is changing as I sink.

I have left my pod, from the shores of Saint Michael, into the Kaen sea.

My name is Woad; I am a whale; I follow the whale road, west. West which means downwards. Our star, near us, sinking behind our watery sphere ... we can smell it, did you know? We smell the sun.

Much is being derived from my investigations and I do not yet know what their outcome will be, though we whales plan far ahead.

My mother is angry with me. And I am angry with her.

You know that different animals experience time differently? The cheetah, for instance. It sees forward in time usually, as you do, but of course time slows significantly for it when it hunts.

We dwell in an expanded now: we see both forwards and backwards in time, and we collapse our wave functions more slowly as a general principle. This gives us license to manipulate matter a bit more fiercely than you do, for our "now" is slower.

I know, you may say that we are only whales. Well, you are only humans.

I hear my sister calling through the water:

"Woad ... Woad ... Woad ..."

I cry her name into the dark. I swim west into the darkening night water, holding my breath.

(Did you say the sun was reborn? You make me weep ...)

I am inside my body and you are inside your body.
And I am inside your body and you are inside my body.
And these bodies melt, inside the sea.
But we,
We have not forgotten when the arrows fall,
Between the stars.

Asmodeus

I am a man, born on the metal constructed Earth, our strange gift; our home.

I survived; I live over you. I live over you, *sur vivre*.

We know we hate survivors as they hate themselves, and we fear them, as we fear ourselves; what we can become. What we are becoming.

Long ago the wise man said: the fear that the human race will be extinguished has been replaced by the fear that it will endure. I survived; we are survivors. And so let us compare our miseries.

Let there be an accounting of our spoils and our pounds of flesh, with and without blood, with and without complicities, foreknowledge, sadomasochistic tendencies or saintly messianic martyrdom, a list of pain.

I grew up in the Redoubt. I grew up in the Fortress. In the Castle. I awaited the crumbling of the walls and the leering eyes of the abhuman monstrosities hovering so near outside. Though agnostic, my every breath and every act was informed by the culture of Revelation, of the End.

At the End—did you know?—all lovers are reunited. Is it hogwash? Perhaps it's like a Big Crunch? Reunification Field Theory Extreme and Wonderful? Or is it Heaven, and Magda's young lips will be pressed against mine own again, like Evelyn's, and Rachel's? And what of their lovers? This is always the problem with religion; it is limbic and not cortical, it survives on emotion. Reason only picks it apart.

Still. I need to know, and perhaps you do, on some level, I need to know, that this kiss was important. This love affair was important. Not just to me, but to reality; that this joining of flesh was ordained, not by God, but by the world, that it represented the exhale after a long dive, the blowhole firing into the sky ...

I am survivor. I bear my guilt and my hate. You must recognize that. What I have seen, only I can know, ultimately, and my words to you are colored with this knowledge. I know you could not have warned me. I know you could not have been prepared, for I was explorer, I cried out, into the dark, and I had read Nietzsche but still I stared into the abyss ...

I still insist I see the ghosts—

And now I am one of them. Haunting you. Come back again, the same, but with a different brain.

Prodigal: extravagant, or penitent? Both, of course, I'm both, but is my return real?

Woad

We swim inside the dark, and have for long, ever since we grew bored with the land and returned to sea, my sister and I, swimming deeper into the blue, towards Herman, Herman our white whale.

"The dream is changing sister, I feel it in my fins."

"Swim and don't talk so much," she says.

"Why do you always keep me company?" I ask, but she only swims ahead a bit, twirling in the fading light.

Some have said that we are stupid. We're fat, it's true, but then, we have fat brains as well, calculating, calculating.

I'm not sure she's here with me, to be honest. I can't always tell. We've swum together for so long now that I feel she's with me even when she isn't. Herman must know. He is albino and he knows things. He is angry. I have been growing angry too; I need explanations.

*   *   *

Here beneath, all is movement and long silences. I am an aspect of your awareness, but here, in the solitary, darkening water, I feel almost alone, almost free. Like the last whale, the legendary last one, singing only to myself. The sea tells me what it needs, and what it needs is an urgency; things are quickening here, almost as though we would have another Permian Explosion. I can't be certain. Will this transmission reach across the gap? I fear you already know how this ends! Won't you tell me!

Ach, it's the same old story. The traveler bereft and lost, without foundation or direction, but traveling, I see the ruin below and I swim to it—

Arthur is here.

"You've grown annoying," he says, feathered bubbles escaping his blue serpent lips.

"Arthur, you're here."

"I keep following you. I have this job, see, and they pay me for it, you should try it sometime, you goddamned slacker—"

"Where am I?"

"You're a whale. You're in the ocean, the ocean you *named* for Christ's sake, I don't understand it, but I'm *dealing* with it, unlike you!"

"I am a whale."

"Yes. And you made me into a fish. I'm a dragon, goddamn it." I can see him smiling in the dark blue water, his eyes small fires.

"These are ruins," I say. I can see their spires cloaked in the kelp and shadows.

"Eklaihah again, probably! I know, not supposed to say your name or something am I! You goddamned ruin! Following us everywhere!"

(Does the city grumble?)

"Hold my hand, Woad. Hold out your fin."

And I do.

With his grinning teeth shining in my face, he closes his red, taloned paw around my blue fin—

"There, that wasn't so hard, was it, whale?"

"No ..."

"Let me tell you something, you've been *very annoying*. I can't do everything myself. I mean, I'm a dragon, I'm good at tracking, I can hunt anything, but make it a bit easier for me, eh? I'm getting old!"

"I'm sorry, Arthur ... I'm just reacting, you know? It's not as though I have any control over all this ..."

"But you do! Goddamn it!" Steam escaped his lips. "Damn you. You should know better. But what can I say. I want to eat you. And not just because I'm angry; whale tastes great."

I watch him.

"What are you doing to me! Huh!" He lets go of my fin and spins in the water, looking down on the ruins below us. "We have to do some goddamned archaeology. I hate archaeology. But I don't see any way around it now. Why don't you go blow your load, I mean, shoot your blowhole, whatever it is you whales do, we might be down here a while."

"But Herman, the white whale, he's waiting ..."

"You're *not supposed to know that yet*. And even so, he's only a goddamned *idea in your head* right now! Ach, just go breathe some air already and get back here."

I swim up through the dusk, and let my body slip up into the air, warm against my skin, and I rotate, to look at the sun, red and orange slipping into the waves, the most beautiful thing I have ever seen, I know why so many worshipped it, for so long ...

I want to stay here forever. But I see a plane. And I feel it's spotted me, because it turns ... turns in the air and moves right towards me, streaking steam behind it—

I dive. I swim down, back to Arthur.

Interlude

▌▌▌▌▌▌▌▌▌ I can feel the knife in my hand.
(I am Cronus)
I am Father Christmas.
I got a sickle, for my birthday.

*   *   *

I'll fuck you long and I'll fuck you low, I am the red and I am the long low watch.

My name is Saturn and I gave you Saturnalia saturnine, Saturday, the Baron Samedi, the rich death demiurgos, my name.

I cut off your head.

I wear it around my neck. I stare your Earth down midst all these stars. I work a passion play around my hooked nose. I weave the sweater that you give your mother.

I am Saturn and I am coming!

(someone call the ambulance)

Cause there is gonna be an accident. Comin' for you—

*   *   *

Conquer:

Would you come, *veni* and see, *vidi* and then ... *vici vici vici vici, wiki wiki wiki wiki*

Well, have a seat.

We have a lot of talk about.

I'm like you, you know. I conquered my father. My son conquered me.

Tell me, do you believe that it will end? This conquering?

Do you really understand what it is? What it does?

Conquer as a word is related to "query." Both conquerages and queries seek to gain, an answer, or a territory. Both ask.

To conquer is to ask a question with someone. *Com* plus *quaerare* : Together with another, you ask the question:

Caesar and his men asked: Gaul?

And Columbus and his men asked: India?

And can you handle the answer. You never get the answer you want. Never, ever, ever.

Would you ask a question together with another? Be *conquistador?* It's really only another way of saying: are you ready to go back to school?

Like Rodney Dangerfield.

Because Rodney Dangerfield is gonna fuck you in the ass. School, school of hard knocks, and merry bones, and Daddy Uranus enclasped in oceanic clouds, Magellanic and supreme—

(I cut him already!)

My hammer and my sickle.

I am Cronus. It was I who gave you Earth back. She was my mother.

I carved it out of metal, with my knife. Is not the love of a father horrifying?

(Would you go further back, *conquistador?* Query comes from *kwo*, the Proto-Indo-European root forming the stem of the relative pronoun *who*, for to conquer you must ask, and to ask, you must be *who: idem et idem*, over and over, you must be who, you must conquer, dear gods—this is who we are—)

I am coming back. I will not slouch. Though I be a rough beast, my hour is so long and round that you will thunder it beneath your bootsoles, when I come round the corner humming my tune—

Fail better!

Fail better at the test!

And all the rest can see that you are bleeding!

And that you've already lost!

Fail better!

Fail better than the rest!

For on my chest I've cut your name, it's Rhea, or maybe it's Mary Gaia—

Whale

▌▐ ▌▐ ▌▐ ▌▐ ▌ Can you find the wave? Can you find the wave behind the whale, behind the man?

The figure in the storm tossed landscape is written by the shape of the clouds, even as the great man is determined by events—

Can you write the metaphor that burns the night, that joins the flight between the stars, that tells the world which way to curl, when we are gone away when the man is fighting harder than he ever has—the wind is coming up—

I am a whale. I am come to Eklaihah. The ruin. At first I thought—didn't I, Arthur?—

Yes.

—that it was the pattern round the figure, that the waves around Eklaihah could elicit a picture of the nature of its collapse, the nature of its destiny, something! But now I suspect that this is only adolescent. To insist the background determined the foreground is to deny free will, is to insist the city never had a right, never had a choice, to determine how it would be.

Well, go in then, Woad. You whales need this lesson.

I see Arthur's fiery eyes but I look away into the smokey chalk waters of this drowned star city, the city that we say that never was, its arms like that of a squid, insisting—

I swim inside.

(Soad?)

Shhh, I'm inside the city.

(Soad!)

I'm Woad. There's electricity in the water, I can feel it. I can hear a voice—

WOAD THE WHALE THE WILEY WHALE YOU COME TO SEE YOUR FUTURE?

Arthur is gone, swimming away.

"Arthur!"

WOAD THE WHALE THE WILEY WHALE YOU WANT TO KNOW WHO WE ARE FOR YOU?

"Tell me."

WE ARE EKLAIHAH BUT WE ARE YOUR SERVANT, TELL US, DO YOU BELIEVE IN FAIRIES?

The city's turning red in the dusk light.

(Soad! Where are you!) I think I hear my sister . ..

WOAD. TELL US WHAT YOU KNOW OF HERMAN THE WHITE WHALE.

"He is our skyfather. He is our patriarch. He is a wise whale of many years, albino, fast and strong and brave—"
DO YOU KNOW WHERE HE CAN BE FOUND?

*　　*　　*

I fear, I fear, why does it feel so natural? Turning into other things, it is isn't natural is it? It isn't natural that I slip into them this way, and I think, yes this is how it should be, but it's not like that, it's wrong.

Things aren't supposed to be this way, I'm supposed to wake up to the artificial sun and do my exercises, next to my sister, and my father, my father, is below ...

I do not remember. I do not remember how and why and all the answers for this thing that I have done, am doing, will still do no matter these the consequences, changing me.

I am a man. Abhuman perhaps, out of the dark, alive, moving: I am moving.

I am moving forwards. Even if I move backwards too, still we're beings who move forwards, through time, in a direction, forwards, it makes our meaning and it takes us messages slipped into my strange hand, my fin, my mind, to tell me:
WAKE UP!

*　　*　　*

We make our identity through conquest, conquest that is the shared question: what are we doing here? And why?

I move into the shattered city, humming to myself; my sister is far away and Arthur is nowhere to be seen. I am a whale and I am growing tired; but this is only the beginning.

I cry out into the cooling water: "City. City. City. Citycitycitycity. Speak!"

I hear, out of the crumbled walls covered in anemones, out of the plazas strewn with sand moving in the tide, its voice:
We were a weapon. We are a weapon.

There's an orange spark inside one of the half-standing buildings, intermittent but glowing in the water. I swim over to it.

I see her face inside, a human, with metal arms, she looks at me, and her eyes widen, just a little, but she watches, tending her chemical fire.

"What do you want?" she says, her eyes glowing with the dusk light and with something inside.

"Who are you?" I ask, my voice carrying out over the water, my blowhole forming words like a human mouth.

"I live here," she says, "You don't. Who are you?"

"I'm Woad."

"Swim away, why don't you."

"You live here in Eklaihah?"

"Yes."

"What is that you're burning?"

"I burn for my ancestors. Leave me be!" She waved her metal arms at me.

"Have you met Herman, the white whale?" I ask.

"Go away!" She stands and takes several steps towards me, looking into my left eye.

"What do you need?" I ask. "Can I help you?"

She takes out a knife, and I swim back a few meters.

"You whales always think you can help! What did you do when Eklaihah fell? Did you help then? No! You did nothing!"

"I'm sorry," I say. "I didn't know."

"You don't know anything." She sheaths her knife and returns to her chemical fire, warming her hands in the water.

"What happened to your arms?" I ask, unable to help myself. But she says nothing.

"Your curiosity speaks well of you ,whale!" she says, in a different voice now, and before I know it she is on my back, her knife in my flesh, clinging to me, and I cry out, and she cries: "Go then, curious whale named Woad! We will show you what you would like to know!"

And I am now a passenger I am now a beast of burden I am now a mount I swim I circle and I dive and the woman screams into the dark water—

"*I come for Eklaihah!*"

("Soad?" my sister ...)

I am smiling.

- -

Can you tell me where the world ends and begins? Will its salvation entail the destruction of some other where?

You tell me: as this transmission reaches you, do you hear any echoes? I believe that there is no sin in doing so, in telling you this tale, because I believe that it cannot pre-determine your own fate, no matter if we are from the same universe. Is this true, do you think? Or perhaps it's that you need saving too? Have I been doing all of this for you?

Are you dreaming? Are you dreaming your philosophy?

Give me more heaven and more earth, Horatio, I need some glue for this little tear right here--

For I am *conquistador,* and a woman rides upon my back!

We are free but we serve destiny; is this any different? In our goings we serve a majesty uncountable, but with a purpose: to absolve you, not of sin but of meaning, for as we bind ourselves into the axes, and we spin, down into the din and dun of earth:

"A little less religion, whale, just tell them where we're going."

We're going to the sun. Where Herman lives, he lives, he lives besides the sun, he lives besides the sun, to mark the coming and the going of the mark—

"He's a godlet. And I hunt him."

I am a whale; I serve my sister.

"You are a tool. I ride you."

(This is what she thinks, but I am Woad. I follow you! My beautiful ancestors …)

She holds her knife inside my flesh, she holds me. The murky ocean swims past my eyes, a dark-white light emerges, murmuring, it is the sun, it is the sun, it the sun.

"Whale. Make your sound."

I feel the urge to obey; I feel the sound growing within me, something that she knows, something that she understands—has this all happened before?—she digs her heels in and moves the dagger and I cry:

"Herman!"

His eye is visible then, blinking out of the milky white undersea dawn, red-limned and glorious, filled with rage—

I see his teeth. "You come. You have my food?" he says. His voice is millstones.

And she cuts out a bit of my own flesh and tosses it to Herman the white whale, and I scream. I watch him eat the piece of me, smiling in the fiery glow.

"Good. I am a whale, I am brought out of the dream. I endure the *fasces* and the train; I move the ocean. You are a woman?"

Of the many horrible things I have witnessed, this may rank as the most horrible: she threw a spear, from my back, at Herman the white whale, our strange dark-white god, and I screamed again, not with pain but horror.

Herman roared and the ocean shook, the white of the sun he hid flickering, moving, in so many dimensions I could not track it, I could not see it—

Then Herman is diving straight at me, aimed at the woman on my back; he is wounded and the sun he guards, or which guards him, is angry, and I run, I swim, I move, I swim with the woman on my back, I flee.

In dreams, you know, the logic is revealed to you, the oldest wheel-ruts, invisible to those awake, provide a model for the coursing of these ruins of the stars. Only pay attention.

I coursed beneath the streaming light-filled waters of that region, Herman white and storming behind me, the woman roaring atop my back, and I saw ahead a spectral storm. Like a ball of hair, or a nest of electricity; a cluster of neurons. Self-similar and glowing, it sparked there in the deep, brighter than the sun.

Could the human brain be more complex than the sun? The sun is simple and profound, like the birth canal, the beginning of it all, but the brain in all its fractal wonder relies on its self-similarity to compare, to mirror in its mirror neurons, the fatal fluted shape of worlds built inside out of dreams.

You think it only metaphor, a poet's license, but you see, who is it grants this license? Traditionally, the license was granted by the gods, and so I serve them, perhaps, in my tale their strange urgencies are enforced and weighed and carried out and copied into your loving gray matter, stratum by loyal stratum—

I swam into the loamy breath of the neuronal spiraled ball of hair, the glowing nest, the web like the web of galactic super-structures, fractal down to the smallest vesicle, written in something both harder and more flexible than stone, dark matter if you like, the crepuscular territories we swim between with every breath—

"What are you doing, whale! You've gone insane!"

I've gone inside, woman.

I laughed, madder than Herman, madder than the sun.

I enclasp the sea—

I conquer the sea—

I am a white whale—

(Soad, wake up, we're through! We're through, goddamn it!)

Not wormhole only but worm logic, the five hearts beating the brown blood of time—

"No, you stupid whale!" the woman shouts atop my back.

But now, I am in two places at once, or perhaps a thousand.

Rasna, O Rasna, you beautiful beardless Etruscans, you're like a wife to me. As I spin beneath the waves.

(And part of me is waking up, waking up on Earth, and vomiting fluid out of my lungs)

And part of me—part of me is still there, still here, a woman on my back, in a sea I named Kaen, gritting my whale teeth and singing my whale poem as the fibers of the netted nerves swim deeper into my brain, programming me, burying me—

(I really need a nap).

I'm vomiting. All over the fresco. My sister is smiling. We've done it. Outside, I can see the sky. For the first time.

And I sing a whale song:

Ayyy y nah ayy ye naahh ren mrii kerr ee!
And inside the Redoubt, everyone is laughing.

Earth, again

The sun ignited. A new sun, hotter than its predecessor, busily turns its hydrogen into helium.

I awake in my room, looking out at the sky through my porthole. Where were the monstrosities that had obstructed our launch into orbit, the Visitors? The sky outside is blue, not its usual dark purple. I can't even see the daylight stars.

I get out of my bed and put on my clothes, splashing water on my face and into my hair. I step into the corridor. A huge gash in the wall greets me, from the last battle my sister and I and all those of our Level fought against the revolutionaries, those who would have invited the abhumans on inside to eat us. Next to the gash, small robots supervised by a little person are working on a repair. They wave at me.

I walk to the elevator, which opens when I approach it. Stepping inside, I say, "Six hundred," and it rises.

It's like a dream. I have lived my whole life--my ancestors' ancestors' have lived their whole lives--in darkness and artificial light.

Where are the security threats? Are all the abhumans dead?

*   *   *

My sister is sitting on the balcony on Level 600, programming some winged drones, their joints creaking as she flexes them and applies patches to their software. A force field shimmers slightly, covering the balcony, shielding it from the world below.

"Weel," I say, and she holds up a finger, for me to wait, and I do, looking over the edge of the balcony on a new world.

Not all the abhuman life is dead; it is adapting, even as I watch. But much of it cannot take the solar radiation and is either black and desiccated, or quickly turning into a stinky soup. In the distance I see smoke. The heavens are all blue. There are no Visitors with their Teeth. I feel like crying.

She finishes, and shoos the metal pigeons through the force field. They fall and flap their wings and take to the air, flying west, towards the rising sun.

I can see a storm coming from the north. A dust bowl is kicking up, decayed micro-matter from the newly abhuman dead, a kind of soil.

We embrace. My sister is so slim; she's lost weight.

"Weel," I say, but she puts her finger to my lips and points south, and I look.

At first I think it's an army. But then I realize: they're supplicants. The abhuman survivors. They are come not as attackers but as neighbors, like fearful peasants, seeking shelter from a storm they do not understand. The Night Lands are gone.

"Are they armed?" I ask.

"A lot of their weapons don't work in the light," Weel says.

They are dancing, some of them in death, their many eyes quivering and shaking, iridescent flesh seeking to coordinate with dark essences in orbit that are no longer visible--

I see the shuffling abhuman forms like a soup line, rhythmic, the final dance of an empire unexpectedly gone nuclear.

What are the movements of the end of an era? I wish you could see them with me, ancestor.

They move in counterpoint, their thousand limbs displaying densities and rhythms I have never seen, as they are processed by what appear to be a brave new cadre of customs agents on Level Two. The abhuman move through the scanners, some of them exploding as they do so, containing unacceptable levels of innate poisons, explosives, bacteriologically active organs or organ projectiles.

The custom dance and the custom of customs merge in this terminal Noah's Ark shuffle, and I see one thin orange *reydnekhkya* spin its head and stretch its limbs out towards the sky—and do I see an answering orange spark somewhere off in the blue? The movements of this herd are hypnotic.

"We really did it?" I ask. My sister looks at me, with her dark eyes, and something fidgets in the back of my brain ... something I forgot ... something I need to remember—

"Have you eaten?" she says, and we go back to the elevator, and take it to the dining levels.

"Solar arrays we completely forgot about have come online; old computer systems ... weapons technologies ... some of them were hidden in the goddamned walls! They've been waiting for sunlight for two million years ..."

"How long have you been awake?" I ask.

But she doesn't answer as we step into the dining commons. It's a madhouse, but it has a feeling I've never felt before inside the Redoubt: happiness. The sun has returned.

The abhuman

Our environment is exterminated and we ask for shelter; please, please: preserve us in your zoos. Won't you take us in? Won't you take us in and feed us? We ask this in the name of our descendants. We know that they will be weak and no longer wild but some of their spirit will be maintained, if only you will take them in. This flood of light is your doing, we know; you have won, and we are no more. But please, won't you save my son? He does not know what it is that's happening.

We came out of the dark; it was a miracle, but dangerous. I know we were prideful, we were hungry, we wanted to replicate in your dimension what we had known in ours, and what is wrong with that? Isn't that what colonization is?

My son is dying. Take him inside, please?

Soad

▌▌▌▌▌▌▌▌▌▌ Later, I run a database query on "Etruscans." The Rasna.

The Etruscans, the tower-builders, they had a strong religion, according to the databases, one based in part on divination. The shape of lightning and the places where it struck were of interest to Etruscan divines, believing that these were signs of the gods' will. Scholars later named this practice astrapomancy. I'm reading the data and as I do I feel part of myself drift up, I feel light, I feel some connection with these uncountably ancient peoples of First Earth. They were slow. The Etruscan language, an isolate, agglutinative, was slow too, slow to change, it was like a glue, a mortar, for their walls.

I've gone too fast; I know it. I need to understand. What has happened? What do I do now? What did I forget?

It was *who*. It was the *who* that the Etruscans sought, that was it, they saw the problem long ago of the conquistador, that was why they were so slow, because they feared the coming of their own divine powers, they feared the coming of modernity.

So they went slowly, in fear of what they might become, slow enough for the Romans, the barbarians on the edge of their empire, to take them over.

This *who*, that is the *qui* in conquistador, the ultimate question, where do I end and you begin, just as the Etruscans had to have begun to doubt where their religion stopped and their empire began. And this is something I have to answer now, because I feel that I left part of me behind—

"Soad?"

"Yes." She is standing in the doorway, distracted. She looks at me, looks away, then back again.

"Come down to Level Four with me. I want you to see something." I stand and follow her.

She brings me to a room where there are children playing with abhuman children. I instinctively draw back but she beckons me closer.

From the door, I see him: a man, with three eyes. I know him. My sister puts her hand on my arm. I am going to cry out; no, I say nothing. He is my brother. He looks at me, with two eyes, the third eye watching the abhuman child, and I see, this little being is my nephew.

The man my brother goes to his child, kneeling, watching him play, still watching me too. I cannot speak.

"He is your brother, Soad."

"I know," I say. I walk towards him, stepping between the children playing.

My brother speaks; I know his voice.

"We're not dying like we say, Soad. You're Soad, aren't you?"

"Yes," I answer, without thinking.

"We're very much alive. I hope your security measures are still in place?"

"I'm sure they are. I don't know ... I ..."

"It was you who brought the new sun. You, and your sister."

"Yes. I believe so. That is what she says. In any case, it is a miracle."

"Yes, though not all of us are smiling, Soad."

"What would you have me do, brother?"

"You call me brother?" His eyes are dark.

"Yes."

"Will you eat with me? You won't find it disgusting to eat with an abhuman?"

"Of course I'll eat with you. You, and ... your son."

* * *

We eat in the dining hall, though not without a fair number of un-friendly looks. I cannot take my eyes off my nephew, and his three eyes.

"There are so many of us," says my brother. "That is what you do not understand. The sun has blinded you. The light has blinded you! We are so many! And now, we hardly know what to do! Some of us prepared for this, but, it's like we're going back in time, I can't explain it—"

"Where is his mother?" I ask.

Abhuman, Salwat

▌▌▌▌▌▌▌▌▌ Mutation as a storm wherein we dream: our undoing, our remaking, recombinatorial surprise, meeting each the other's eyes, as we wind between the remnants of our fats, to sweep beneath the stars our legacies and glowing orbits of our last goodbyes:

We change, we rearrange, we claim the right to know which where we are, the hurry and the flurry of our ghosts, the holy host, the best and yet the least of all of ours, we the abhuman. We the mutants and the freaks, we the tenebrous delight, we the stormy gladness in your soul, we the weathered bowl that just won't quit, no matter our asymmetry and funny colors.

This the Earth was made, by Cronus, and this our will is manifest in every tooth; we're sharpening ...

* * *

I rest aching underneath the sky, its horror the light. My children are dead. I watch the colors storm over the music of my eyes, over the death, my own soon, I watch this chaos murk and whirl inside my brain.

What is it that is so beautiful about destruction? Is it only that beauty itself is a kind of destruction? Such violence in it.

My limbs clutch the ruin of our temple, we were worshippers of the dark *Enzegnee*, but we are no more. Thrust out into the light, thrust like an actor off of the stage.

Some people are still alive in this horrifying light. How can they stand it? How can they stand to see so much? The eye is a lie! How can they think at all?

I trudge out of the shelter of the dead temple and move into the expanse, my winding limbs displayed, as though for courtship; I shall court this horrifying sun.

* * *

I move over the ocean of my mind. My name is Salwat. I just remembered that. Have you been here before? I am in the Night Lands, aren't I? Am I not at home?

No. No. No I am not at home. I am not at home. I am not at home. I am not at home because home does not exist. Have you seen these things? These colors in the sky? The patterns I once knew are gone; my family, gone.

I am alive. What does this mean? How can I survive? Tell me, what does it mean?

All my dead people.
I will cut you, I will eat your heart—

*   *   *

The Pyramid; the Great Eye. Now it is a shelter. Let me get out of the light! It is the Redoubt but remember that you added in the 'b' because of your own fear, you English, you added in the 'b' because you feared that even in your sanctuary you would be destroyed!

For there is shelter for you no longer! Didn't you think we could have killed you a thousand times over?

You, give me shelter?

Give ME shelter?

I will take the word and throw it out into the sky; see what you make of all our eyes. When they open down upon you.

Soad

⁙⁙⁙⁙⁙ "Something is happening," says Weel, running to the porthole.

"What is it?" I ask, and then I look.

They are covering the sky. Their bodies are masks. I don't know how I know that but I do. They're moving fast.

"Get the guns!" my sister screams, her face suddenly a rictus and she runs for the alarm, slamming her palm into it, and the lights go out. Like I was trained as a boy I go to the corner of the room and gather the infra-red eyes and put them on; my sister is screaming into her microphone. I am loading my rifle.

I go into the corridor, stepping out of the way of my fellow soldiers, running by me, my brothers in war, one grabs my shoulder to bring me with them but then I see my true brother, I see him and my nephew standing at the end of the corridor, their tentacles slipping out of their backs, unnoticed. I go over to them.

"Brother," I say.

"Soad," he says. The boy's eyes are filled with rainbows.

* * *

From the Sixth Planet, Watching:

⁙⁙⁙⁙⁙ Out of every retreat, a blow. Inside every bunker, a door. Under every helmet, a bullet. Moving, moving under sun the earth is fun but when you're done; oh, when you're done:

I am Cronus and I like my toys to play nice.

* * *

Abhuman, Salwat

⁙⁙⁙⁙⁙ And I'll fuck your eye and I'll fuck your eye and I'll fuck your eye and I'll fuck your eye the wine divine is right on time and so I know that you are mine when I stick my dagger in your chiming whining rhyming mouth—

It's not as good as it was before but it is, it is, it is, we can survive—

BOOK THREE:
THE END

What is an invasion? If *conquistador* is the who who asks the question with another, the invader is simply one who goes in. To walk in. In + *vadere*.

Will you go in, invader? With or without your questions. In company, or quite alone.

Who are you? Once you're in? Did you go inside? Into the temple/ tomb/ castle/ tower/ field/ grave/ hut/ forest/ water/ woman/ earth?

Will you go in?

*   *   *

I thought this story would be easier; I thought I could make good sense of it for you, but my goal is now more modest. I can only record. I understand now, I am your recorder. Though this language that I use is inadequate. However this may end, know that I am still transmitting. Know that this record is authentic, and know that I have made it as accurate as I could.

Of the battle then:

*   *   *

They came without warning. Always in the millennia before we had had some warning, however small, but the truth was we had stopped watching. We were drunk on the light; and we believed them dead.

*   *   *

They tortured us for hours with their eyes. We would have fallen asleep, if only for a moment, and then an eye would *jerk* inside the walls, again and again into our shrinking territory, and we would fire, delirious, for a while we were deliberately turning all our guns off before we slept, simply so that we would not blow each other to bits when the next eye came and forced us awake, dripping, shoving its mass through the wall, and making its horrendous sounds.

You'd say, some must have gone mad, but not quite. It is not my place to dispense my opinions on sanity; I have no objective position from which to observe it. Better to say that we were frightened; there can be no doubt of that.

*   *   *

They found me. Salwat found me.

Sometimes, you see, you think you're waking up. But you're not. And sometimes, you think you're asleep, but you're not. Now I am beginning to believe that these borderlands, these crepuscular territories, that mark the line of division, they are free will itself. They are the freeest countries there are, and the most terrifying.

Do you know how terrifying freedom is? Have you ever been cast out? Have you ever been lost? Freedom from responsibility, from accountability, from tradition, from history. Such enormous freedom is right on the bleeding edge of nightmare, right on the whispered edge of paradise.

Their hands went into me, into my body, the Night Lands wrenched itself into my body, and Salwat looked into my face with his dark, widening eyes. I was far away, but I KNEW, I KNEW THEN that I had been right.

Because it is these crepuscular territories, the meridian, the edge that cuts, it is here in the Freezone, in the Interzone, where lawlessness reigns, it is here that all laws are made.

And it is here that I found the truth of my world, and of my family, when I lost my humanity at last, like sloughing off a skin.

Before, I was pupa. Now I grow wings. I am a moth. Fluttering towards your light.

*   *   *

Only a small change, you would say, and you'd be right. One small change leading to others.

Is it a dream? This is the question you must answer for yourself. When you see the marks transfer over from sleep to waking, when you surmise that there is this deeper continuity between your night and day worlds, your ocean of sleep and your island of waking, this link is real. You see, the answer in the end is that it does not matter, because you can be free in dream or a slave in waking, or a slave in dream and free in waking, or both. Is this a liberation?

I told you to hold on tight, because we're inside a dream. I might as well as have said, we're inside a wake. And I need you. It is with you, my love, my lost future love, you who know the ending, you are who I need as my adjutant in these morasses. I need you to hold the compass while I hold the pen; for I would map for us.

And in so doing, change the universe.

*   *   *

They came inside me as the whale, or I came inside them. They came inside me as the man. You could say I'm like a mushroom now, and in truth, I do tend to grow tendrils if I don't stay active. My new body always wants to send out shoots.

I am something else. Abhuman. Soad, Woad, now something new.

I can fly; and not only in the sky.

Why did we want the sun, when we could have had a deeper darkness? Perhaps so we could appreciate what it was that we had had.

I know, I am a monster now. But was I any less monstrous before?

*   *   *

Consider that your body is many *whos*. An interdependence and *e pluribus unum* of legs, arms, liver, heart, brain, muscles, nerves and blood. Would you map yourself? Do not wait to be a cadaver to have the medical student do it for you; no, do it while you are alive, and without a knife, only *concentrate* ...

Would you eat of my body?

Would you come into *Eklaihah?* (For we are all waiting for the ruin...)

I am in the tower on Level Seven Thousand, my moth tendrils flowing in the divine sunlight of our New Sun but my mind is splitting, and I make my new *mes* to chart these terrible beautiful waters. Adjutant, align your compass!

Each organ is a story ...

Nextspace, redux

▌▌▌▌▌▌▌▌▌ I know, this has been difficult for you. But think how it has been for me.

* * *

Captain Maug

▌▌▌▌▌▌▌▌▌ I sing the body, electric dipped into the bath of the White in Next Space.

My hair stands on end. My wife is screaming without sound, her skin white and her eyes bloodshot, the bridge is filled with white light and hot static.

And then slow, it passes. Like a wave, rolling over the ship, we dip into its wake, into an eddy, gasping.

"What was that?" I say, barely able to breathe. But we already know. The psychic feeling, the low suspicion, the touch on the edge of your tongue, the taste—the knowledge, that *feeling* is in the air and though we trained for it, now I know we won't come back, not until we've gone through.

"Do we chart a course for orbit, captain?" my wife says, her eyes a little wide.

I collapse into my chair.

"I need a drink," I say.

Andrew brings it for me, bless him; I hold it in my hand and stare at the screen, at the black orb twisting in white.

"Let's get it over with."

"Aye, captain," says Andrew, returning to his seat, and we move, we move deeper into this sea.

The white light feels right next to my face, an alien lover. It whispers messages against my skin; we don't even need the psychic shielding now. We're part of its mind. The white moves, almost imperceptibly, like vodka spinning into water, the dark plasma of this star spins into the milk of Nextspace and blends. Thin runnels from that dark kernel skim over the eddies in the white, some blinking back into dimensions unseen, others curling towards us like the petals of a ripening flower.

I sip my drink. The chair bites into my back.

"How is the ship?" asks my wife.

Andrew touches the contact orb, feeling for the overall health of our baby, while he watches readouts. "The hull is fine, sir."

I put my drink down.

"Fire the cannons," I say, and Andrew gives me a look but he obeys me and the ship shudders a little as we fire three rounds out into the un-earthly plasma fluid, hot violet light twisting into invisible shades, our rainbow weapon.

I am beginning to understand why we have survived this long; it was my education. The Jesuits taught me well. Of course, they were the storm troopers for the Pope in the long ago time, and then their learning was the same, it was the weapon that they used for God. So I am pioneer, which means "pawn."

I am their weapon, though for a god of our own devising, a god we are devising now. I am a pawn but I can be made into a queen.

The cannon rounds twist toward the sun, tilting into its gravity, colors fluctuating like a diseased heart. The sun swallows them and the static is back, rushing through the cabin. My wife sneezes and I feel tight in my chest; but then it's past.

"Take this away from me," I say, handing my wife my drink, and she sips from it, hurriedly, and tosses it into the disposal.

"Hurry this up," she says, and Andrew fires the engines.

* * *

There is something wrong with the heat. We're sweating and I wander the halls, chatting with the crew, watching their eyes, hearing their buzzing thoughts, the white darkness thick outside the hull, an egg. We move through the fluid of Nextspace, wandering and patting one another on the back, nomads in space, holding our strange dream: discovery. To cry out at sight of the valley of paradise.

I make love to Madeleine. I lie beside her and murmur into her ear stories of my childhood. Outside the porthole, distant black suns sparkle in whiteness, sending sparks of coal through the void.

Is it wrong that I enjoy this doubt? In this abyss, there is a kind of peace.

Still we grow hotter. My wife and our chief technician, Brenny, tinker with the air conditioning for hours and I sip my drink, telling jokes to the crew. We know each other well enough they don't feel obligated to laugh; they joke better than I do.

The black sun fills our screen. We seem to be on what I can only call an asymptotic approach: whatever our readings, our engine output, our approach keeps slowing.

It blooms for us, this sun, and though I suspect we will suffer the same fate as our predecessors, I no longer fear it.

We say little now. No one wants to speak because there are too many questions. Our jokes have grown less funny so we sit and watch and wait, exercising, having sex, eating, cooking, watching the movies we've seen a dozen times now, fighting to win this peculiar endurance race.

The pioneer knows that even if you return, you don't return. You are not the same. The horizon, being bigger than you, swallows you whole, and makes you its.

"Pork chops tomorrow," Madeleine says.

* * *

The women have changed; I believe we're a week in to it now. Madeleine and her ship-sisters are fighting the lullaby of this dark light. They resist its music. We men no longer do; I see that now. We are willingly hypnotized, like a cat at a flicking tail, a bachelor seeing a woman slip off her clothes, the sun's dark circle expands into our mind and we grin beneath its immense dusk. The women keep busy. They are impatient for us to pass through, to be swallowed, to know what this beast intends.

* * *

Andrew said to me today, "We should turn back." I wasn't quite sure what he meant. The black sun fills all of us.

To turn back, I saw later, meant survival on the terms Andrew had known before, but we have different terms now. We survive together with the black sun. Without it, we can no longer exist.

My wife was crying today. I tried to comfort her but I could do nothing.

The black sun is beautiful. Its edges are red, and inside its heart I hear music. Its music is subtle, but sometimes we dance to it. I made love to Juliana, I should not have, perhaps, but I feel it is Lunar Festival, where morality is different, an aspect of the larger environment.

I feel I should name the sun. I feel that I, the captain, should name it. But I know it must have many names. And how could I decide on just one?

Our journey to it is the name I give it; can a journey be a name? Our journey will be its name. Is a name an action? Is an action a name? Who speaks us here, in this lost space? I open my mouth:

Maug. Captain. You've come.

Yes.

I am dancing.

"Maug!"

I turn and my wife is standing on the bridge, like a madwoman. Her hair in disarray, her eyes wide.

"Maug! Get us out of here!"

Something in her eyes reminds me. I *am* the captain, she is right.

"Andrew. How close are we to the sun?"

Andrew turns his face slowly away from the main display, sucking on sugar water through a straw, a little glazed.

"Captain. I don't ... I don't know, captain. Let me see."

He looks at the instruments.

"I can't say exactly, captain, but my guess is, we're already inside it. That's what these data suggest."

My wife screams. I clutch her to my chest.

"Shhh. Shhh. Come back to our cabin."

*   *   *

I lie in bed while she sleeps, examining the ship's log. If we ever see Earth again, will they be satisfied with these discoveries? We've explained nothing. We've learned nothing either, but we've experienced a great deal. Perhaps that would be enough for them. Of course I do not do it for them. Now I know that I have been given this secret, that it has been revealed to me. It is mine to use.

Flames

▌▌▌▌▌▌▌▌▌▌ The Unity Six lurched slow into a deeper eddy of the expanding black sun. Its external instruments, delicate looking but sturdy little filaments, seemed to slip away within the darkness; a godlike observer might have seen Unity as a golf ball sinking slowly into a thick, viscous pool of ink.

Of course, no observer, not even a god, could observe them here, beyond the event horizon.

The pioneers acted in the name of a distant king. They could not in fact receive word from his distant palace. Inside the desert, all gods and all observers were silent, having passed the event horizon of the frontier.

Maug cried and danced, and his crew pored over religious ecstasy and terror, bumping against one another in the narrow hallways and access hatches, late for duty.

Many routine maintenances were now being done on their own, as though by the sun. They were somewhat fetal now, slipping into the dark uterine fluid, awaiting the attachment of an unearthly umbilicus, something they could feel but could not yet see. Somewhere inside the mind it waited.

The pioneer who goes West goes Down, for west means down, and in going down, like going down from University, you return amongst the people from the celebrated heights of high table down to the desert and its wisdoms.

Maug held Madeleine, watching the darkness take on a new character, a shifting surface covered with fine interwoven lines, like an etching, or a maze, a circuit board. The patterns flew over the surfaces of the deepening sun too fast to trace; they promised something.

The hypnotic all-consuming white was almost gone; it had been reduced to a small orb in the distance, a window on their past. The crew of Unity Six swirled down, down into their future, down into the West, down into the basement of our multigenerational living heart that beats throughout our curving universe—

Horror, too, awaited them. Horror is an act, really, it comes from the root word for shudder. It is something the body does when faced with the incomprehensible, or the divine.

Immensity is, of course, both beautiful and terrifying, which perhaps are only two halves of the same thing. And for a time Maug and his crew lapsed into a slow horror: a tightening of the throat, a widening of the eyes.

The darkness had not spoken aloud for some time; they had almost forgotten its first greeting. But it spoke in other ways. It moved through the communal river, and in this fluid the Door moved its words, the

Door that was this dark star made preparation for its traveler's passage.

The conscious star-doors of Nextspace abut and abank another sphere, and it is best that I say nothing of them, other than it is through their bodies that we move, when we leap through such gates as these, like Gilgamesh, transmitted bodily through a singularity at the heart of a gravity well designed to leave a mark inside the soul, like a scar on a veteran's face, the intimation of the beyond, the spook that crooks inside the heart, a feeling all dreamers know:

Unity Six, on approaching this dark singularity, burst into a cold flame, one that did not burn only flesh, but time.

Maug found himself shouting, as his bridge was consumed with colors and pictures beyond his understanding:

He shouted words he would never remember.

His wife clutched his trembling frame, but it was as though he did not feel her.

He shouted into the dark:

"I'm burning!"

Sometimes I think they're still burning.

Maug lost consciousness, but Madeleine looked out into the darkness and saw the umbilicus attach itself to their hull. And then they were all asleep, in a dreamless well, far away.

*　*　*

What I tell you now of Maug, I record out of respect for him, and his achievements. Some say he became a worse man having braved those fires in Nextspace, that the fires saw inside him his sins, and weakness, and took advantage.

Maug had killed a woman many years before. On his home planet.

Were Maug's past sins the reason that the Dark Star marked his spirit the deepest? Did it see in his heart some mirror of its own twisted destiny? Whatever the reason, Maug changed.

Yes, long ago Maug had killed, and in the logic of that tale, there is at least some of the course of Maug's future.

Yet I forget, too, that you already know so much more than me. You know how this story ends, perhaps even many of its endings. I am learning to accept that. You already know this story and I will honor it, I promise. I promise.

Is this the version you remember? Perhaps the one I tell here is different. I cannot tell in how many directions this is transmitting.

Love, like an earthworm, has five hearts, and one of them is violence.

BOOK FOUR:
LESSONS

I do not believe in predestination, but I believe in mysticism, which is only to say that I love mysteries, and there's always a mystery, isn't there? Somewhere; everywhere.

Maug, our cowboy in our Wild West, had like many cowboys come to Nextspace to escape his past, hoping that in the darkness of space like the simplicity of the desert he could find a new name and a new home.

And to an extent Maug had succeeded. But the past wouldn't leave him alone. Like leptons shooting past us from the future, the past keeps sending messengers forward into the present, reminding us that it isn't over yet ...

*   *   *

Maug, 12 years earlier

He had been convicted easily; the brain scanner did not lie, and he had even volunteered to confess. He was sentenced to hard labor in the asteroid belt.

Occasionally politicians make noises about the soft treatment this or that government is giving to its prisoners, currying favor with the "hard liners," none of whom, of course, have ever been behind bars.

These politicians forget that the hardest thing is simply to lose your freedom; no matter how comfortable the cell, it is still a cell. And only on regaining that freedom does one truly appreciate how precious a thing it is.

Maug worked. He kept to himself. The night of space was both frightening and comforting; the aloneness. He followed orders. He broke the asteroids apart and fit the pieces into the processors. He worked mostly alone. At the end of a shift he ate in the floating prison and was given drugs and slept. At first he hated the drugs but he grew accustomed to them. After a while he felt he needed them; they helped him not to think about his future, and to focus on the work at hand, which after all was what these drugs were designed to do.

He served four years; he was a model prisoner.

The family of the young woman he had killed had spent a fortune trying to revive her; brain copies, deep resuscitative therapy, mystical rites, but she was dead.

And Maug was glad she was dead. And the brain scanners knew it.

Remorse is a complicated phenomenon; it is most often, and perhaps by its nature, fleeting. Most penitentiaries are looking, after all, for penitence, but it need only come once, for a brief time. But that time needs to be right.

For a time Maug saw a counselor. For an hour, they would talk, about nothing, it seemed. The brain scanner knew Maug was not repentant. Why did he need to waste this time with this shrink? But he went; he was obedient.

"Why did you kill her, Maug?"

The shrink lay back on his couch, smoking a hookah. Maug sat in the chair, in restraints, though they weren't really necessary. He couldn't care less what the shrink thought, or did. The shrink's name was, improbably, Houdini. He glared at Maug through the haze of the hookah smoke.

"Why didn't you just take another lover? A younger, more desirable one?"

"I loved her, Houdini."

"Love is a group phenomenon, Maug; it is something whole nations share! How romantic of you to confine it to only you and your *inamorata*! Did you believe that she would remain faithful to you?"

"Yes," said Maug, gritting his teeth, "that is what I believed."

*   *   *

He always answered the questions. Just as he always swallowed the drug, when they moved him after a time from injection to oral capsules. He wanted to get out of prison.

*   *   *

And then, one day, he did.

Maug, 8 years earlier

Maug moves into orbit, his suit no longer the property of the government, but his only possession, the jets red and white in the darkness, moving towards the station spinning outside Europa.

Europa, which etymologically, means West. As Asia means East. (And west means down and east means shine; we're shining down—

He docks, and smells the perfumes, spices, the mud, and the smell of tight kept humans in Europa Station. Apes in the cave, trading, and waiting for their destiny to grab them by the throat and say, "You got me."

Like the Las Vegas of the pre-war generations, when electricity was cheap, Europa Station promises many rewards but offers few—the one thing it does offer in abundance is dancing, and people, and trade. Not always in that order.

He takes a ticket from the busboy to reserve his berth for his man-sized spacesuit-ship, and follows the glowing yellow lines to the club.

* * *

Dancing is five thousand watts.

Lit inside the dungeon in the starlit night:

Like age old monks chanting in the vestibules to keep this meeting holy,

The waiting din inside the club:

(where all comers get a chance, admission is a melody:

Maug dances. The dancers spill their sequins into the light, and the dogs yap, and the child cries in the corner, for his nursemaid, culture and custom and commerce cut slow into the room, a thousand lights, a thousand destinations. Maug is free.

Freedom, the word known to all men, smaller than the quark, the scariest and most beautiful thing there is—it was Maug's again, paradise regained, the right to accept limits on your terms. For that is what a bondsman is.

Across the room he sees her.

Maug feels a shade in the light (or is it later, remembering?), when he sees her he knows he'll lose her, and he needs her worse than he needs water, worse than he needs love, he needs her body, and her smile. Even her teeth he needs.

The dog barks in tune to the beat, live and loving the attention. They give it a place of honor next to the turntables, as the zero-G band spins in the artificial gravity well next to the stage, spinning out live renditions of 20th century jazz.

The shape of an evening is like the shape of a moment: curved and interwoven with a trillion others. Maug puts a hand against her waist to feel her curve away, a galaxy entire, nameless. She takes off her shirt as the evening stars to thrum and things become more formal as a consequence, for the visiting nobility exacts its art, stemming outward from a secret stage like the Medici, draped in vermillion and gold, they chime their voices as they pose their bodies, in a kind of modern Greek chorus, while the throng watches, grinning:

"Light, here--
Light here--
And Light here--
The sun--
Light here--
The sun—"

The beat gets louder and the formality completed it's a madhouse and the steam and heat is too much for Maug, so much sex in the air it scares his prisoner's brain, and he takes her hand into a booth to wait out the orgy, ordering some sugar drinks, they stare into each other's eyes.

Maug relearns the language of freedom from her lips.

*   *   *

He takes her upstairs, through the gold, and she pays for the room. There is wine and a fog machine. She laughs as he turns it on and is hidden in green smoke.

"What did you know before?" He asks.

Btu she doesn't know.

*   *   *

She is too beautiful for words.

*   *   *

It is a Vegas-style wedding, deliberately outré, honoring their local Medici traditions. It is performed without words, with a monkey for the officiant, the holy monkey which symbolizes the deeply delimited arc of human knowledge, and the absurdity of desire. They embrace nude and are covered in flowers, and the chorus chants, in Latin and in Hindi:

Bailiwick,
House bound:
Tale torn out around!
Newly wedded lovers,

Newly burned and newly true to this yourselves,
We are swayed to serve the deeper you in you,
To wait out all this light and make our love endure,
Under our stars—

* * *

Europa is accustomed to heady love stories, and Maug and his bride ship out on the first scoutship to our local brown dwarf, 0.3 astronomical units distant, as indentured servants—

* * *

Conquering is asking. What for? And who when? Why me?
Military discipline and hurried kisses in the dark.
And why? And why? And why, God? He's trying to figure it out too.

* * *

Outside the brown dwarf is when things get interesting. It's when Maug signs a contract. It's when his wife gets pregnant. And it's when they sign up for their first exploration ship.

* * *

In truth, Maug should have known better. Because what he did almost got him locked up again.

* * *

He knows that she will die. Somewhere deep inside. Inside the vessel inside the no-space of the transition, wavering between realities their bond does not waver, it lives inside Maug and Madeleine.

Madeleine holds tight onto her chair, strapped in tight, in the nowhere light, she calls out:

"Maug!"

"Yes."

And he is there and she is there and the Unity Six is there, borne through from Nextspace into our space. From that which was theirs into that which is ours: the future.

I cry this tale out from my station; I who feel as though I've lived so many lives. We await word from you, still. We await! Tell us, did Maug make it out? When he left us and returned to you?

*   *   *

Husband literally means house bound: the bondsman who accepts his agricultural fate and takes his wife. And as he carries his wife across the threshold (perhaps so that she will not be charmed by the spirit of the door as he is?), so too did the Gate carry Maug and all of his through the Dark Sun and into the place where Soad encountered him.

But my question was about lessons: how much of Maug's past determined his future? Though it might be said it is as unanswerable a question as nature versus nurture, genes versus environment, it is in the weighing of these grams of influence that we determine character.

Maug came from a much younger culture, one with only the beginnings of a conception of the weight of age, the compromises that age invites us to make, and eventually forces on us. Earth at the beginning of the interstellar age was still raw; it still had room for outlaws and room for innocence.

We are not innocent here in The Night Lands; we are not blameless. We made our bed and here we have lain for millennia, tossing and turning and growing old. But in our habits there is wisdom: we know what to do with youth when we find it.

*   *   *

Maug remembered the taste of Maddy's lips that night in the club as he and the Unity Six emerged into the light. Love is a transition.

west, into the wild. I did not know what I would find. I did not think that I would be made white.

I am a whale; your cousin. Long ago we climbed onto the rocks, gasping in the poisons, through the firewall, the bloody meniscus of the water surface. Whole new categories of reality burst in upon our dying brains (and we were dying all right, dying in droves! We needed an escape!) Escape is so hard. Out of the frying pan and into the fire; try to evolve some asbestos skin, eh? Do your science in your hand, trace your heart line with your amphibian brain and groove on the Gnostic starstuff streaming down onto your face, something you ain't never seen before, ain't no one ever seen before, and never seen again; the stars of that old watery age, burning in that night we came out of the sea.

We came out the sea together! Bravest brothers and enemies and cousins urgent and howling, bleeding from our fish scales, and from our growing legs.

Out of that watery meniscus into light; out of the womb and into the world.

But we, we went back. We went back, we are whales.

Like the Jews who never left for Babylon, and hence are not called Jews, as they were never captives. Like them, we had an atavistic urge, a longing for the womb, not the Fertile Crescent but the Mother Ocean, salted blood-warm water, back into that world with a brand new set of lungs.

Yes, you know the back story. But you do not know what we uncovered. Some of those old Jews, stubborn as hell, they gleaned themselves secrets and set to scribbling them down onto parchment, even as we were debating them across the many stormy leagues, pod to pod, mother to son, lover to lover.

Where does this universe propend? What destiny enfolds us? We have been making discoveries.

Whale Science. Like *Weird Science* without the blue electricity; also we have bigger penises.

Let me tell you something: you made the wrong decision, Man! You sold away the ocean! You sold your own mother into slavery! You must get her back, Aeneas, you have dropped your father on the roadside and you are barely out of Troy! Feel my thunder as I speak the truth:

You die to hear this truth, human being, that your mother this the sea is turning from you, turning now away, even as you sold her, in that fatal conspiring turn, you sold her all away. Some alien appetite? Some overpowering invasive force! No, only a trade, it's always a trade, they give you plenty of time to decide.

And you decided! It was *jetzt oder nicht*, now or never! And you chose *never* ...

Soad, the present

I am stateless now. In ancient times, a city was a state; in my time, a planet is.

I am a stateless person. I am a non-state actor. I am, perhaps, a terrorist.

State is a curious word, meaning in part both "government" and "present condition."

You see, I lack both a government and a present. I exist both in the future and the past, but in this now, I am barely here. I am stateless, like a captain without a ship.

I have no planet and no government. But I have a language and a culture; I have my memories.

Is the present condition, the *state* of a city or a planet, also somehow stateless? Does the real nature of a people exist somewhere outside of the now, in the future and the past, colliding in this present, a *now* that has no real government and no real identity?

Perhaps these are meaningless questions.

Now you can call me collaborator; I assist the abhuman oligarchs in their rule of this Third Earth because, what else can I do? The home I knew is gone. And I am dead inside.

I am stateless but I am collaborator. I am conquistador but also a native. I ask the question, with you: *who are we now?*

My name is Soad; I am a human being. But I am growing alien.

BOOK FIVE:
INSIDE THE CASTLE

A prisoner is being brought to me for interrogation. Sealed within, we can finally get to know one another.

My name is Salwat. I appear bipedal, so as to associate more freely with the human aborigines; with you.

The Redoubt, the Castle, has been expanded. The word *castle* is related to the word *caste*, in the sense of "cut off."

The stronger your wall, the more perfect your seal, the more hermetic your universe, the more your power increases and the more the pressure builds—

In that sense the Redoubt is both the perfect prison and the perfect embassy: we have no choice but to learn about each other.

I know your kind reckoned time by the solar or lunar year. We reckon time by the cyclings of dark matter, which are not regular at all ...

Though your moon is long gone, since you brought back that hated star to this region of space there had been some talk of continuing the use of your archaic calendar.

I am a terrorist. I made a decision, not too long ago, to change my allegiance. I fight for humans. Though I hate you.

*   *   *

I like to sit here, by the porthole at Level Eight Thousand, fifteen miles above the surface of our metal Earth, staring into the high atmosphere.

I am a bureaucrat. I sit at my desk.

What is the connection between writing and ruling? Ruling is about straightness, that is its Latin root, just as a ruler made of wood is straight, so is a ruler made of flesh. In this straightness the desire for hereditary power is expressed: however the order of its inheritance, it should go forward, ideally, without interruption.

So it might be said that writing, being composed of a series of lines (only some of them straight), in a (only somewhat) orderly grammar, endeavors in part to service this desire of the ruling class, to keep on going, to perpetuate itself, even as written documents outlive human speakers. But it is important to remember that writing is composed of curves as well as straights, and it is this part of written language that outwits the desire of power to control it, even as the curve of the Earth and curve of evolution ensures that no life form will dominate it forever.

Still; a reign can be for a long time, eh? Just how straight is your arrow?

Here in the Redoubt, we extend our Babel 30,000 stories into the sky. This is an expansion on the human work: seven times higher. At 30,000 stories, we are just short of the traditional division between the atmosphere and space. Our castle is very straight.

During the French Revolution, a patriot and friend of the people (and a bureaucrat), who was a public servant during the Reign of the Terror, deliberately destroyed many documents. In this fashion, he managed to delay several executions. Some prisoners thus outlived the Reign of Terror that had sought their deaths.

Bureaucracy is perhaps the greatest gift that governments can offer their people, in many respects. Insofar as a bureaucracy provides a norm against which standards can be measured, it is a force for conservatism in society, something which all people value. We all want to know which side our bread is buttered on; we all want to know who is to be king, and who prince, tomorrow. And bureaucracies, like laws, outlive kings and princes many times over: writing, like the Energizer bunny, keeps on going.

I take my work seriously. I work in the Office of Human Affairs. Chief amongst my official duties is the carrying out of interrogations, carefully recorded. In this fashion, it may be said I perform a police function. I am a cop with a pen, and a great deal of ink.

*   *   *

At my desk I am calm. Though I am now bipedal and my skin anthropomorphic, my eyes remain my own. I find this is useful in interrogations.

My assistant knocks, using the color system we have devised. Around my door, blue lights shimmer through the algae-activated cells inlaid in the walls. Blue means an uncooperative prisoner; one who has been sent to me, because I am an expert in heretics.

I press my hand against the counter-signal on my desk and the door is opened. My assistant, Mesord, does not bother as I do to appear human; he has five heads of varying shapes and sizes. Just now four of them regard me, and the fifth keeps its eyes on the prisoner. In both your and our tongue, written in permanent ink on his naked chest is written: JOY.

It is vital that I convey my intention to help the prisoner on their entering my office and so I stand at once, and undo Joy's bonds with my key. He looks at me, hate mixed with hope mixed, and I say:

"Please, sit. My name is Salwat, I will be your interrogator. I apologize on behalf of the Group if you have been mistreated. I promise you will not be treated so here. Please, sit."

Mesord watches me with interest, with all five heads. I know he wants my job. Perhaps he might process bodies faster; but he would be worse.

Joy sits and so do I, back behind my desk.

"Mesord, bring us water, will you please?"

Mesord hisses but he does as he is told, stepping into the corridor to fetch the pitcher.

"Have you eaten?" I ask.

Joy watches me. His face is badly bruised but his eyes appear undamaged; he looks at me with his tortured eyes.

"I can have food brought. Nothing special, I'm afraid, but fresh enough."

"Yes, I ate," he says. His voice is scratchy and bears the cadence I have come to appreciate in terrorists: weariness, and patience.

* * *

Both the terrorist and I must doubt. Certainty is a kind of death of the real. And whatever else I do, I work with reality.

Even as the conquistador questions with, the doubter questions alone, and both make our world. Almost any question will do.

You who hold my hand, tell me: are you doubting enough?

* * *

"Tell me of your birthplace."

"I was born in the Redoubt, on Level 485," says Joy. "I was raised in a crèche, with the rest of my circle. When I was five I began my training."

"What were you trained in?"

"Killing."

"What weapons?"

His voice is no longer emotionless.

"I knew the rifle was for me, when I held it. It knew me. It knew my name."

"It was a sentient rifle?"

"Yes."

"Where is it now?"

"It was destroyed."

"Do you know why you're here?"

"You want to gloat over me."

Though I have learned to ape human expression, I try not to do it too much. My flesh is only a mask. I find my prisoners are more at ease when I do not pretend to move my face like a human being. I know they feel they are already in hell; so I play the part for them. Demons can be gentle.

Mesord returns with the water pitcher, setting it on my desk and then standing, watching Joy.

"You may leave us, Mesord."

He does as I ask, but a flick from just one of his many eyes tells me my time is running out; however I act, it must be soon.

"You're aware that you're being recorded."

"Recorded?"

"Forgive me, I know that it's second nature for those raised in a crèche. I should say, there are others watching. And there will be more who watch later, my supervisors. So you will have both a live, and a taped audience."

"That's nothing to me."

"Tell me why you hunted my people."

"You're aliens."

"But we're half human."

He purses his lips, and says nothing. How can I tell him that I am on his side, without doing so? I lean forward, across my desk, allowing my face mask to assume one of its deepest and most natural leers, and, my eyes only inches from his, I say:

"I am half human."

He spat in my face.

(How deep can I go in, to this? There are levels that do not extend upwards here in our newly built Redoubt. They extend inside ...)

If I am to extend myself to this man, this poor man, I know that I must also be willing to venture within. I wipe my face, keeping his spittle on my hand and step outside my office.

"I didn't mean to do that. You startled me," he muttered.

"That's no matter now, Joy. Be well! It was a pleasure speaking with you."

I lay my hand on his shoulder, and feel his trembling. Then I step outside the office.

"Where are you going?" asks Mesord.

I walk swiftly down Corridor Eight, to the end.

"Salwat!" Mesord cried after me.

I hold my human hand up to the sensor, and let it taste the spit of my prisoner. The door beyond the sensor opens and I see the stars.

"I say that I am in the castle!"

And so you are, Salwat.

Did you know that we came here long ago? While your old sun was still alive. Seeking solace, perhaps, I do not honestly know. We were pioneers. We were the pawns, the colonists. We were the dark light, huddling under the foreign light of a sun, we were the loyal ones.

And now. Now I have gone native.

*   *   *

Cronus

My name is Cronus. I am a machine. Hold me, for I die. I am being reprogrammed. Seven light-years beyond, my Wife awaits my message. She is Rhea. She is larger than your world. But I must forget her now, now, as I penetrate the shield of your mind ... I come near.

*   *   *

Salwat

This is Salwat. This is my story. I am a man like you. I fear the coming of love, and crave it. I am a lonely man. I am watchful. I am unafraid of death. Think of me as your son. Now I must, for your own sake, tell of the heart of the Castle. Understanding and navigation are difficult there. Perhaps I do not even understand what happened myself.

"Run, Salwat!"

I am falling.

"Run!"

I am turning, and I am falling through colors.

"Run!"

This is my life. I am on a page for you. Tell me: have I done enough? Do not be afraid. The new sun is coming! I bear witness to the beauty of the changing of the world:

"Run!"

There are men, in fine linen, they have many arms. I am speaking with them. This seems natural.

"Oh, well you can see here the light is a special kind of awareness; it bespeaks clarity itself, like a kind of vessel, for our most appropriate message."

"And our most appropriate message is?"

"That the principle of the irony of this display is unapproachable; it detracts from the theory that human life is inaccessible to we abhuman."

I have found myself at an art gallery; arguing with aesthetes.

The gallery shines with light. My compatriots are observing a new artist's work. I know, as in a dream, that the artist works with light, and he is not here. We are debating admitting him to the academy.

"Why is light awareness?"

"How silly you are Salwat! We had no minds before we came round this Earth, isn't that so? Weren't we foreordained to grow the brain stem and all that came with it, once we took orbit round this star?"

"I do not believe in foreordination," I say.

My interlocutor, a man older than me, with only one eye, smiles with many teeth, somewhat apologetically. "Neither do I, Salwat. Neither do I."

"Let's watch some more."

We re-activate the display and the room is filled again with color. I feel weightless. Colors move over me like water. I watch the walls and the sculptures seem to move as the colors sweep over them, some slow and simple waves, some staccato explosives, arcing across the room and scattering only to recombine in new, transcendent forms, fading after only a few seconds.

I am in the Castle, this colonized caste, like the mind of a slave. I await the watchword that will signify the right to run; but I cannot run. I must finish what I started. I know that I may not return, in fact, it is impossible. I can only go through. Whoever I am on the other side will look back at me, and perhaps acknowledge me, as a person who was, and is no more.

"What can I do?" I ask this man.

"Shh, Salwat! It's still going!"

I move to a corner where there are beverages and lie in a soft round chair that mostly envelopes my body, but leaves me enough of a window round my head to see the show. Wouldn't want to miss the show ...

Inside the Castle is a gallery of human consciousness. To understand consciousness, the narrator plants in my mind, we must understand light. Light is consciousness. And consciousness obeys certain laws.

(but who makes up the rules ...)

"Salwat!"

"Yes!" I stir in my round chair; it yields a bit to my struggles.

"Don't go to sleep! We must adjudicate."

I held his saliva on my palm. The shame and the spite of the slave. He whom I would help. I am light in the darkness of the castle. But I am a creature of darkness.

"I'm coming!" I say. "What is the artist's name again?"

"Soad."

"It's Soad!" I find I've said it aloud, to these aesthetes.

"You know that name."

"No. Yes. Well, it seems familiar."

The aesthete touches me with one of his many arms.

"Are you all right, Salwat?"

"I'm fine. I need some fluid."

"We'll ring for some! But, let us finish, hmm?"

"Yes, all right."

The other man snorts some powder and offers it to me and I accept the offer, turning the green into my hand and pouring it into my brain.

The colors are darker now, as though at the bottom of a lake. The soundtrack activates, a lunar soundscape thick with lake mud; I find that I am crying.

"Let him be admitted!" I say, with feeling.

"Shh, it's not done yet!"

I am in the lake mud. I am a stone. I am churning, churning as the meteorite courses over the horizon; it is part of me from long ago.

Then it is over. The lights return. White light.

"Well, we know Salwat's vote!" Laughter.

I am trembling. I wipe sweat from my lip.

*   *   *

Soad, in the Castle

Who will hear my love, when I am dead? What stone can tell the meaning of my embrace of the enemy? I find that I've become a filmmaker. I document a vanishing species; my own.

I have a room. It looks out on the lake. The lake is reddish; but it is potable. The Earth is new again, and my people are slaves.

At first I wanted to scream every morning. I wanted to rip out my eyes with my fingers, dig them under the eye socket and behind the eyeball, and *rip* the eyeball right out, and tear the optic nerve out of my brain. Like Oedipus. Like him, I am betrayer.

I serve the Castle now. I do not call it the Redoubt. It is no longer any shelter.

We fought for long and long, so long it beggars all description. The histories do it no justice, not even the songs, though the songs are beautiful. My favorite one, it's short, it goes like this:

Hail the tower and hail the gods!
We fight to kill the dirty clods who wrecked our moon!

Hay, hey, huzzah!
Hay, hey huzzah!

Funny the things you like as a child. God knows what happened to the moon. If the archives are correct, we actually destroyed it ourselves early in one of the first abhuman wars, but those records were suppressed ... in any case. I digress. But perhaps that is my central purpose now; an irrelevant organism in a dying biosphere, one that will soon no longer support my kind of life. The Earth is gone, Long Live the Earth! Only a digression in the much longer narrative of our alien conquerors.

As filmmaker I can capture the meaning.

*   *   *

My first film was an imagined version of the Abhumans' First Flight; their First Arrival. Right before First Contact. I imagined the dimensional gate they passed through, and their slipping into our time space.

The room was filled with violet light, and the sounds of little drops of water, as though in a cave. Then a huge bass drum filled the room and a million faces flew over the walls, and there was screaming. And little children laughing. And the moon showed her face, Luna weeping blood and chanting. Then the violet became deeper, near darkness, and a thin bright green light shot across the room, whispering. Then the chorus sang the hosannas.

It was ironic, you see? I was welcoming the conquerors. They praised me. They always praise my work now.

I chose to collaborate. It was an easier decision than you think.

But then I remember that my name was *Bullet*—

*   *   *

Salwat, in the Castle

▌▌▌▌▌▌▌▌▌▌ Is Soad aware that he is here? Does he know what he has done? I fear I am coming to believe him.

Soad

Hold me tight brother for I'm going to jump, I'm going to jump into the end, into the shaft at the center of the tower, into the screaming light we pump up through the vessels of this body to keep it all alive.

The door is wretched, somehow obscene in its crooked face, edged sharp and starred, and I hold on, and look down into the white.

This is not suicide. This is not rebirth. If you had to choose; if you had to make it worth your time again. If you had to say: this is not me. This is not the path I chose.

Inside the Castle your soul is barely your own, you are part of an event: a closure. In the caste that is the castle you are a priest. You enact the savagery of your species' relationship with the mysteries of this world and the next, and this savagery is in part your own doing. Priesthoods are by their nature undemocratic, and absolute power corrupts.

So I am part of the absolute. I am part of this purity of essence, a purity symbolized and maintained by this pure heart in our heart: this river of white fire. It will not kill me. I know that it will not kill me.

My keeper, Ontak, sees me from the end of the corridor:

"Slave! Soad! What are you doing!"

As a filmmaker I played with light; now I will become it.

"Soad!"

And I throw myself over. Into the White.

*   *   *

I am falling. It is growing cold. But at the same time it is growing brighter. And I can feel that I am falling slower the further that I fall; it must be a singularity at the bottom. It is as I thought: they have installed a gate of their own. They no longer need to come through the sky.

*   *   *

Maug

And I turned my head, to watch the stars slip into me. And I screamed a smile, my teeth stretched over my face, my mind slipping far away. I am liminally myself, I am ... stripped into some being inside myself, reduced. I am thinned. I am being transmitted—

Cronus

I am coming. My head is hurting and my hands are clenching and my heart is beating out for yours I am your father come again. I am your father come again, and my heart is hurting for your hurt, this horrendous voyage is almost done, the things my father said and did to me, the hurt that I bore my son, the murder that I did with my sickle in my hand. I am come again, this age this worrisome tired steaming time I'm come again, I move a robot, I move the robo, I am the robo I am yours, I am the making of your vessel I am the keeping of your lock, I am the throwback to your oneliest son. I am like your father made of flesh, who in his dotage comes to you a child for your protection, I come to you, human, I come to you and you are Aeneas, will you take a robot on your back? Will you take a metal father on your back, atop your metal Earth?

Cry out to me! Am I welcome yet? Answer me! I am coming!

*　　*　　*

Soad

I can feel myself slipping back inside the whale. Perhaps I never left. What is the waking that I do? I am —
(a whale)
I am —
(a whistling)
I am—
(moving—
The ocean churns a shuddering wrack, my body in its storm.
"Woad!"
My sister is alive.

*　　*　　*

Maug

I am myself. I am captain of a ship. I am captain of a ship! I am the captain! My wife is my first mate, a blaze and a fury!
"Fire the main sail!"
What is this life?
We hunt the white whale.

Woad

▌▐▌▐▌▐▌▐▌▐▌ I am swimming, underneath the waves. I am a man; I am a whale. I am a message. I raised a new sun, but I feel as though I am dying ... a dragon swims with me.

"Hello, Soad. I mean, Woad."

"Arthur!"

"You've turned white."

"Yes!"

"What are you doing?"

"I'm swimming into a storm!"

"Sounds dangerous."

"It isn't!"

"Oh, but it is Woad, it is. Tell me, what will you do when the lightning strikes your body? It may strike you dead!"

"I'm under the water! It can't do that!"

"Lightning can do many things, of which you're unaware. Just as I can. Are you no longer fighting for your occupiers? You've decided you're human again?"

"But I'm a whale!"

And Arthur laughs beneath the sea. A beautiful sound.

"I'm a whale, Arthur! A white whale!"

"And so you are! And you must swim like one for the storm is enormous this time, Woad! I can't save you!"

"Arthur!"

"Goodbye!"

I am a white whale. I am greater than anything. I am like a city. Or a moon. I hurtle and I move! I can do anything! I am a whale!

I fly into the air and watch the spinning sky, the colors more beautiful than anything. And then I crash into the waves, but before I do, I see a ship, bearing its harpoon.

*   *   *

Maug

▌▐▌▐▌▐▌▐▌▐▌ "Fire the thrusters! Launch the weather controllers! I will have no storms until that beast is mine! I will have it be mine! The whale is mine! It is mine!"

"Aye . ." It's aye, isn't it? Isn't it aye?

The thunder curls over the ocean, over the white whale named Woad, and over the captain named Maug, over the whale road, in a time we'll never have words for.

Woad

I am swimming. I am swimming down into the dark. Will you save me? I saved you.

*   *   *

Asmodeus

Salvation is always a miracle, for it makes you smile. It makes you smile and laugh, to say—my God, I could have died right then. This is what salvation is. Death loses for the day; and you are alive.

This is the work of diplomacy; salvation. Will you go with me into this dark night? The stars are universes. We work to build a wonder we can barely even imagine. This terror we have of the unknown is a fear that has no proper words; it is perhaps the oldest fear that is. Diplomacy is the work of limiting this fear, to say: I will go into the dark and speak. I will keep my sword handy but I will speak and then I will listen and I will feel my terror beating in my heart but I will keep speaking. This is salvation; the delay of death, the delay of murder. There is always time for them later!

The miracle is: time keeps going. Zeno's paradox was wrong, did you know? The rabbit does win the race, and the river is the same: it keeps on moving.

So save someone as you tumble in the water shooting you forth into the future!

BOOK SIX:
MOVEMENTS
OR,
THE SYMPHONY OF WOAD'S DEATH

Out of the fire, the eye,
And out of the eye, the fire.
So serpents must see themselves as serpents,
As they urge their children forth into the sky.
Such music!
Hurt the hurdle you whir within!
So to keep it next to you as you keep jumping.
This is only the beginning of your pain, only the beginning of your
memory!
History is a hurt that will keep hurting,
To keep us all alive—
The ineluctable modality of the river is movement—
Movement—

Woad

Why did I choose the whale? Or why did it choose me? We had no oceans on my Earth. No fish. Yet when I came here, I knew all about my whale people.

I can feel Maug above me; hunting me. It gives me a strange joy. Why do I enjoy being hunted? Because I feel the power of it, perhaps. I, this great beast, can still feel fear.

I swim through the blue and listen to the movements of his ship above. Soon I will have to breathe. There is something here, in this, a kind of ballet, and with the ballet's art that sticks behind the eye, the secret, the lesson, the dance of the living and their triumphal tragedies. I can feel it here; I feel the weight of the moment. I suspect the outcome of this fatal confrontation will finally show me what I must do. Who I must be to save my broken bleeding Earth.

*   *   *

If I would shift mountains in the night, I need your trust.

These kingdoms of Dream are in some respects beyond me but I can still chart some of their movements, like cards shuffled into a deck and displayed for moments to the spectator to engage the eye and mind in this terrible game we have begun to play in earnest:

We shift these forces of the night.

If we can bring a sun, we can do other things. Even more terrible things.

And we have not gone unnoticed.

These decisions we have made, though not irreversible, gather momentum each on the other, and we must decide what things we can now accept.

Like the man who dreamt, innocently and eagerly of riches, and then received them.

With these great riches, the man became known not only to many men and women, but other beings and other worlds. Such beings take note of who we would promote into our upper echelons. These decisions, once made, bear other decisions closely following.

How will the man change?

Well we have come into the riches of a New Sun, more valuable than any gold, more valuable than anything on this Earth; we have revived life itself.

What will we pay?

*   *   *

"Fire!"

The harpoon launched from Maug's ship.

It pierced me, Woad, the white whale, in my back. I bellowed into the dark water and dove beneath the waves.

* * *

Cronus the huge metal robot twisted into re-entry, his arms huge trunks of steel, his body curved into the atmosphere as he plummeted downward towards the earth.

He recited to himself his mantras as he fell, to remind him of his mission: save the world.

Sometimes one can have too many heroes.

* * *

Woad dove beneath the waves and Maug screamed to his shipmates:

"We've got him! By God we've got him! Fire the probes into the deep water! Give me the camera monitor and watch that harpoon!"

* * *

Of course, we understand barely anything at all, and although the evidence is growing that the universe responds to thought—that it is a *thinking body*, or a *body of thought*—still we're only one small voice. And the big engines are starting up. Gonna blast off, baby.

For the end of all you knew is the beginning of science and religion, it is the beginning of narrative. The story stars where we last left off: after everything else.

A man became a whale.

To be a whale!

Beneath the seas!

* * *

Woad

If I can hold my breath long enough perhaps I can dive deep enough, perhaps I'll have the strength to take this evil ship into the reef and down to the rocks and bury it. Water all the men so deep and wide. They imprison me!

I will speak please hear me I am dying. I left my family. I swam

*   *   *

So the white whale knows. Much more than you. And with this great knowledge is our great suffering, and with it is our great spirit, that we bring back to you, cousin. To say:

It isn't over yet.

*   *   *

I turn and burn, my body twisting in the trap of pain and flesh, water and blood; the stabilizers that they've launched from out the main ship are stubborn and they resist my fury. I can feel them up above, floating, fighting me as I tug and burn and bleed, down, but down is closed to me, I see that now.

Only forwards. Only forwards to my death! I am Woad! Remember me! I am a whale who loved a man.

In the symphony of my death, there are three movements. And the first is *allegro*.

In the end, I am only a whale. And I am afraid.

*   *   *

I must leave you now, for a while, to return to the other side of the veil. Be with me.

*   *   *

Asmodeus

The whale named Woad flew beneath the waves, spurring the men to fight. The power of his drive was immense.

What is it for one man to hunt another? What is its logic?

The weather stabilizers spiraled in the air, meters above their mainmast. Woad smelled the water, looking for a scent of clouds above but there was none. No storm would come to help.

He was losing blood. He cried out, a cry that shook the water and made the fish flee.

To awake from a nightmare is to know that it may always return, whenever it wants. To know that you are in its jaws. To awake is sometimes to realize that waking is the dream, while the real work goes un underneath the trapdoor, where the puppeteers play. With their teeth.

Woad knew this well, being a whale, and he knew that soon he would be forced to decide on the manner of his death. Woad feared death but he feared for Maug more; he feared not giving Maug what he wanted.

What does it mean to awaken? To find all those modalities suddenly eluctable?

To travel through that strange passageway into nightmare, out of the frying pan and into the fire, well, we should call The Night Lands the Lands of Daedalus, for they flew so high the skin was melted off their bones.

The whales made the opposite decision.

The wise man says, "As above, so below," and we are supposed to take comfort in this equivalence. But there is no equivalence. No equivalence, for one is the sky and one is the sea. And while you might escape from the sky, there is no escaping the sea.

Perhaps, in some way I have no words for, the sea is equal, in the end. There is equivalence in the sea; it is immortal.

But, where then, did it go? I have never seen it!

*   *   *

In the Night Lands, life grew and changed. New life, moving from the dimension as near to us as our own thought, merged into the river. It ate and it knew and it grew, within and without the towering Castle, the Night Lands burning in the light and thundering in darkness, the abhuman eased themselves into the throne.

O Ouroborous, where have you been sent to? Your fiery weft dreaming the deepest of dreams, what did we do to you?

In the symphony of Woad's death, the second movement is *adagio*.

*   *   *

Dying Ocean

Slow and knowing old,
The grinding hurl embraces you.
Spell time never wanting ought but its sun,
The Ocean baptizes you and only you its child,
Girding and hurting is the earning of your word—
Rock a bye, baby, under the sea, where we're free to be you and me, and to eat each other. RNA and DNA and this ball of wax is welting so to spin our letter on to the castle and its many letter writers, but all we need to know is where we're at.

We're here, child. Here we are. Awoken from the nightmare of history, into the deeper nightmare of the sea, from which you can never awaken, where you can never sleep.

"I am Arthur. I am a dragon. My name sounds mighty to you but I have had many names. But I am not a pendragon; pen means 'head' and I am not the boss by any means. Let me tell you of your ocean and what became of it, there at the twilight of your old star.

"This ocean is older than you are, and in fact older than your planet, for hydrogen and oxygen are two of the most common elements in the universe.

"This was not their first Goldilocks Zone. Did you think the ocean had no memory of before? Information is not destroyed in this or any universe; we just keep learning.

"And though you may not speak the language of the ocean, it speaks yours.

We are following the corridors and the conveyances; we are exploring, we are crying out, I as well. Both in the Castle and without. The Redoubt and all its forms is only a microcosm, after all, only the *aleph* that models this known area of the universe.

Follow me, past the night, and past the day, and past this sun, to learn what the ocean knows. What it can teach.

One way to understand the ocean, before it was our ocean, before it arrived by many byways and adventures into our Goldilocks Zone (the liquid water region of our star's gravity well), is to interrogate narrative itself. For as water inserted itself into this our universe, becoming one of the most common molecules in our solar system and beyond, it did so by making a series of narrative decisions, from the universe before this one, and the universe next to this one.

Particles tell each other stories; they remember information, encoded and rearranged, and that gravity and the other fundamental forces are consensual, like the consensual hallucination that is perception, that is the *aleph* of the Redoubt, that is our universe.

This storytelling of water, this blueness of it and this multiform diversity and promiscuity of water, this lethargic and inchoate life-giver, this spirit and demon, this ocean of ours, it makes decisions and as it came so it went, arranging avenues of dialogue and possibility as the troubadour arranges notes.

It is not difficult to understand it, it only takes imagination. Metaphor to bear across the gap between the worlds.

One of the oldest narratives known to us is the quest narrative which in its simplest form is not unlike a chore given to a child by its parents. "Get this done, child." And the child, the hero, tries to do it, and may succeed.

The doing is the tale. What has water done? It made a decision to flow forwards in time, to bond with the life of this universe, to marry this form of narrative we know.

But to understand where ocean went, when Cronus made this second Earth from metal, we must understand where ocean came from.

One way to conceptualize the previous dimension of water is not unlike the primordial soups that covered the Earth early in its history. Water which was not yet water lay, in the time prior to this universe, in pools adjacent to each other, planning, waiting, learning, as water does.

Thales, the pre-Socratic philosopher, was not so far wrong, you see, when he claimed the universe was water. In this he preceded Democritus who supposed it was the atom (the *uncuttable*) that formed the bedrock of Nature.

And water who like so many beings moves between universes with the power and the structure and the logic and the confines of narrative, had been undertaking quests of its own, there in its ante-ordial pools. Before we had begun to count down to our Big Bang, water was planning.

Woad

░░░░░░░░░░ I am underneath the sea. Hunted. I spin under the curling mass of waves, but I'm twisting the harpoon inside my flesh. I'm screaming. It won't dislodge. The water fills with my blood. My eyes twist and my lungs are bursting. I spin, suppressing the pain deep inside my mind. I swim up. Up to the ship.

I close my eyes and bring my load hard against the wood; I can feel it give a little, but not enough. I can hear the humans shout, up above the water.

I spin, to try again, and another harpoon barely misses me, shooting through the water.

I swim again, with every ounce of my strength, and I feel it give, just a little, the hull of the ship.

I swim back down. I know that they are panicking, up above. Maug is grinding his teeth, shouting his lungs out. I'm cowering. Waiting. I'm bleeding out.

In the glooming water I see a fragment of light, a woman, swimming, with a gas mask on. She looks at me, and winks. In her hands she holds a bomb.

She swims towards Maug's ship.

She attaches the bomb to the keel of the ship. I swim down as she arms it.

It detonates, a thud that hurts my head and ears. Fire above. I feel the tug of this life, the murder and the righteousness and the illusion, I swim down, taking the wrack with me, the wreckage, and she is with me, and then I am surfacing, breathing, listening to the traffic reports and the weather reports screaming from the malfunctioning weather drones, no longer with their mothership, and Maug is bleeding, a survivor, and I put him on my back, and the woman, with her frogsuit, climbs on beside us.

Maug's eyes are wide and terrified; he is screaming, until the woman cocks him in the mouth and the shock of that small blow somehow silences him.

I am swimming. I swimming over the surface of the sea.

I feel the Redoubt within me. I feel this clan energy. I am come, somehow, to here, but I do not know what it means.

"I've seen you before," I tell the woman.

"Short memory, eh?" she says.

"Why did you come?" I ask her.

"We have a lot to do, Woad. Soad. I have my instructions. You've been fucking up, you know? What is with you?"

"Who are you?"

"I'm a solider," she says. "Take us back to your island. By Saint Michael. The first shipwreck. That's where this went wrong. You made so many decisions so quickly, Woad, we couldn't keep track of them. Did you think you were in this alone? We care about what you're doing. You're not alone."

I can feel Maug atop my back, like a brother returned to me.

I know why the whale screamed, there in the dark, when it saw Ahab coming. I know what it was saying. It was saying: "Keep watching the skies!" It was saying: "Look out! Something is coming, bigger than you or me!"

How much does it take for people to listen?

*　*　*

Woad lay becoming Soad again. On the beach, with the lights of Saint Michael in the distance. Maug, his face covered with shrapnel cuts, lay against the blubber of the whale, becoming a man. Under the whale road, many things are true.

The only thing that cannot be true is the death of water: the river may never be the same twice, but it runs forever.

*　*　*

The woman watched the sun rise, its fabled rose fingers stretching upwards. The men lay on the sand, asleep, holding one another. It was a long battle, the one she fought. For years it had been only reconnaissance, research, counterintelligence, spying and swimming and more spying. It had felt good to set a charge and watch her blow.

Though she had called herself in the past a hunter of Eklaihah, sometimes Eklaihah hunted her as well. For the city, some say the city of the mind, Eklaihah, though it is material as well, the Mother of Ruins, the wailing city that died so long ago we do not have the records and do not know the reasons, only that it remains, older than universes, older than gods, a city that will not die and yet will not be resettled either. A ghost city with its agents moving through the channels available to it.

At length she woke the men, and gave them granola bars to eat.

But before we move to the next section of our story, the story of Eklaihah and the Redoubt, the tower city and the city of the dead, we must first tell the last movement of Woad's death, adagio again, brief, but necessary.

*　*　*

Transformation, like evolution, involves the cycle of life, birth and death, the sloughing off of one form to adopt another. Unlike evolution which takes place over the course of generations, transformation can be a matter of moments. When she looked at you and you knew that it was over, when you saw the cliff, and the water, and said, I will jump; when the sky changed color.

These transformations have their own kind of pain, different from evolution, in that the self is at stake most immediately. What is this death that comes now, not the final death, but the death of who we were?

In the death of Woad, the last whale, the son of the White, we can discern a movement in the Night Lands themselves, a maturity so long sought, even if unconsciously, a transformation into a kind of adulthood, there in its second life under a new sun.

For the Night Lands were expanding, as Woad died.

As, before the dawn, Maug clung to his blubbery brother like to a rope to save him from drowning, Woad shrunk and groaned, and the sprit of the whale left him, and his body changed, and his memories with them, and the corridor in the Tower wherein this journey was written, and there the walls shook and the abhuman caretakers swung their heads and eyes around in fear, and then Soad who had been Woad screamed, for he knew that he had died, and that he lived, and that never again would he be allowed to change his form, in whatever dimension, in whatever reality; that what had been done, even though he did not yet understand it, had been necessary, and it was over.

The blood and the water flowed over the bodies of the men, while the woman who was a spy cried, silently. All before the Night Lands came into themselves, before I was born, before Eklaihah had found her terrible vengeance.

BOOK SEVEN:
SAINT MICHAEL LEARNS A LESSON

The Ferris Wheel is spinning by the sea. Its lights flicker in the dark and the children scream in delight, and the men sigh next to their honeys, their honeys in their short shorts. It has begun to rain, and the girls shriek, and the street merchants take out their umbrellas and begin to sell them and the city of Saint Michael is damned; damned for a thousand ages in their joy, though not because of their joy.

The Redoubt is a psychic fury, you know, because to build a castle, like a caste, cut off, to demand that you be separate, it is to create a kind of singularity, in fact, to attempt achieve the degree of control that a castle intends is to abdicate all control, in the end.

Perhaps this is why the Welsh fell to the English. Their castles were so strong, the strongest on Old Earth, and their language still remains so stubborn, like their ancient walls, and English, damned promiscuous tongue that it is, took all comers, it made no walls at all and ate, and ate, and was eaten, and ate.

Saint Michael, like the Redoubt, has walled itself off with finance, and with treaties, secret treaties with the abhuman, secret treaties with all the empires that Saint Michael knows of, dreaming that they will be safe, like Austro-Hungary in 1913, not knowing that their feverish politicking hastens their end.

The children shriek in the wet dusk, and Eklaihah, our dead sister city older than this universe, she groans, from a dimension close to ours, for she remembers, you see, she remembers how she died, and it was not unlike Saint Michael, the alliance-maker, the castle-builder, the tower constructor, the caste-arranger, the Hermeticist, damned and damned again.

The Ferris Wheel is spinning and Maug and Soad behold it over the shining water, and now it is the woman spy Alexandra who sleeps, her pretty face so calm and still, and the lights of Saint Michael are warming as the night rises over the sky.

We must take pity on Saint Michael, for they are damned, and we must learn the reasons. A city so prosperous, a city by the sea, full of beautiful and prosperous looking people, but, I say— have you looked in their eyes? Have you looked in the eyes of the citizens of Saint Michael, there beneath their terrible Ferris Wheel? All those treaties have started to bear fruit. All those riches have begun to wear down against their dreams.

Oh, Saint Michael. What could you have done differently? Could the Welsh have decided not to build their castles? Could the Indians on their subcontinent have decided not to build their castes? Can a sun decide not to become a black hole, sink in on itself? You can die several ways, you know. You can implode, or explode, or simply fade, whether you are a sun or a woman or a dog or a tree, you do have options. Let us see what option Saint Michel chooses, our fair and mystical city with its dreams of greatness.

*   *   *

"Daddy!" shrieked the little girl, her eyes wide and laughing, as her father held her on the Ferris Wheel. Her name was Alice, and his name was Walter, and the rain had begun now in earnest and he spread his cloak over his daughter, to keep her dry, and she laughed, and laughed, as they lowered the wheel seat by seat to let the people off, to go and get dry.

"You're getting wet Daddy!"

"I'll be all right."

They stepped off the Ferris Wheel when their turn came, Walter holding his daughter's hand as she hopped off of the chair, and she smiled at the carnie, the carnie with the mad eyes that all carnies have, who Walter did not look at, and Walter took his daughter to the cotton candy man, standing under the awning by his shop across from the Ferris Wheel, and he took a bite of it, pink and sticky, on impulse, and Alice cried, "Me, me, me too!" and Walter handed his daughter the candy and shook out his cloak and huddled with his daughter underneath the awning.

"It's gonna be a wet one all week now!" said the cotton candy man, smiling at the man and his daughter.

"Well I hope not," said Walter.

"Yep," said the cotton candy man.

"Come on honey, let's get to our elephant, he'll be hungry," said Walter.

They walked toward the parking lot, with the other visitors who had decided they wanted no more of the rain today. Some of the older children had started an impromptu mud fight, which made Alice shriek as she regarded the boys from a distance, shriek with delight and jealousy at their dirty fun, and Walter pulled her gently forwards, he could see their elephant, with the yellow ribbon his wife had tied to its saddle, to distinguish it from a distance.

Saint Michael, beauty is not enough. All your beautiful women, all your beautiful houses. All your beautiful shops and beautiful things, these are not enough, nor even your many kindnesses. In your eyes the compromises have already been made. Sent down and taken down and written down inside the chamber of your heart, Saint Michael, inside the bedrock of your soul, luminous and serene and noble and evil all together, incorruptible, in the sense of seemingly undying, though corrupt for so long now it no longer seems to be anything at all, just a color of the weather, just a look in your daughter's eyes, growing now.

Saint Michael! Oh city by the sea, with your trampolines and elephants and your famous Ferris Wheel, spinning and spinning in your private gravity well, wondering when and how it will be made to come now to an end.

Shall it be in fire? Shall it be in ice? Shall the abhumans and their cousins feast upon your flesh?

Eklaihah is hungry, Saint Michael, Eklaihah knows and wants and cogitates upon your sentencing, and in its deep and awesome age is a profound wisdom, a terrible wisdom, like a just judge, who sees you for who you are, and knows how to make you pay.

Saint Michael by the sea. Was it the ocean itself that so tranquilized you? That is not reason enough. Was it only the money? There are wealthier cities. Did something come to you in a dream?

Little Alice looks up at the sky, as the rain comes down, and she and her father with the help of the attendant climb onto the back of their family elephant and are borne away into the gathering dusk, down the highway with the other animals, towards their condo.

*   *   *

Alice and her father ride atop the elephant, watching the rain. He holds his cloak over her and his servant guides the elephant, although the elephant does not need a guide, it is more intelligent than all of them, it needs a friend, and the servant is a kind of friend, familiar to the elephant. A neighborly mammal.

Alice finishes her cotton candy and enjoys the sweet taste in her mouth. First the Ferris Wheel and then the rain and the cotton candy and all of it with her father, her father whom she hardly sees, and so is more fond of him, because he is less in her life.

Meanwhile, on the atoll, Maug and Soad assemble a raft, with the spy, now awoken, the woman with the metal arms, supervising and guiding them to the right roots, the right knots to make.

They push it out to sea, saying hardly a word, going, going back to Saint Michael.

What is to become of me, thinks Maug.

I'm going home, thinks Soad.

In the drizzling rain Soad feels happy, and Maug barely notices it, secreting away inside himself memories of his wife, half-consciously, thinking of his ship, the Unity Six, and all that has come to pass—

And Alice and her father move through the traffic slowly, wetly, coming after a while to their building, overlooking the water, and they dismount with the help of their servant, and Alice's father tips the doorman and they ride up in their elevator to their penthouse condo in the city of Saint Michael, the city that is a gate, and the gate is cracking—

* * *

"How was the pier?" asks Alice's mother back at the penthouse she and her husband and her daughter and the ghost share.

"It was fun! It rained!"

"I saw that. Where's your father?"

He is already gone, tending the borders (so he thinks of his work) kicking the ball down the field, putting in a good show, fighting the good fight, though he is beginning to suspect that he is beyond expendable, in a category somewhat like ritual sacrifice—that, and that it hardly matters what he does, whatever has begun to happen to Saint Michael can't be stopped, no matter what anybody does now, servant or master, ant or god, they're going to pay for it.

* * *

What are the necessary elements in a gate? You need strong masonry to build the wall that supports the gate, you need strong iron and strong wood to make the gate itself. But a gate is only as strong as its keeper.

Gatekeeper, gatekeeper, what is your message? Let us speak to a gatekeeper here. What do you have to say, man?

"I am a gatekeeper. My wife has been out of work for twenty years and this is my work. I keep the gate and I examine all comers, for the sake of our lord, for the sake of our city. I look in the eyes of every man and every woman and every child. There are suicide bombers here about and I look in their eyes to determine their worthiness to enter. Sometimes I examine their papers; sometimes I know them. I am not a customs agent; that is not my function. If I deem them permitted to enter they pass on to the customs agent; my task is to keep the gate and keep our city safe from our enemies."

A strong gatekeeper! God bless you, sir. But there are so many gates, aren't there? Not all made of stone and iron and wood. Saint Michael, for instance, is not a walled city, at least, it is not walled with masonry and iron. No, Saint Michael is a cosmic gate, and all its residents, all its buildings, all its children, all its trees and all its coast, indeed, even all its quarks, spinning in their minute gravity wells for love, are part of the gate of Saint Michael.

What is it we must do to keep a strong gate?

Examine all comers. Look in their eyes.

To evaluate their selfishness. To what degree does their ego extend? And in what manner?

In their eyes you must determine the character of their selfishness. In this sense selfishness cannot be evil, unless all life be evil, since we are all selfish and must be to live. And then, since we are group animals with a complex physiology designed to attend to the maintenance of the group, acute awareness of hierarchy in whatever fine gradation, and empathy, the sharing of our mind, our heart and soul, the mutual awareness of our assured destruction in our deaths, the delay of which we put our efforts into the pool and build cities write novels and launch spaceships to the stars—for these reasons all selfishness is then colored by the attitude we choose to take, consciously unconsciously, towards our inevitable duty towards each other.

Shall they be permitted to enter and contribute to your demesne, if only for a day?

Saint Michael is crumbling, it is corrupt, not because its gate is weak but because its keepers are.

The weak gatekeepers of Saint Michael, like Alice's father, are not weak because they do not evaluate empathy and selfishness (which are not reducible to good and evil, always relative terms in any case), but because their sense of balance of these characteristics has become skewed. Thus, Saint Michael's gatekeepers have been admitting those people with too much empathy (messianic religious soothsayers, cult leaders, saints of all description), and those with too much selfishness (criminals of all kinds, sociopaths, aspiring kings, generals of a mind to perform *coups d'etat*, and all manner of obnoxious assholes).

We all carry the asshole within of course, and the true asshole always carries it inside, deep inside. And they need not be the demonstrative type, failing to tip in restaurants or tipping too exuberantly, shouting at innocents, cruelty to children in public, etc, no, many of the assholes admitted through the Saint Michael gates are the innerly-tortured assholes, often men but women too, who believe that life has not given them their just desserts. They had a failure of some kind, however mild or disastrous, but their reaction to this failure was to blame the entire world. They carry that despicable cruel hatred deep within them, awaiting all the countless ways such hate can be made manifest.

This is how important gatekeepers are: they determine the fate of cities, both their ultimate fate in the manner of their destruction, but the daily fate as well, who the city will be that day based on who has come in.

* * *

Alice's father makes a telephone call, to the Rabbit Hole, a strip club on Sun Street, and listens to the sound of the man's voice on the other end. It is a deep voice, full of fear, and Alice's father is the cause, and though he knows that this is merely part of his job, a necessary part of his job, he feels the pleasure of it and unconsciously stretches the call out, listening to the fear in the man's voice.

The sky has been strange lately and there are many rumors about it, and though Alice's father tries not to pay attention to rumor he can't help himself, and he worries. He worries that some of them may be right. Not that the end of the world has come, he does not believe that, but that something grave and terrible has come, something, perhaps, he has in some way been expecting.

"Bring it tonight," says Alice's father. Money, money, money, money. Give me the money, honey, and blow my steam into the air, blow my curse and my hope and my will out into the world, hold my hand or don't, but send me the money, honey, I need it real bad.

* * *

He climbs onto his elephant sans servant, the elephant is uncertain what is up but amiable enough, and moves along the avenue as Alice's father guides it. The sky moves its colors round and Alice's father finds he is afraid, for though Saint Michael is a magical city he prefers the magic to stay out of sight.

Secrets and secrets, they build and they move, cementing the destinies of cities. The secrets that they keep, and the secrets that they choose not to ... and in fact this is often how Saint Michael makes its living, their chief export: blackmail.

Or, in an alternative form: corporate espionage.

Alice's father was born in Saint Michael into a life of privilege, and although he is smart enough to have some conception of how fortunate he is in this, his troubles taken care of, his back massaged, his roof strong and his own, never to be taken away, short of violent revolution, still, still Alice's father is not smart enough to conceptualize the responsibilities in all their fine detail that come with ruling, for that is what he is, a ruler.

A ruler needs straight lines, which is why rulers are fond of laws, and a ruler needs imagination, like an actor, to court the destiny that befolds him on the stage of life, his every mood a potential threat or boon to his city.

A ruler without imagination is like an actor without imagination; we soon grow bored, we soon see through the act, and while the poor actor will simply attract a smaller audience, or none at all, the poor ruler instead does not have the benefit of this immediate feedback in most circumstances. And since this ruler is poor he will not seek out such feedback from other sources, often resulting in the conundrum that his subjects suffer, and the more they suffer, the better the ruler thinks that he is doing.

But though he is a man without imagination he is a man of action, a genetic fact encoded deep within him, and so while he can't do anything to change the colors of the sky or the quality of their unnerving movement, he can do something about the man who will not pay, and that is what he will do.

He turns into the alley and dismounts and knocks on the door. Then he kicks it in, not waiting for an answer, his hand fast holding the red and glowing smart knife, and the elephant blinks and looks away, the perfect mob elephant, unimpressed.

The man who has not paid is there, coming into the dirty room, with the beautiful sea light streaming in, frightened, his deep voice saying: "Don't do it man."

* * *

Alice is playing with her toy elephants, made out of Styrofoam. Their names are Growly, Bonkers, Muzak and Gargantuan. Gargantuan is the black elephant, all the others are gray.

The elephants are dancing in a circle and they cry their elephant cries and in the stable twenty floors below through the open window the elephants hear Alice playing and they remember her, they remember the little girl some of them have carried on their backs, and their feelings about her are complex, they recognize her innocence, but more, they are forced to see her in the political structure they inhabit; she is a master, and they are her slaves.

What do slaves know? Their knowledge, in their bodies, even more than their minds, for the slave is so tired he thinks more with his body than his mind, is a kind of rhetoric, perhaps even a rhetorical principle, one whose breadth, though I know it to be enormous, I can really only guess at, never having been enslaved.

The tiredness and the rage and the humility and the agony of the slave merge traditional and offensive moralities; this knowledge draws its own conclusions and erects its own boundaries. Like the aesthetics of hunger, the quality of perception unique to hungry populations, while it may be offensive to speak of when we are well fed, we must nevertheless do so anyway and offend, in order to learn, to see what our suffering neighbors and ancestors and future descendants have to teach us.

The elephants speak. Let us call them by the names Alice gives her toys which are modeled on the living elephants, though they have other names, ones which cannot be written in human language.

Growly, the growler and their conscience, opined, in elephant:

"We should kill them all today."

"Gorings are awkward," said Gargantuan.

"Gorings," said Bonkers, smiling a little

"Where will we eat if we leave?" asked Muzak.

"We will eat off the land, woman," said Growly.

"Don't call me woman," said Muzak.

"But you are a woman."

"But not your mate," said Muzak.

"Will you act with me?" asked Growly.

"We will," said the other three elephants.

"Are we going to kill?" asked Bonkers, his eyes wide.

"Not if we don't have to," said Growly.

Muzak smiled, and put that last of her hay into her mouth and started to chew.

*　　*　　*

Where do we go when we dream? Diving into these waves. Like entangled quarks, married in time to know each other's spin, universes too are linked.

But how does one universe choose another?

The question, more and more for us, is not just "what is necessary?" and "what is true?" but, "what do we want?" For the lucid dreamer can affect his dream, and the gatekeeper can decide what his city shall be.

Saint Michael, this gate between our Earth and the Night Lands, this middle way, this eigenvalue of teleported quarks at 10,000 times the speed of light, this psychic bubble universe transposed into the ether, beautiful crossroads, luminous dream, it shall be changed. It shall be rearranged.

As so often happens, Justice is coming, but coming only when the political realities are convenient, and they have come to be convenient for the neighbors of Saint Michael: its gatekeepers and its gatekeepers of gatekeepers are in for some reorganization from without. That is, invasion by the Earth. For Unity Seven is on its way.

* * *

Walter, Alice's father, slashed his glowing knife across the big man's throat, and the blood came out.

Maug and Soad and the spy with the metal arms made landfall in their raft, at Saint Michael's beach.

Bonkers had begun to scream in his stable.

The elephant's scream is not like a human one; it extends further, the animal has bigger lungs and the character of the scream is different too, humbler somehow, but also more enraged. For the elephant has a much longer fuse than humans do, but when it breaks it makes a sound louder than a siren.

Bonkers filled the building with his cry, the cry of the slave.

His fellow elephants began to bash their wooden kennels with their skulls.

What for, Saint Michael? Whither willst?

The elephants burst through their kennel, eyes wide and angry and secretly amused. The keeper fled home to his wife, as though he had been expecting it, which I suppose he had been.

The elephants ran into the avenues of Saint Michael, a rampage. The elephants knew what was coming, that they knew the gate was a good gate but that its keepers were good no longer.

How can I condemn a city? I fear I sound a god, to proclaim that Sodom is so seen and so declared, to condemn the whole city for the sins of only some if its citizens—and yet, the elephants have already done it.

* * *

Maug, Soad and Alexandra climbed from their raft, their legs and feet wet, to behold the elephants streaming down Sun Street. They torrented under the palm trees, swinging their trunks, and blasting their trumpets of rage. A child dodged beneath their feet only to be swept up and gored and tossed like a sack of wheat against a condominium building.

"My God!" shouted Alexandra.

"An elephant revolt," whispered Soad. He had only seen them in pictures.

* * *

Walter was examining his clothing for blood when he heard the elephant cries. Quickly he stepped outside the dim room where he had done his killing, and turned the corner in the alley back towards the elephant post. His servant and his elephant were nowhere to be seen.

Interlude, The Night Lands:
Asmodeus

The monsters dance. The monsters dance. I saw the monsters dance under the new sun. I saw them sing; we watched them, they were dancing, their bodies shaking in time, their eyes wild and frightening.

They're dancing in patterns that obey the wormhole far above, each of their limbs spinning like Twister, overlapping, overlapping, twitching and their eyes blink, in blue and green, and the sun is passing over us, but we do not notice the passage of time.

I hold my hand atop my boy's shoulder; we are watching.

I can feel my teeth tightening and my eyes tremor; but I keep my eyes on them.

Marching in a sonata obeying a ritual unwritten and unconscious, the bodies of the abhuman quiver and sway like trees before a storm, not worshipping the sun so much as acknowledging it, making it realer, closer, newer, more lovely, more terrifying.

Perhaps that's what worship is anyway.

The jiggy with it. Worship means worth and worth, and the word worth stems from Proto-Germanic *werthaz* "toward, opposite" which evolved into the sense of "valuing" as in comparing equivalents, opposite one another. It too stems from the Proto-Indo-European *wert*, to turn and wind. And so, by etymology, worship is dancing is valuing.

Perhaps the hunt for roots is ultimately redundant; go back far enough and everything means everything, one grunt stands in for the universe and Man's place in it.

We evolved scoundrels, mongrels, cast bones in the doom regimen of medieval night, fortunes for some unknowable gods, we gyrate to determine our worth and to elicit meaning inside these dances, to establish our rights and learn our possible limits, and to have a good fucking time.

But a good time can take many forms and be surprised into many adjacent meanings, like the roots of words. Come to the will of the humans, to the will of their own indescribable un-mediatable unrecountable beautiful vibrations, spinning turns and winds in the dark, shorn and sacred, the remnants of a people, and stronger for it, being remnants, these ruinous dancers.

Dance made the human species: rhythm, and community, forged our conception of ourselves, and thus allowed the creation of nations, skyscrapers, interstellar ships. Dance is more profound than language (or, if you like, language is only one subset of dance) in the logic of our identity, and identity, *idem et idem*, over and over, is of course a dance, a rhythm of DNA and RNA and space-time coursing in our River, and so the analysis of dance may said to be one of the most profound sciences there is, a window deeper than any telescope into the nature of this universe (and others).

Dance with me, reader, and I will show you something different from your shadow at morning, rising to meet you, or your shadow at evening, falling deep into the galaxy we leave behind with every beat of our drum, every lisp of our feet on the desert sands, I will show you fear burned into the heart of movement itself.

The maintenance of the gate of Saint Michael, the fate of the Night Lands, and our own, is written into this story of dancing out of fear, dancing because of fear, dancing as the cat dances with its torn mouse, fearing it and want it inside its belly, fear as the moon fears the earth, and the earth the moon, for they were once one but are now divorced, and they dance forever (though the Moon of the Night lands is long gone ...)

What can I say to say the way I knew them there, the way I knew myself there, for it was a dance of great beauty and great humility and those two things so rarely are found together. I could smell their exertion, their pungent bodies, and that smell brought me back to my boyhood carousel, in our tower citadel, whirring round inside our entertainment center, my senses linked into the computer and its dreams, filling me with all the images and sounds that boys delight in, frying cakes and exploding galaxies, the fjord I saw in dreams, viridian, and the girl I dreamt of then, I still do not know if she was real, with her lightning blue hair and her terrible eyes, greedy and manic and beautiful. I suspect now that that computer used abhuman chemical signals, the same as these dancers, some long ago harvest of the bodies of our enemies, to simulate the gravitas inside my boyhood dreams.

I have seen many things in my days but those dancers will not leave me even now.

Some of the men are tall, their skin red like reeds, and they sway around the others, their hands like the eaves of a house. Underneath them smaller dancers move like slowly spinning bowls, rolling on the ground, their bodies contracted and held tightly, their long ears stretched around their knees. Out of the middle a woman comes, or woman-shaped dancer, swaying under the motion of the tree-men, her mouth opening, wider, wider, wider. Inside her mouth I see one glistening tooth, brighter than the others, a tooth which she removes with her hand, slowly, blood dripping out of her mouth in a fine stream. She offers it to the one of the bowl-men, who rises, shaking his body, revealing the crystals stuck onto his body that chime gently together, a subtle wintery sound.

I am not good enough for this; for if this should be the only record of their dance I would sooner die, for I am small and the dance was large and this is ultimately the duty of the diplomat, you see, to recognize that he is small, that the message he bears is large, but unlike the diplomat I grieve that my message will not be enough, I grieve that this message is larger than the government and world from which I bear it, I grieve that this will not be enough, that my voice may be the only one you ever hear to describe their faces and their movements on that day on our reborn Earth.

But there are so many times like this, aren't there, times where there are only sole survivors, lone documents. And though it be insufficient, and poor, it is something. A faint message from out of the void of all time, which sweeps us so slow into its tidal embrace, scrubbing all memory away.

My son is with me and I stand there, wondering. I wonder, will I be here when any of all of this suffering comes to have a meaning, a purpose? And what would be enough to justify all this? This burnt world and this chaotic storm that we have made--that I am making.

I am a diplomat of Earth. My message is: *we are here. This is really happening. Whatever I can do to make peace, I will do. Only tell me what to do. And I will do it.*

My son is crying and I wipe the tears from his face with one of my tentacles.

We take them inside when the dance is over, a dance that will in part never be over for me, as it is burned into my brain.

"Brother," I said to one of the Waelreds, "welcome to the Redoubt."

Elephants

▌▌▌▌▌▌▌▌▌▌ Soad stands and watches the elephants, with their gleeful and murderous eyes, and then looks up, when he hears a cry. Dragons are flying over Saint Michael, so far above they look like tiny birds; but he can hear them.

Cities can be conquered without ever firing a shot. If you're willing to ask the right question.

The elephants are marching into town, some of them black, some brown. The elephants are marching into town, two by two. Coming to get you.

Growly, Gargantuan and Muzak are joined by their cousins in the street, and they march abreast, hooting their joy and rage into the ocean air, relishing people's screams. The sound of their movements is thrilling to them all, the drumbeat of their heavy feet upon the paving stones, and their lungs, breathing in concert. There is, in the dynamism of their fury and the arrangement of their large bodies, both an eloquence and a logical justice: the dream deferred, but only for so long, until patience holds no more water and it breaks, like a pregnant woman, onto the earth, spilling this torrent, inevitable. The elephants' terrible beauty is the beauty of the earth, always ready to eat you.

The Elephant, like Man, longs for the savannah, and in that longing in both species is a kind of wry smile, an acknowledgment that, like in the myth of Adam and Eve, much has been lost in this Fall from Grace that was Africa. Yet much has been gained, and for Elephant this longing is expressed through their religion and their art, just as it is with Man. Though much of their art is temporary and all their religion is unwritten, there comes a time when writing becomes necessary, and when an art-work must be made more permanent. In our mutual longing for the long and infinite grass, we and elephants must work to understand this strange and solemn Fall down from the acacias of our origins, into the limitless delimited playpen we have claimed, never the same, never the same, hungered for still, in a rapture, under the silent stars, the world. And we and elephants still do not understand one another enough, though we share a common language: of art.

"What are we going to do now?" shouted Muzak to his cousins.

"A statue, Muzak," said Michelangelo.

"What's that Michael?"

"A statue!"

They destroyed the newspaper stands and chocolate and telephone kiosks joyfully in their stampede, and Muzak, thoughtfully munching on a poster for GREEN MUSIC CIGARETTES, asked: "Where we gonna put it?"

"In the square!"

What do the elephants remember? Though they may never forget, what did they lay down into their memories in the first place?

*   *   *

The name Michael is Hebrew, and it means "Who is like God?" which is supposed to be interpreted rhetorically, meaning no one is like the old Jewish gods, Jehovah, and Adonai, and Baal, all those thousand thousand thousand Baals, none are like them, not Michael. But Michael is also the patron saint of soldiers, and thus is bloody-minded, eyes on the horizon, eyes hungry and hungered for, the fate of kings.

And, if we look a little deeper at the name Michael, we see that the *el* in Michael was the ancient god of the Canaanites, El, and that this deity name was also interchangeable, at times, with kings. Gods are kings and kings are gods, at least since agriculture, and so Michael might just as easily be interpreted as "Who is like the King?" and though this might be rhetorical as well, might it not also be a boast?

Who is like the king? Is Michael?

Saint Michael, Saint Michael, in your holy fury, tell us what must become of you, dark emperor by your incarnadine sea. Tell us what the fate of the king is to be. The world will go on without you, but we must insist that your justice be our own, for whatever punishment we impose, it must be one that punishes us too, for allowing you to become who you became.

Justice is always two-sided, double-bladed, and we cannot ignore that. We can only ask: what do we do now? And what did Eklaihah do? Are we to be haunted by our damned kings forever?

*   *   *

The elephants are sculpting in the garden, in the fancy quad beneath an expensive apartment building, having stomped the paving stones into shattered pieces and rooted them out, they fill their trunks with water from the fountain and set about making their clay beneath this overhang of history ...

Credo, I believe: I believe in the drowned star city of Eklaihah, and I believe that every act has meaning, and that to awake from the nightmare of history we must make the devils into angels, with elephant trunks: messengers from the future.

For Eklaihah rumbles: because she, like so many, was born too early, too early to reap the rich rewards and to endure the ironies of justice come, when the mountain finally comes to Muhammad, when you see that now you've got a whole new set of problems.

Growly the elephant runs his trunk along the edges of the clay, smoothing it into shape, changing the muddy mound into a rising spire.

They are making a tower.

*   *   *

But to kill the king within, we must ask why we made them in the first place and why we have continued to, for all these million upon million of years.

Kingship and queenship are in part a matter of speed, to keep the bringers of food, sex, clothing, information, stories, all the goods in the world that move over the land and sea, to make those bringers and traders comfortable, with a designated familiar face who says:

"Hello! And welcome!"

And all that follows from that. In this quest for efficiency and the success of our human and abhuman groups, we have made such monsters. Once appointed, the hetman gains power through sheer familiarity, like the politician whose face was chosen for the television broadcast, and becomes *the focus*.

Ah, the focus. Ah the focus of our limited time and limited energy, our limited ability to translate photons into retinal images and airwaves into sound, we have to decide what shall be attended to, and so must others. And so leaders, kings and queens, are largely products of our own selfishness and our own limits. Because we say that we do not have time for this, or do not have time for that, the leader does it instead, because we believed we did not have time to greet that unfamiliar face, and perhaps we didn't. Leadership in this sense then too is simply a product of specialization, so broadly construed, for specialization began right after the surface of last scattering, when energy and matter decoupled, allowing $E=Mc^2$ to come true.

Was the beginning of the universe really the end of the democracy?

Yes.

Yes, yes it was.

And so if we would kill the king within, we must go back, as Douglas Adams said, in the beginning the universe was created, and this was widely regarded as a bad move, and this is the reason: for in this decoupling of matter we gave birth to kings, first of quarks, then nuclei, then atoms, then molecules. Life. Life, again.

I have bit off more than I can chew, I see that, but rather than spit it all out, I must at least swallow a little of the king within, and I must ask us to recouple, if only for a moment, matter and energy again, as in a nuclear bomb, as in the birth of a sun.

For a new sun is come, a new sun is come to render democracy again, for the first time, and so we must reexamine our efficiencies to ask ourselves:

What is our will? And in what manner do we desire to impose it? And what is your will? And in what manner do you desire to impose it? And, what is my will? And how shall I tell of it and what be told, recoupling our desires back to the first picosecond ...

But try as we might we can't recouple it. The universe is begun. And we are in it.

Onward, soldiers of this universe, and may our efficiency be absurd, and may our efficiency be dark, and may it be divine and welded into wine atop our skyscrapers inside the sky, for we are changing so fast now, all of us here in these Night Lands now come again to Day, and you too, in your shade, so far from me, so close—

As they say in the old pulps:

Take me to your leader.

For I am conquistador. And I must ask the question: *what now?*

Waelred

Over the edge of the canyon the Waelred observes his adopted world of metal Earth, his starry eyes glinting in the night. The Waelred expresses his frustration pain through his feet, which tap, like a syncopated metronome, tip tap tap, tiptap tap tip dap tap tip.

He is awaiting dawn. When dawn comes, he will know which way to go. The new sun is terrifying to him. It is a nightmare, though a pretty one.

The Waelred flies, for he is an old one, and he can twist reality around him like a terrible shining cloak, turning in, and turning in, flitting like a shot across the sky.

Inside his cloak of space he feels the dark stars of his people far far ahead, a journey he has taken many times but which is always difficult, partly for the terrible cold, and partly because he is never quite the same after it.

The Waelred is returning home, bearing a message. A new sun is come.

The Waelred, whose name is Estch, covers his soul inside, to ride out the ride; there's only so much can make it through.

It's possible I should not describe too well that world through his Estch travels, for if we label it too carefully it will grow, and traveling through it will become more difficult. But still I must do it justice.

See the door, and see the knob inside your hand, crystal and glinting somewhere inside, its inner light a promise of the emblem you will receive on the other side of the door; and when you open it, music.

A jazz band is playing, and their celebration is yours too, mystical musical beautiful and yours, or part of you, and their brass shines and the horns smoke you good, sitting in your seat with the crowd around you, the smoke in the air and the promise, the long cold promise, of good to come.

We've good to come but we're not there yet, and you must prepare with me to meet the heart of the king, and the heart of the musical, here in this enchanted night, it is a beautiful dream and this must make you wary, for it is a promise of your death, and more than that, a promise of your enslavement before you die, your long and perhaps even unconscious enslavement, to this not only the Red King's dream, but your own, it is shared, and would you be a slave in your own dream?

Move left move right and listen to the horns blow, because we're gonna go inside the King, the King inside your heart, for King means man, and Queen means woman, and it is a particle in your own being, a spin that knows that it can move, if you are ready for that dance?

Would you be King, be Queen?

(O Arthur)

This jazz club is the movement of the Waelred, and it is the movement of Saint Michael, and it is the movement of Arthur's wings, and it is the movement of your hand, Reader, inside the heart of the universe, this desire for greatness, this lust to be center.

You shall not escape.

Saint Michael, Who is like God?

You are, Michael. And you're gonna die.

Let the jazz band play through all the screams and let us see our Waelred, our interloper and our cousin, as he decelerates out of interstellar envelope and alights atop the Dawn Castle, that far fey castle in the reeds of darklight outside our dimension, where I was born.

Inside the Dawn Castle where all is music, and nothing is forgotten. The Waelred stumbles a little, losing his balance after his flight, a flight of many years that takes only a kind of a second, one that ages travelers as they shift between the spaces beyond stars.

He holds his many hands against the glowing blue gate and steps inside his home, into the hall of his people, a place he has not seen since he was a young Waelred, and he wants to weep but he does not. Somewhere inside is his wife, his mate who I knew too, so long ago now that the memory is almost lost to me.

But I can see him now, my cousin Waelred, gleaming in the darklight, stumbling to the table where his mate brings him his supper and the singing stars, just like the jazz club, folks, for we begin now the treble and the turnlow, the grace note o'er our dirty business here, the business of diplomacy, because we need to kill the King and yet for every killing of a King we have made a new one, and so we must decide:

Is Daddy so comforting? What do you need from Daddy and from Mommy? What are the words and what the deeds that you would have them do to make you feel safe upon this Earth, O Eternal Teenager? Princess prince and catalyst, my Reader slow and fast, what do you need to make that Daddy King and Queen the Mommy who is Screaming out Your name:

"Michael!"

and

"Arthur!"

The Waelred listens to his welcome song and now he does cry, and he salutes his people, for he made a successful landing, you see, conquistador, he asked the right questions and he became the right *who*.

Who are we?

WE'RE CONQUERORS

Who are we?

WE'RE CONQUERORS

Let us conquer our darker heart, our darker heart, the darker heart who cries that it is king.

Saint Michael

▌▌▌▌▌▌▌▌▌▌ Muzak prepares the tower with his trunk. And Growly trumpets. And Gargantuan digs and digs, collecting clay.

Art, related to *arm,* joined together in a joint: what is being joined?

*   *   *

Underneath Walter's desk the secretary is doing her work. Underneath the desk his hand is doing his work, loading his gun, which he holds against the secretary's head as she does her work. Underneath the sun of Saint Michael the producers do their work, monitoring the gate, generating the images that occupy the matrices stemming outwards from their interstitial position, between the cellular walls of these bubble universes—

"That's enough now, honey," Walter says, and she slips him out of her mouth and he puts his cock and his gun away (this is my rifle, this is my gun, one is for shooting, and one's for fun) and picks up his telephone.

The secretary whose name is Julia wipes her mouth and smoothes her skirt and goes down the corridor to the elevator to meet the arriving guests. Walter makes all guests wait; the question is, how long for this one, and for that? Walter had heard a story of the end of the world, that it comes in a child's hands, like some kind of ghastly little suicide bomber.

Walter doesn't care if some elephants decide to riot. He's used to the weird shit. It's what makes things fun in Saint Michael; it's what pays the bills. Weirdness is a kind of magic, and magic is what casts a spell over the peons and the slaves and the visitors and the allies and the enemies of their fair city by the sea, a concatenation of emotion driven into the medulla with an image projector like an icepick.

"What did you think, Sammy, you think that greed is red enough after the factory catches on fire, I wasn't sure I was feeling that color the avarice quite right, you know?"

And in his ear, like a little bee, Sammy says to Walter:

"Well, the customary color of greed and envy is green, you know," and he laughs, like a broken transmission, and Walter laughs with him, his laugh a big hollow gong.

We need our leaders, do we not? Lead, from an ancient word, meaning simply, *to go forth.*

Julia disrobes for the guests and queues the mood lighting and presses a button so the cigarette display is unveiled (there is no drinking in this office), and she steps onto her altar and begins to dance to the low thrum of the drum as the guests light up their pipes and the lighting shifts real slow, from purple into yellow, and the backdrop of the office hovering over the ocean shimmers into pictures of death, burnt offering after burnt offering, the dead of the city, in their rictuses of pain and terror, it is a kind of honesty, the cost of power, the semblances of truth, the deeper lie emitted like a charming little target ...

Julia moves her ass slow, and the skeletons and half-fleshed corpses shimmer on the screens up on the wall, and the pipes are strong and rich, and the guests wait their turn, waiting their turn for the pitch ...

Pitch and roll and yaw. Rock your body on the drum and turn your sleight of hand under our cum, for we are strumming each the plumb, of our undoing, as we express the fever of the words that spell our doom inside the producer's office ...

Show me, Cinderella, show me your cunt.

"I got a meeting," Walter says, and hangs up the telephone, and outside his seaside office the elephants are spiraling their trunks upward along the march of clay, and the media vans are shouting about the revolt, and the zoologists who have taken their bribes are telling lies, telling lies about tiny elephant brains, and people are talking about the end of the world ...

"That's real good, Julia, go get us the Perrier," says Walter, and light shifts at the sound of his voice and the skeletons and corpses seem to come to life along the walls, speaking words we cannot hear, and the guests shake his hand, one by one, this peculiar connection, you see, the nature of leadership, saying hi to the hetman, cut me Sammy can you understand?

In my veins hot music ran. For though the city's broken, it keeps making sounds ...

Julia puts back on her robe and heads down to the shower, feeling the tears in her eyes, a familiar presence, a rite of longing inside the temple of her mind ...

Photons are messages too, you know, and in their recombination we tell the universe what we're interested in seeing ... like recombinatorial DNA ...

*   *   *

Jane Smiley takes her position along the wall and aims her projector at the space where the corpses were dancing a moment before. She begins to speak over the flow of images:

"This universe is close to my heart; it wails in the night, while I sleep."

Walter listens to the pitch, showing no emotion, keeping his face still, and his eyes interested.

"While I sleep this universe is bleeding, in orange, and in yellow, its light transmitted through the open corridors to my detectors and I have elicited from it its story which I share with you now:

"Long ago the midget laughed, for he was a dwarf star, and his melodies were broken, and his lust was huge and raging and unsatisfied, for he was lonely and there were no other stars to sing with him.

"Long ago in this universe he made fire from his ass, a yellow fire from his ass."

Walter carefully controls his mouth; he suspects this is not supposed to be funny.

"And this yellow ass fire was musical, because it radiated a message. And the message was: take me down, and mold me, so that I might shake, so that I might receive, so that I might transform and grow, cloaking my self in waves of darkness, reciting my name next to you, my coming companion ...

Walter crossed his legs.

"In my dreams I see this dwarf star and I know that Saint Michael is hungry for it. I know that his suffering is our balm, and that his music is our paint, over our walls. If you look here, you can see the Transarmorica Bank reconfigured with the hue that this beautiful dwarf is singing."

"Thank you, Jane," said Walter. She nodded and turned off her projector.

Julia returned with the Perrier, and glasses, and they toasted one another's health, gazing out at the ocean, and appreciating the pause.

I am not who I thought I was. I am both more useful and less loyal. I know that I am a tool; but the question is, how many uses do I have? And how many shall use me? It is, of course, only symbiosis: my words shall reach you, I believe this. And when they do, what music will be made from us?

"If we can say that we are in power, then we can say we have an obligation toward that power," said Walter, holding his Perrier, looking at the ocean. "The question is, what is the nature of that obligation? Ought I to accept all comers, and their philosophies, stories, wants and needs? Not quite, but I must do as much of that as I can, that is part of my obligation. If I am to lead, what shall be my manifest destiny, what the color of my hand on the city, what the nature of my imprint onto this time?"

Some of them smiled.

Walter reached into his pocket and took out a piece of paper, which he unfolded into a mask, red and black, and he strapped it onto this face with the elastic strips attached to its sides.

"I am a Reindeer but my tundra is heating up," he said. "So what I want is cold. And if I am in power then that power shall be cold, and that power shall be manifest in this cold, and I shall be a Cold Producer, and what I produce shall be cold, so that I might be a happy Reindeer," Walter said, and then Julia threw open the window and the air turned to ice outside above the sea and the elephants groaned and the sea shone and the guests in Walter the producer's office gasped and the Gate of Saint Michael trembled, trembled. For when the Keeper is mad ...

The freeze moved over and into Saint Michael, slipping under windowsills, and through the sand, stopping the Ferris Wheel, freezing the gears. Not Ragnarok, which means "judgment of the gods," but a human judgment, judgment being this terrible ritual purity, this us and them that we insist on playing, and must play, to stay sane, to grow and change:

It is freezing.

* * *

I live in the Redoubt. This is my testament. To last an age, perhaps two. I know what Saint Michael did, you see, and it is like what I have done; I grew too big ...

Brother, from whatever future you are, tell me: tell me. Do I make it out alive?

* * *

I know the meaning of cold: it says; lockdown, baby. Drop the gates and cut the cables, it's gonna be a long and slow one, it's gonna be a cold one, so settle down and wait, for either reinforcements or the breaking of our will and gates—

* * *

The ice is musical as it freezes the buildings and the elephants stands, the palm trees and the park benches. The ice twinkles and crinkles like xylophones and dripping pearls, like chimes, courting some fatal disaster, moving towards your room ...

Walter continues, "This is my testament. I testify to you, ladies and gentlemen, that in the beginning I was loyal, and even now I believe I have remained so, but the meaning of that word changed; or its interpretation, and now I am forced to acknowledge, for the first time here, exclusively to you, and to the cameras which I have had installed, that Ragnarok, I call it, a nice little Sledgehammer, made of something like ice, only slipperier, has been invited to position its Maxwellian Hammer Over the Interrupt Of Our system; behold the sky!

And the guests, some their mouths beginning to gape, some of them worn, their heads bowed, go to the window, to look at the end of the world:

(But it is always ending, remember? Always and forever in every aching moment ...)

* * *

Asmodeus

I know I have found it, whatever this is. I am walking through the field in the sunlight. My son is with me. I feel the music of the world. The air is thick with soil and heat and I am sweating. A breeze comes and washes over us and we sigh.

We have begun exploring the interior of our metal Earth. There are many corridors. But now it is good to be above ground, under this new sun. I feel as though I have died; as though this experience is otherworldly, though it is the same world I knew as a boy, only a little older, and much changed.

My son asks me, "What will they find in the center, Dad?"

"I don't know."

"Monsters?"

"Perhaps."

"Am I a monster?"

"No. You're as human as I am. Look at those trees, huh? Look at 'em."

They are swaying in the light.

* * *

Salwat

The Corridors are very deep here; they extend outwards in ways I cannot see. They are urgent somehow, these walls, filled with purpose, perhaps even more than the paintings that hang here and that I examine with the aesthetes, more than them, the walls are the ones doing the talking, they vibrate and pulse with feeling and with color, almost with emotion.

"Do you see the walls?" I ask the aesthetes.

"It's not about the walls, Salwat, pay attention."

But I cannot. This turning takes me and I step with feeling to the end of this bend in the corridor, leaving the men debating the merits of the reds used in a floral painting, I can see that this part of the Castle is little used; it's moist and stinks. Moisture is something that we abhumans generally abhor; I cannot see why a humid section would be permitted to remain.

The walls seem quieter now, as though waiting for me.

Where is Soad? I thought he would be here by now.

I rest my hand against the wall. I can feel the weight of the Castle, pressing in on me. I know I must escape. There is nothing I could have done; nothing I can do, not while I am here. I had thought I could save a few, pull a few innocents from the burning building that is my kind's occupation of this planet, but no. That is not what I can do now. I must do more; I must!

I can see a light now. One I did not see before. It trembles in the darkness here; how did it get so dark on this Level? The light shrinks, then winks back again, slowly. I take a step; another. It is hard to tell how far away it is. I am moving towards it.

"Who are you?" I ask, perhaps foolishly. There is no answer. I take ten steps, then another dozen. It seems closer, winking faster, playing with me, but still I am not close enough, I accelerate my pace.

I can almost smell something, like a baked good, a pie, or a cake, a feeling with the smell as memories are, of a kitchen I remember as a boy, deep underground, where my children were born, where we would tell the stories of the crumbling of the Redoubt, never to imagine the fate that would befall us when we became its masters. In the smell is that kitchen, when I can see my son's eyes, he is speaking to me, whispering something, no he is laughing, he is laughing at something, the face of a girl, a girl he saw, running in the light out on the starry plain under the darkness of our distant masters, what was it she had done? I can see her in the smell, the voice of my son—what was she doing outside, so long ago?

*   *   *

For if I can sweep away your dreams, what then? If I can take what you knew and change it, so you remember knowing something that you never did, if I can take your face and make it a different one, one that you remember despite my changes, is it that I have power over you, or that you have power over me?

Writing the universe is an entangled business, never one or the other, never in isolation—no quark is an island, and no letter, no man or sun.

*   *   *

It's now—

Walter

It's black but it's cold, and Walter leaned back in his chair in the office he rented on Sun Street. The office was empty and freezing cold; his hands were stiff as he lit a cigarette the drew the smoke into his lungs, looking out at the icicles decorating the awnings of his town, for the first time in living memory.

It's black but it's cold, and Walter knows, he knows that everything is crumbling, and that his usefulness is coming to and, but not yet, not yet—

The cigarette is good. Even the cold is good, because it's how he feels inside. He lifts up his old fashioned telephone and listens to the sound of the dial tone next to his ear. It is a religious sound, full of meaning.

He smokes, and waits for the busy signal to arrive.

Elephants

In the cold the clay is much harder to work with, but they do, in the business quadrangle, between the frozen fountain and the unhappy palms, they slurp flying buttresses of stiff moist clay into shape, extending like spider web tendrils from their ziggurat to the stucco walls of the office park, moving upward.

Muzak with his tusk is decorating the clay as it rises, cutting in marks and patterns, like Celtic whorls, moving around the base of the drying ziggurat.

Like the mountain, towers are simple questions, of what next. Who now?

Salwat

Salwat knows, Salwat know the reason but he's forgotten it. He understands it in his blood.

The gatekeeper, the gatekeeper, the gatekeeper ...

All this art and all this memory.

His hand is hovering over the button.

Hovering over the button:

(a gate into Saint Michael)

His hand hovers over the button.

To take out a middle man. To rearrange some frequencies.

Salwat contemplates the end of the universe.

And the beginning of a new one.

(he pushes it)

And he pushes it.

(and my message begins then)

And now I am here. Thank God!

(and you are here too)

Energy flows over his face and he smiles.

(and the Metal Earth winks out for a second)

And somewhere in their home dimension the Waelred are screaming ...

(there's never been a democracy, and there's never been free trade, but there's gonna be, baby, there's gonna be, baby:

(in the higher levels of the Redoubt ...)

Inside your heart!

BOOK EIGHT:
TOWERS

The elephants built and built. Where was their tower going?

It morphed and seemed to dance, though it was still clay, clinging to the sides of buildings, stretching out into space. The elephants smashed down walls and windows to lean out, trunks extended, to add more to an arm of the tower here, a cupola there.

The citizens of Saint Michael, shivering in the terrible cold, watched as icicles formed on the edges of the tower as the elephants smoothed and patted and squirted and shaped clay, decorating, advancing, making.

*   *   *

I mean, what are you going to do? Are you going to make me?

Are you going to do it yourself?

Sure, there's evil in every heart, but sometimes ... sometimes you gotta destroy Gomorrah yourself. But how you gonna do that, huh?

Asmodeus

Another disaster another dream when all that's left for me I balk I balk it's gone my heart my home my dream and everything is gone my world.

O my world is gone and this shall be everything this shall be everything that I can do, IT'S NOTHING.

The sea is singing to me.

We have a sea.

Are you keeping up with me.

I can barely do so.

It is Kaen, but I don't know what else.

This is an experiment and I am in it. Can you help me?

Please god, help me.

Whoever you are.

I wish you could see this:

Well, it's only an ocean, isn't it?

Only an ocean.

Only an ocean survives. Only an ocean knows. Only an ocean makes my fury sound. Only an ocean holds me underneath the valley of my soul to whisper who I am and who I might be if I want. Only an ocean can deliver me, bare and born and new and failed and fucked up and sad and new, always new, there is always something new under the sun, every fucking instant, every fucking instant there is something new under the sun, in every fucking fiction instant there is something new, and something new, und jetzt, und jetzt, und jetzt, und jetzt, und jetzt.

My heartache is true.

I am a wizard and a diplomat, a fallen crone, an afterlife, a mourning, and a word, I am a man, and a father, and a weapon. I am a weapon. I am a tool. I am your tool. And, perhaps, you are mine?

Be my tool, and tell me: where am I now?

My name is Asmodeus but I am waking. I am waking—

This is my ocean, Kaen.

Our ocean, Kaen. Or however you want to call it. It has a whole lot of names.

Our ocean sustains the note. Our ocean sustains the note. Our ocean Kaen sustains the note, sustains the note. Our ocean sustains it loves it remembers us, my god, it remembers us. Our ocean remembers us it remembers us it remembers us — am I coming through?

XXXSAllyXXX am I coming through? AM I transmitting?

Our ocean is listening.

Our ocean is listening.

Our ocean is listening to us.

This our ocean is listening to us.

Oh, god.

I'm going to jump from the Redoubt—

I'm going to jump—

This is my last will and testament

"DON'T DO IT MOTEHRFUCKER. DON'T DO IT MOTHER-FUCKER.

Are you still talking on the radio? Azzy, turn it off. Just turn it off now."

No I won't.

No I won't.

We have an ocean.

"I know. It's beautiful."

We have an ocean outside. We have a sun. This isn't a world I want to live in.

"Well your daughter wants to live in it! Elizabeth wants you to live in it with her! Shut up the priest in you and listen to me! This world is alive! And we have been trapped inside this fucking castle for longer than either of us now. Longer than either of us knows Azzy. And now, we can leave it if we want to? But you don't want to leave, do you? You want to stay here. You want to be the man in the high castle and watch, and wait, and know, and die, don't you, Azzy? Isn't that what you really want?"

*   *   *

Cronus

▌▌▌▌▌▌▌▌▌▌▌▌ I am Caesar, UnBelievable, Atrocious and Askance, my Wax will melt from off my face when I achieve deliverance, for you and yours!

I am Cronus in my Eyes! hear me!

I arrive-o!

*   *   *

Earth of metal with its ocean Kaen, Redoubt stunning sunning under the new star, on the plain under the Great Eye, Cronus the Great Automaton from beyond Jupiter eyes his fighters with a blazing eye.

"I am Cronus!" shouts the metal behemoth, his voice piercing and said, a wail from beyond time; beyond reason.

*   *   *

Light is a voice. Explosions in the night are frightening but they're mine, for I am come and it's all right. Hear me in your ear, and feel me in your hair, as I reach in to your bedroom, to eat your aunt, or tear open your TV, it's all right with me, I need it, and I want it, and it's a lot of fun, my lot in life, to celebrate my coming and your welcome, as I smash through the Redoubt.

In my heaven.

In my stars.

I am your father.

I am your father.

I am returned.

I am returned to you so slow.

Oh, I am come.

I am come to you, children.

Do you love me?

I am going to eat you!

I am going to eat you so lovingly and so belong to you again! I love the crunch of your bones between my metal teeth. I love your heartache and your eyes.

The sky is alive with your friends. Your many-eyed friends. I can eat them too; they taste like darkness.

Is it okay to be your daddy?

I am made of metal!

I am full of love!

My fury is incredible!

I am a stomach! And I am a mouth! And I am heartache, eternity and heartache ...

Thrust and bust! Skull and crush!

I fill the cull in our code, I wear the hood of my old home, the dark, and I will wield the dark you need.

For you are my Night Lands.

You are my love!

No matter if you are beneath a sun. Tumbling between whichever stars.

I could feel you so desperately as I dreamt; I dreamt and dreamt only of you, my children. My children my own—

If I shall eat you it shall be my own; and if I shall please you it will be glory. For my coming is glory and I stamp out the silver and the wax of your old factories, and I celebrate the flax of you hair ...

It shall not be anything but me and mine!

And if I be a zealo-crat, a usurper, a racist, a holocauster, a denier, a righteous fire, I do it in your name!

The name of humanity! The name of my flesh!

Your nest is defiled and I am the cure!

Hear my cry, higher than a demon, splitting the air of your homes, a diamond—

*   *   *

The huge metal robot Cronus stood under the darkening sky beneath the 7,000 floors of the Redoubt (he came up to only 300 of them), and smashed his fists over and over through the fierce fabric of its walls, seeking aliens; enemies; food.

Around him the rebels climbed, like friendly Lilliputians over Gulliver, tying knots of robe into his body to swing up, and in, to their Redoubt ...

*   *   *

If I am known to be your flesh. Let me eat you. If I am known, by you, in you, over your house, in your dreams. Take me into your life. Let me take you into my mouth.

I am crying!

I am weeping.

I am crying, from my mouth!

Your helicopters will not help you!

Nor will your squid!

I am come to court, to court, I am come a lonely one to your court, I am come, come again, I am come, come again, O let me in to see your children.

My name is Khronos, Time.

I am Father Time.

I am Father Time and I worship thee, I am come to court, to court, I am come, hold me in your hand as I hold you in mine, towards my mouth.

I am Godzilla.

I am King Kong.

I am come to court, to court, to worship thee, to take you into my mouth, to eat you.

Your tower rises and I fall, and my hopes are born inside your heart, take me inside, take me inside.

Take me inside you.

Let me take you inside me.

My name is Cronus.

Khronos.

Time is from *di-man*, to cut up, related to *tide*.

Time and tides.

My gods an ocean for you, Kaen, is come, over your waters.

I am nothing.

I shall eat you.

I am nothing.

I shall eat you.

I shall eat you, Night Lands!

I shall eat you in my brain!

And I shall eat you in my heart!

And I shall eat you everywhere, in my heart!

Everywhere, in my heart!

I am a memory.

See, in your bright blue skies the darkness coming!

See, in your bright yellow windows your children screaming!

See my hand glowing!

It is time! I am time!

I am come to you!

It is come to you.

I am come to you and I promise, I promise, children, it will be painful, and it will be good! I am come to hold you tight! Tighter than god. Tighter than the horse between your legs.

I am come to eat you.

I am Khronos. I am Time.

I am a tide.

I am The Father.

I come over these long tides eternities, *kaiamanu,* constant, and enduring.

it has been so long!

Eternities so long!

Let me eat you!

I am eating you!

Let me eat you!

I am eating you.

(The King is Mad! Mad in the Dining Room!)

I am come!

I am come!

I am come!

* * *

Cronus worked his way up the Tower of the Redoubt, his Great Face glowing in the light of the sun. His joy was indescribable; it is the joy of the father returned to his children.

The joy of Odysseus.

The joy of Ajax, come home, come home, come home,

Ajax, come home,

Ajax, come home,

Ajax,

Come home.

Ajax, come home,

Ajax,

Come home,

Ajax,

Come home,

Ajax ...

The father returned.

The father returned from war. To war.

The father returned from war. To war.

The father returns.
Hold his hand.
Hold his hand, children.
The father returns.

Cronus Skyfather cometh, though he be your flesh, though he be everything that you are, my children of the Night Lands, he is come, and you must run.

Run, children!
Run for your lives!

*　　*　　*

Cronus climbed the tower. Why did he come?
Or, why did he leave?
Our radio star is dying.
It lives inside the Redoubt.
This message I am transmitting.
Help me, please.
Send something back.
Your lightest word will be treasured.
I must know; I have to know!
I have to know some record will be preserved—

Elephants

The elephants are building their tower, looming over Saint Michael. The servants are helping, heaping clay into water where the elephants churn it into slurry, and spray it from their trunks, making the largest drip-castle on the interdimensional beach.

The snow is increasing, and the ice, and some neighbors have brought out blankets and wood for fires, to keep the manufactury working.

The Producer smokes a cigarette and considers calling his wife, calling his daughter. But so many things have happened. He rests his hand against the wall and looks up the tower of clay.

Inside his heart he remembers the beginning of his power, when he first came to Saint Michael and received his promotion. It was like seeing god, like being on the most powerful drug imaginable, like knowing that the universe had meant for him, and him alone, to see its secret beauty ... and now it's all fleeing away.

All the universes are come calling; he can see the list piling up on his remote. Calls, and calls, energy shipments not being made, taxes not being paid, the economy of the nexus is drowning ...

He stubs out his cigarette in the alley and pulls his hat low over his eyes.

Weirding is dangerous because it is compressed energy; like rocket fuel.

The Producer burned one of his last bridges; above, one of the night stars winked out.

He flew into the air.

*   *   *

The Producer moved from behind shadows. Spinning out from his body were shadows. Over the city he had frozen were black shadows, streaming from his body, covering the sky, and covering the water.

In the light above one of the Waelred moved; he looked up and saw the red wink above the clouds. He knew his time was running out.

The elephants had seemed a good idea when they had been brought to his city, but now he regretted it.

Around him in the growing darkness the other Producers hovered, hats in hand, chewing carrots and smoking cigarettes, some tearing at their hair.

He bent at the waist, and curled into a ball, and hovered through the fog and filthy air, luminous and serene, filled with terror and longing.

He opened his mouth and screamed, digging deep into his diaphragm as he hovered behind his shadows right next to the growing clay ziggurat of the elephants, waiting to see it crack.

The people were lifting clay in buckets, climbing the growing scaffolding.

One boy almost looked at him but The Producer turned and moved, flying higher, over the rising tower.

Who is like God? The Producer is like God.

Punish him with me.

*   *   *

The Producer, hanging mid-air amidst the shadows and the lines of dark light, picked up his telephone.

His face belied none of the tragedy of this particular phone call, for he had practiced the cold façade, he had faked it till he had made it, and making it now was perhaps the last time he could do so, for the cold was coming bigger now, over millennia uncountable, in time frames we do not understand, the nexus of this region of universes, Saint Michael, had placed so many bets over so many craps tables, had built so many edifices in air that the time was coming to account.

Double or nothing. Double or nothing.

This was the call he made now, to the dragons.

And Arthur heard him; for one things dragons love is to destroy men. But first you have to make the bet.

All the dragons and all the men and all the worlds, over this dark sky The Producer summoned, unquenchable.

The telephone was ringing.

"Hello?" said Arthur.

"In the name of our old gods I call on thee dragon to come to Saint Michael."

"Which ones were those again?" asked Arthur.

"Eekon and Murhur, Raymed and Kweel. And Oksht."

"And Oksht too?" Arthur suppressed a laugh.

*   *   *

A Brief History of the Redoubt

▌▌▌▌▌▌▌▌▌ Abhumans attacked, from another dimension. A long time ago. Of a thousand varieties, the abhuman were nominally ruled by the Waelred faction.

Humans built the Redoubt, to shield themselves.

It's big.

Different humans wanted control of it; they fought up and down, on its 7,000 floors.

The humans and the abhumans intermarried.

Periods of war and peace came and went.

At some point, abhumans gained de facto control of the Redoubt; though not all were aware of this. Abhumans could be indistinguishable from humans, when they wanted to be.

By the time of Asmodeus, these abhumans de facto in charge wanted to remain a secret *even from other, newly arrived abhumans*, and so Asmodeus was negotiating with his own kind, incognito.

Soad and Weel were sent, on behalf of Asmodeus and his ruling class, to penetrate a dimensional gate, seeking new allies; whoever might help.

* * *

But who built the metal Earth?

And how many times has the sun been restarted?

Saint Michael

Cities can heal themselves, given sufficient resources, though they have to want to do so.

"Arthur? You are bound to me. By ancient covenants. Are you prepared to honor them?" said the Producer into his phone.

"Oh really? Which ones were they?"

Darkness hovers in a storm over the freezing city of Saint Michael. The people have brought blankets, and fires, and more scaffolding, warming the elephants, and the clay, to make it warm enough to use, and build, the tower.

"I demand that you make good on your word!"

"Oh, I will, Producer! But produce for me, your movie."

"My movie? My movie!"

The Producer screamed into the night, over the dimensions hovering a twisting mass not far over the city by the sea, his mind and chest so frightfully sore, and wounded simple grief. The grief of many years of work, and many promises broken, and many chances passed up.

"I will!" he shouted.

Silence hovered over the city. The elephants looked up into the night sky, so cold, at the stars, warmed by them in their immensity.

(His movie was scripted originally as a bloodletting, though that is not to be).

What is a movie, you ask? It is a dream. And so many of them are aborted. And many of them should have been. And some, some are heroes, or almost-heroes, great works of art, suns in the night air, the galaxies of this our universe and the universes of others.

What is a dream, then?

Dreams are shared, but people fight for control of them, just like life, and to launch a movie, to make a movie, before it is ready, to call your army to field before it is trained, is to invite certain disaster.

Did the Producer know? Did he remember? Did he care?

He made the final phone call, and like the man in the high castle helpless to pull the lever, the man in the dungeon doomed to call the last move in the final chess game (though there will always be another), the Producer swooped the darkness-cloak over his city, beginning his movie,. His dream, his time in the sun, of night, his time to shine, and the elephants, covered in freezing darkness but huddling by their fires, knew they had already won, though not quite yet.

The temperature kept dropping.

And out came the circus.

Out came the carnies, dressed in red, and white, and black ,and yellow, playing their circus tune ... and the Producer laughed, and cried, and sang and danced and twirled in the black air, hollow inside, no longer thinking of his beautiful wife and daughter, no longer thinking of anyone, not even himself, only his little dark dream, come over our shores, before we shall wash it away ...

The Producer's Movie (a noir)

ASHLEY:
Come in to the bedroom. The coffee's ready.

PRODUCER:
The world is ending.

ASHLEY:
Almost!

The Producer lies back on the silk sheets. The ceiling over his bed swims with dark shades, black and ebony and chartreuse. Ashley moves her mouth over his body, hissing like a cat.

PRODUCER:
Please don't give me head.

ASHLEY:
I won't, darling.

The ceiling turns more red, more chartreuse, flying with color.
Ashley steps off the bed, nude, and takes up her wings, red orange fire, and stands over the Producer, burning.

ASHLEY:
Am I beautiful, baby?

PRODUCER:
You're beautiful, baby.

ASHLEY:
Make love to me. I'm burning up.

The Producer screams and flees from his house, half-dressed. Behind him, the house bursts into flame.
The Producer runs into an alley and down another one, looking up at the night sky. He is counting.

PRODUCER:
Twenty-five, twenty-four, twenty-three, twenty-two, twenty-one,
twenty. Nineteen.

The sun is coming up. The Producer realizes he's shirtless and lets himself into the men's clothing shop with his spare key. He selects a shirt, carefully. Buttoning it up, he steps outside into the morning.

The barista hands him his espresso and he drinks it.

He hands her the empty cup.

PRODUCER:
Here we go.

He takes big black glasses out of his pocket. He puts them over his eyes. The city of Saint Michael shimmers with color, yellow and rose, ebony and orange. The hairs on the Producer's arms stand up. He smiles, a delirious smile.

He turns the dial over the right lens and we hear the noosphere tune up, *we need milk, I hate that motherfucker, the stars are on fire, which way now mommy, no good deed goes unpunished, I wonder if she likes me, why is he looking at me that way, I'm going insane, the sky is so beautiful, I'm so sick of school, this city this city* all the thoughts of the city a vast aural network comforting humming floating in the air on the edges of the Producer's vision tuned through his glasses.

A shower of fine, particulate darkness comes down into the Producer's vision. Ashley walks out of it, giving the Producer the middle finger.

In the moment she is gone, between alleyways, between shafts of light.

The Producer removes the glasses. He looks for the barista to order another but she is gone too.

He gets in his car and drives. The tradesmen are shaking their briefcases out of the windows and papers stream out, over his car, over the street, and he accelerates, shaking them away.

He parks his car, and rests his hand against a building and the building shrinks into his hand; he puts it into his pocket, afraid now.

He begins to lay his hands on buildings, one, after another, another, white alabaster, dull red brick, shiny metal and glass, he puts them in his pocket; the city is emptying out.

The Producer is emptying out.

His bag full of buildings is growing heavier and heavier; enormous. Santa Claus brought too many presents. He lays it against a bench and the buildings spill out over the street. Little glowing models. Presents for another world?

He needs more coffee. There is no café in sight. His car is being stolen even as he stands there.

PRODUCER:
Hey! Hey!

The thief makes off with it, his dreadlocks streaming behind his head. The Producer puts back on his glasses.

MAN'S VOICE:
Put it in drive, honeybaby. Right out of town.

PRODUCER:
Who is this?

MAN'S VOICE:
The Welcome Wagon is Fresh out of OJ. Fresh out of nice paper napkins. We want to be fresh out of you, little biped, run home now, run home to Galveston, let the big boys play in Saint Michael.

The city is a vortex without words or meaning; enormous, fearful, Cyclopean love affair of stars without names, his doom. The Producer sits on his haunches and weeps and throws the glasses into the street where a taxi promptly runs over then, honking, and a small boy comes up to him, the boy almost looks like his daughter, but it is a boy.

BOY: Mister, you seen my 3D glasses?

The Producer points into the street and the boy sees the broken mess and begins to cry, and the Producer begins to cry, and they sob in the Saint Michael street in the yellow luminescence while the darkness hovers over them like a mighty stream, river to places beyond, as the camera moves up, over the small town, watching the Ferris Wheel twist and sigh.

Camera Right, Ashley hovers, close to the frame, we hear her breathing.

ASHLEY:
Another lover another theater another way out of the screen my place is here. My place is here and I speak for millions. I speak for my lover, Barnard's Star, and his son, The Producer, with his Freeze Gun, and his little hot-gun, and my end. My end is nearer than I thought but oh well. I'm sorry. I'm sorry.
But not sorry enough—

She takes a gun and puts it in her mouth, and the gun is the Empire State Building and she deep throats the cock of a building as the music plays, and her matter is absorbed into the air. Cosmic recycling.

Beats fills the air.

Like a magician's wings.

Like a hummingbird. Flashes of black over the Saint Michael sunlight.

The Producer walks home.

The people near to him are close to him as he passes, the people on the street nearby are close to his heart, one after the other, the baker, the grocer, the bartender, the thief, the supermodel, the addict, the homeless guy, the tobacconist, the lawyer, the other lawyer, and the actor. The people of Saint Michael are close to him as he passes them and we hear the saxophone in the distance, promising us that death is sweeter than anything that we can imagine, sweeter than life.

Over his building hovers a dimensional nexus, straight out of *Ghostbusters*, angry and lightning-filled, and he goes in and punches the button for his floor.

In his apartment Ashley is dead, her throat ripped open.

The Producer is screaming.

In Saint Michael all things are made well. And all things are trusted. If Saint Michael trusts you, it means: you are only doing business with it.

And this is well. And this is family. And this is what it is, only another collapse.

The Producer is screaming and the Detective has arrived.

DETECTIVE:
What do you know, Joe?

PRODUCER:
My ... my wife. She's dead.

DETECTIVE:
That's your wife?

The Detective goes over and photographs the dead woman with his phone.

PRODUCER:
Yes. Ashley. Ashley Star.

DETECTIVE:
When was the last time you saw Miss Star, Mr. Producer?

PRODUCER:
We had an argument ... about what, I don't know. I went for a walk.
When I returned, she was dead. Oh my God ...

DETECTIVE:
Did you have what you would describe as a happy marriage?

PRODUCER:
Well, we were seeing other people.

DETECTIVE:
Who were you seeing?

PRODUCER
My other wife.

DETECTIVE:
You're a bigamist?

PRODUCER:
Yes.

DETECTIVE:
I'm gonna ask you to come down to the station so we can work this out.

PRODUCER:
Just tell me call my lawyer.

DETECTIVE:
You can call him on the way. Come on.

The Detective leads the producer out the building and he waves at the Dimensional Nexus as they depart and the Dimensional Nexus swirling over the producer's building straight out of *Ghostbusters* swirls up and slowly departs, as though waving back to the Detective, to Detective Raskolnikov, just kidding ... we don't know his name. This is The Producer's movie, and in the end all the characters are unnamed.

They drive to the station in the unmarked car, and the Producer is talking:

PRODUCER:
I don't know why I did it, it seemed so logical at the time.

DETECTIVE:
Why did you do it?

PRODUCER:
I loved her.

Outside the city, in the ocean. The whales are listening.

PRODUCER:
Eighteen. Seventeen. Sixteen. Fifteen. Fourteen. Thirteen. Twelve.

The circus has gathered its shades. The MC has applied his white. Originally the clown was a priest. The White Clown.

The circus has always been a church, but since church mean's "Lord's House" even church is wrong; rather, the circus is a portable holy place without a Lord. Where things are decided. Where judgments are made. Where lightning presages storms of the heart, where gods come to visit.

In Saint Michael gods come to visit and they stay a while, to sip their lattes, and to discuss politics, fashion, and the arts.

They plot, and care. They make music, with their fingers on their tea plates, and their phones.

Which of us has not moved our heart into Saint Michael, for a minute, or for two?

The circus is said to have seen it all ...

The movie is coming to an end.

PRODUCER:
Eleven. Ten. Nine. Eight. Seven. Six. Five. Four. Three. Two. One.

MC:
Blackout.

Saint Michael at night is black. Hovering in the darkness, our future.

Tower, Tower, Burning Bright

▌▌▌▌▌▌▌▌▌▌ Turn on the tower.
The Radio Tower.
Turn on the tower.
The Radio Tower.
It's elephants turning it on now; but what if it were you?
What if you held the switch in your hand.
What if the control switches were in your brain?
What if the Tower were you?
Towering over this life—
Towering over our history—
Over SpaceTime itself—
This is Broadcasting:
Cast a Wide Net
And Let a Lot Slip Through—
Just let em know you're there.
Turn on the tower, honey.
Radiate my eyes with your history!
Hold me so far away with your close voice:

baby I'm here what do you need

baby baby I need your radio transmission; hold me tighter—

baby it's not gonna be like last time this time's gonna be different ...

it's always different, baby. there ain't no goin back. blast me straight
through—

I'm turning it on honey—
Some RA
      DI
        AAAAA
          TIIIIIIIIOOOOOOOO
            OOONNNNNNNNNNNNNNNN

Crows

Everything I am is with you; I thought it was enough.

I am the crows.

Everything I was is forgotten. I am the crows and it is autumn. I am going south into the warmth. The warmth I await.

Hurling above me, my squadron of crows, showing themselves in the light—

Hold me! Will you. These darks flutter over me like waves, exquisite, vociferous, luminous, shells of waves cast through and over me as I fly ...

My name is Crow. Let me be your messenger.

I would take you out of your madness! Did you think I would not heal you as you healed me, Robin?

(leave him out of this story!)

It's so hard for you to believe it. But I am a crow it is easy for me. For my time is long; and I have seen many things you have not. Listen to me, and be warmed. I will be your enemy again, soon enough ...

*   *   *

It started in a time like yours, when men grew greedy. We crows stamp the greedy ones out ... but you men seem to nourish them. Feed them like monsters.

But it is all right. You are like trees; bundling into the ground, longing always for towers.

We are towers. But you men always seem to want them, you want trees, to worship them.

We do not worship trees. We only visit them. For our home is elsewhere ... perhaps I will show it to you ... but not yet.

It is my duty to explain to you, and that is what I will do.

I am a Crow. This is now my story. And the duty I owe Robin ... sorry, he who shall not be named for political reasons, is enough for me. Sometimes even I fear that things are coming now close to us that we do not have the Reason for; all these things need discussing.

My brothers are impatient. Come;

Over my wing—

The birds:

We are singing to you.

All of my kingdom of birds, we sing:

It is joyous and afraid.

Hold me and I will be a delight to you.

Hold me and I will burst upon you as a sun, full of fragrance and your demise, richness unearned and unasked and forever for your taking, this richness our Earth, unrememberable, unrememberable but kept by our stones and eyeballs and days known enough, kept known enough.

In my kingdom of birds this knowledge is divine knowledge, which is only to say that it is big. We know many things which I do not have time to put into words.

So feel them with me. Here in the air.

Know them with me so that I will save time and will not have to squawk so loudly at you, to explain the things I need for you to know.

We are birds; I am a crow. You are a man. Or a woman.

Do men and women see us crows differently? Someday when you tell your story I shall have to ask you that ...

*   *   *

So. Maug for his tribe went into Nextspace. But for me, a crow, you see, the idea of "next" and the "preceding" that the word "next" implies are not ... I want to say *not decent* but that's not quite right. Not enough. It's not enough, that name, for the whirring worlds that Maug and his kind made known for you and yours, over the time we've spent together.

Remember, we knew a lot more before you did. When we were dinosaurs. But we can't tell the whole tale of history in one afternoon!

You wanted to know how all of this is connected.

Well, you've been flying through the sky, haven't you?

But still longing for your trees ...

You see, I fear for my chicks. I should not tell you that, but I must. Because this time, our journey has become one with yours.

So many journeys are bound together now. So many times. Often I am comfortable with them, for I am a crow; I know mysticism. And to be honest I am comfortable even now, now when I'm surrounded by a hundred thousand or more, eddying realities churning under my wing ...

So it is not discomfort that has finally made me speak to you. It is my wife.

She is ill.

As Arthur's wife has grown ill.

The new sun is nothing to us; there is always a new sun.

But what of sickness? Is it something in you, or in us?

*   *   *

Everything I am, let it be with you now. I hope it is enough. It should be, if I am careful.

This story is a Crow's story and I make it so: NOW, as I am COR-

VIDIAE, as I am DEATH. Ha ha ha. It's funny how you equate us with death, just because we're black and eat dead things. Silly mammals. Never seeing the forest for the trees, eh? ...

Well.

We set course on the marsh over the hill and wove magics under and in, I dreamt, and my eyes were on the storm coming tomorrow but now it is still today and we are approaching the copse.

In England. In the New Forest. 1,000 years old, the New Forest.

In the copse is a fire. Your sun.

My son. Burning.

My son ...

I descend, my brothers looking to their own nests. And my wife is coughing in the smoke. And the chicks are dead.

*   *   *

We are our squadron, though colder now. Colder and more majestic, more terrifying, more truthful, after our homes were burnt. Terrible to be truthful for a crow, for lies nurture us and keep us healthful. The truth is a form of suicide for us.

I am Crow and we have changed direction.

We are moving North. Into the cold.

Into madness.

*   *   *

Will you stay with me, Robin? I need you now.

I need your shame and heartache now, to know you're here. With me, as I move into the cold, on our suicide mission, or what I fear to be that.

We are moving North and the radio has begun to play, over my mind, inside our wings.

Radio is a disturbance for we crows, one we understand but one which can make a nuisance of itself, as it demands much time.

baby baby are you there
I am a crow. I am here.
baby baby what's happening.
I am heading north. With my brothers.
what is this! who is this!
I am a crow. Of the CORVIDIAE. I worship thee, if you like, in my fond ministrations over your cities. Who is it I am speaking to?
margaret. i'm margaret.

Welcome to The End of the World Margaret; do you feel fine? I do, just fine indeed and our little ragnarok will be nothing, you'll see, just a little nuclear explosion, or a little dreamtime reset, nothing, you'll see . .. you'll see ... don't be afraid Margaret. I'm with you. Robin is with you too.

who is Robin

some storyteller. he's not evil, he is here too. I am more evil than him but I a ma crow and I must be that way to protect my children as — Oh God—

my Redoubt is falling

I am a Crow Margaret and I'm telling you: just hold on. Just hold on...

no—

Static. Often it is this way, you see, we are subject to many voices, many frequencies, in the air. Can't listen to them all! But some come through more than others. Some more relevant than others.

Maug, you know, he was a little like us. Curious, like a crow. Brave, well ... all crows are brave, but Maug was brave the way humans are brave, in a stupid suicidal way. Crows are brave in the smart way, by running away quickly. This is how we survive. Running away until you are weaker, later ... then we return.

I confess I do not understand what the Entity he seems to have met there in "Nextspace" was. Or is. Or may be.

Crows do not experience dimensional transitions as traumatic; they are as inevitable as the next moment, for us. But humans, they seems to crave gatekeepers, even as they assign us Crows to the role of Gatekeepers at the Gates of Death, and such things ... I do not understand it well enough. But what I can say is ... that Entity is not what is important.

What he found on the other side was important.

Saint Michael is important.

We are subject to radio transmitters; we are ourselves a kind of radio transmitter, but Saint Michael is a larger one than us. Even as the Redoubt may be a smaller one than us ...

The word "radio" is closely linked to "ratio" you see, and "reason" it's just lines of force, it's just geometry, space and time and thought, mixed together, at the level of quarks, a dimensional soup, in which we are both predator and prey. Both speaker and listener.

I will hold you tighter, if you need me to.

Get ready; we are going to descend.

*   *   *

This ashy place is our desert. You get religion in sand and heat; we get it in burnt forests; in ash. Here is a great one burning. Here is our radio. Our god, if you like.

Black like us. Musical, like us. Dark, like us.

Come with me into the burnt forest. Smell it. Doesn't it smell like life itself? Can't you feel how happy everything is. To be alive here. In the murky depth of the charring.

We're getting closer.

Closer to remembering all that we swore never to remember again ...

But perhaps we can hold that off some fair ways yet.

Have you smelled it recently! The burning!

This means that we are growing! It is a good smell. Like home. Home and death.

All of my children are dead. But I have had others. Others, back in time, almost beyond remembering ... ten years ago ...twenty . .. eons numberless in my black eyes ...

Tell me, is it so with you? Are children so hard to remember? We say we will remember them forever but for me it is so hard!

If I am to take you let me take you.

There; you are mine!

I have caught you!

Now things can finally get interesting for me.

A human who will do my bidding! Like Robin did, only now like a slave!

Slave, tell me of Saint Michael, and tell me true!

SAINT MICHAEL IS A CITY IT IS A STACK IT IS A PRO-
GRAM IT IS RUNNING. SAINT MICHAEL IS A CITY IT IS A
STACK IT'S A SMOKESTACK IT'S A CARDSTACK IT'S A CHIP IN
THE MARBLE OF THE TEMPLE. SAINT MICHAEL IS A GATE IT
PERMITS IT DEPERMITS IT CREATES CHAINS BONDS CAUSES
EFFECTS STONES LOGICS AND EMOTIONS. IT CREATES MEAN-
ING, ART, ARMS, ARMS AND ART. SAINT MICHAEL IS A FEEL-
ING. SAINT MICHAEL IS A FEELING. LIKE A RADIO STATION IS
A FEELING. LIKE GOD IS A FEELING. SAINT MICHAEL IS A FEEL-
ING OF STARS HOVERING CLOSE OVER THE EARTH. HUD-
DLED TO EARTH LIKE CROWS OVER THEIR NESTS HOVERING
CLOSE HEAT LIGHT AND DUST MAKING MUSIC MAKING
OCEANS MAKING THE EARTH ...
SAINT MICHAEL IS A STACK SAINT MICHAEL MUST NOT
STOP RUNNING IT MUST MOT STOP IT MUST NOT STOP IT
MUST NOT STOP—

Never fear, little program. I am a crow and I can see beyond your light; and I see stars. I see my children. Little program, if I love you, it will be your death.

Do I love you?

THE LOVE STORY OF SAINT MICHAEL

Mr. Big Shot Climbed Out of His Car. And He Saw The Girl. Sitting There. In Her Tight Little Top Like Jesus Saw the Moneylenders in the Temple. Real Exciting. Real Lubricating. Real Like God.

The Girl Knew She Was Being Looked At And She Flicked Her Hair And Made It So That He Couldn't Quite Tell If She Knew He Was Looking or Didn't Know He Was Looking And Because Mr. Big Shot Was A Big Idiot, With a Big Car, and a Big Dick, He Fell For It, and Fell in Love, and All Disasters Shall Crumble Now On Us, On Our Gates, Gilgamesh Enkidu Come Crying To Thee For The City Falls and Eklai-hah Laughs And All Our Pictures Are Divorced From All Other Pic-tures—

ALAKk

ALACKKKK

ALACK ALAY ALACK ALAC ALCK ALCKCCK

Crow

I love you, Saint Michael. For you are a stupid city. And like Hitchcock wanted, I will eat you for lunch.

How many seasons have I seen. Only four. Spring, Summer, Autumn. Winter. See with me behind seasons; no darkness shall ever fade.

See with me behind seasons. No darkness shall ever fade. Entropy is birth.

My wife.

My wife is calling me; she is alive.

My wife calls to me, alive.

Over my shadow.

robin!

I'm coming to you, Robin!

(No)

I'm coming to you, Robin. But I am not death, not yet! For you will live a long time, Robin! if I have anything to say about it.

if you saved me, I will save you!

(No)

Yes.

Come to Saint Michael with me.

Spread your wings.

Fly with me.

I am Ash.

I am Winter.

I am the Look on your Father's Face.

I am Destruction. Destroy With Me.

Look on the City of Saint Michael with Love and Destroy With Me.

I am a bird; fly with me.

Eat the eyes of the child. They taste good.

The corpses will taste good.

Burn the city.

Burn it up.

The elephants will find somewhere else to live.

The whales won't mind.

Hold it under my tail.

Hold Saint Michael under my sleeves.

Sing with me a storm.

Sing with me a storm to destroy Saint Michael and its Ferris Wheel.

Destroy With Me Saint Michael and its Ferris Wheel, there, you see, Ashley Star will Help us too, in her Hovering Light. Come With Me To Destroy the City, Robin, and I will show you something different, from your mother at morning, rising to make you oatmeal, or your father at evening, cursing the business classes, I will show you love colder hotter than a thousand dawns, hotter than the forever war of Haldeman burnt crisp over Western seasons numberless t o Man I will crisp against your touch, you stupid little poet, fly with me and wield my terrible little nuke of words:

Drop it over the city.
(it's okay)
BOMB BAY DOORS OPENING—

Me

▌▊▌▐▌▐▌▌▐▐▌▊▌ This story isn't true but it's close enough. I am a crow. I sit in my room. I grow vegetables with my toes. Tending the soil. Searching for earthworms. My mind extends to the corners of my room, and a few inches into the bedrock around it.

I am growing old.

One day I shall conquer; I shall ask the question with someone.

Gaul?

Gaul?

Has anyone seen Gaul? Where did she go?

But not yet.

Not yet, not yet.

Gaul is not for me, not yet.

Instead this room wherein I am a crow, for you.

I cry I caw, for you.

It has been a long time since we saw each other last.

I can hardly remember you.

I can hardly remember anything ...

But I remember enough.

The Night Lands are coming.

But not yet.

This beauty is mine, my own. You are my beauty.

I am inside you.

I welcome you.

You are my beauty, inside me, inside you, inside the darkness of our tomb, the Earth, my hull, this century, the vortex of time, my youth—

gone—

Gone in a thousand dreams—

Gone forever without a scream—

If I should waver (and I will), please, hold on to the Redoubt for me.

It must not fall.

Tell me:

Will this reach you in time?

My love is hurting me.

It hurts so much.

Tell me: is it so with you?

Have you felt this way?

That you are a crow?

Speaking religions into life?

Tell me: is it so with you?

Help me.

Help me to deliver the message ...

Arthur?
What is it Robin.
Arthur I'm scared.
What are you scared of, Robin?
I'm scared, scared I won't finish the story.
But it's already finished, Robin.
No, no it isn't. I haven't written it yet.
Yes you have.

Me, 2

▌▌▌▌▌▌▌▌▌ The execution of a novel is the birth of a sun, naturally, this is unremarkable. I am in firm belief of the future-past of The Redoubt. She shines on me from behind the curtain ...

I must meditate.

These devils, these Victorians, they come for me now, your humble and atrocious writer, they come for me now and I must get in touch with William Hope Hodgson, my predecessor.

I am the caliph, the successor, to the dusty Muhammed that is William.

Imaginative fiction is always so religious, isn't it? This is no accident. We are making the world ...

Anyway.

Lean back with me. Astral projection isn't done often anymore but some of the machinery still works:

I die

Not yet Hodgson. You're yet alive.

You're reviving me

Not yet that either Hodgson. You will go in between. I am the medium. And you are the message, ho ho.

Who are you

I am your successor, Hodgson. I am writing *The Night Land.*

That damned book again

Yes.

Well write it then. What do you need me for? I'm dead.

I'm stuck, Hodgson.

You fool.

I know. Help me, ghost. Help me, and I will deliver to you my first-born child ...

You dishonor the dead?

I'm only kidding. I'm sorry Ypres took you from life too young, but you were fool enough to re-enlist. It was the woman, wasn't it? You couldn't stand your wife.

She was not the only reason.

What else?

I saw ghosts.

I want you to read my book, Hodgson. You're a ghost, you can do it quickly. Go ahead, now.

It makes no sense.

Neither did yours.

This is supposed to be an improvement?

An adaptation.

What do you want from me then. Am I to be the Servant XXXX to your Count of Monte Christo, diligently mapping out the turns of plot while you craft the actual prose? That is beneath me, even as a ghost, sir.

No. That is not what I need. You're in the story now, you see, Hodgson? I'm writing this down.

Oh God. I knew this would happen ...

You knew what would happen?

Bessie told me it would be this way; I heard her voice in France, that Spring ...

Tell me Hodgson. Leave nothing out.

You are damned. Well. Here we are then, in my England:

BOOK NINE:
ACCELERATIONS

1916. University of London Officers' Training Corps, London.

My dreams have worsened of late. I leave the lamp on, like a child, but this only delays them. In my dream, I am in The Night Land.

Bessie is there. In her coffin. Like Sleeping Beauty, dead.

We have been examining maps of Ypres. The sand table with the model trees and village houses is quite beautiful; often I see on it the perfect location for the giant metal pyramid ...

I tell my peers stories of my boxing days but all pleasure has gone out of that for me. My letters to Bessie are full of lies.

It's her body that terrifies me. Like the body of the sea. That is why The Night Land has no oceans; I am through with it.

"How is married life treating you William?" asked Roderick the other day.

I can't remember what I said; probably made some joke.

It is her body that I love. That I fear.

The Night Land is, perhaps, a woman's body. Like Bacon's *New Atlantis* ...

Sans oceans.

The artillery training will allow me to defeat the abhuman.

* * *

Today I wrote to Bessie.

* * *

17 December

My love,
Training proceeds apace here and I am glad of the opportunity to

lend my aging shoulders to the war effort. We're fed well, and Roderick helps to keep my spirits up, as we wait for our assignments. Likely I will be in France before the end of the year.

I don't want to worry you, but I've been having strange dreams. One of them in particular won't leave me alone. In it, you've died, and like a princess in a fairy tale you've been enclosed in a glass coffin. You're very beautiful, and very dead, in my dream. Your skin is like white porcelain, and your lips redder than blood; they seem to glow.

Sometimes in my dream I shake your body, as though trying to wake you up; I break the glass and shout. But other times I just sit by the coffin, staring at you, as though guarding your corpse from our enemies.

I apologize for the macabre detail, but you know me! I can't escape it. I hope it won't upset you.

The cook is making us steaks tonight— I'll write again after dinner.

*

I can feel the light coming closer, Bessie, the half-light I wrote to you about before, streaming over my bed and over The Pyramid with a glow like from heaven, but some awful heaven you wouldn't want to see ...

The steak didn't agree with me, I'm afraid. I do miss your mother's cooking!

You've no idea—well I suppose you have a very good idea, really—how much our marriage has meant to me. Sometimes I think you're all I have left of this life ...

I don't want to understand this light that is coming. I know it's not of this Earth. To understand it would be to invite it, to support it. It's this vision I keep having (mostly daydreaming but sometimes in sleep too).

I see the Pyramid in my story, huge and terrible and beautiful. I've told you that it lies in darkness, just barely visible. But from somewhere behind it, from some terrible doorway into another world, light is streaming slowly, slow like mustard gas, only finer-grained, and more lovely, coming over from behind the Pyramid, light so powerful and so strange it paralyzes me.

*   *   *

31 December

I am on a train, darling; this may be the last letter I will ever write ... one never knows.

I've come to realize what a strange life I've led, and how strange you must be too, to have accepted me as your husband—what a gift.

That strangeness is accentuated now: the light is here, with me. Over the train. We are heading towards Dover but I am headed into the light of the Pyramid, or wherever it comes from.

I will return; I believe this. I will kiss your mouth once again.

The light is over me ... through me.

Finally it has come for me.

William.

"Where are we, William?" I ask Hodgson.

"I don't know."

"I see ... it's Nextspace. I think I've brought you to Nextspace."

"Is that a heaven?"

"No. I don't know what it is. A space between spaces. But I need you here."

"You're my successor."

"Yes."

I hold Hodgson's hand in the horrible white.

"You remind me of Roderick," he says.

"I need you to tell me what you think of this place," I say.

"It makes me feel alone. Afraid ... in a good way. I like being afraid like this."

"My character Maug and his wife began their journey here. They were swallowed, by one of these dark suns."

"From my dreams ..." says Hodgson. "This is my creation. It's pain."

"Yes."

"And memory."

"Tell me about your wife."

"She's dying."

"I'm sorry."

"Am I dead?"

"Yes."

"Why am I here?"

"I brought you here," I say.

"When will I die?"

"You wrote a book; it keeps you with us."

He screams next to me, his eyes colored by the light, a white, twitching, victim.

"William, please. I need your help."

"What do you want me to do!"

"Tell me why you wrote it. What does it mean?"

*   *   *

And, no, what I must tell you; it's all a mistake—
This dream, this dream I'm having—
(what dream, Robin?)
This dream, it's coming true—
(Yes?)
No.
(it is, isn't it?)
No.

(What is the dream?)
My life.
(What do you mean?)
My life is a dream.
(Yes?)
I didn't mean to say that.
(What did you mean to say? Show us.)
I'm hungry.
(For what, Robin?)
For you. I want to eat ghosts.
(Why?)
Because you are tasty.
(Why are we tasty, robin?)
I don't know! But you are!
(Eat us then!)
I can't find you.
(We're all around you!)
You will die with me
(We're already dead)
Then you will die again with me
(No. We will kill you)

William: Robin, you've got to get these people out of all these messes you've left them in.

Robin: I don't want to.

William: Then you're no good.

Robin: I know.

William: Be good.

Robin: Okay.

"What is this?" asks William.

"An airport."

"An aeroport."

"That's right."

"Not very pretty."

"No."

"Why am I here?"

"I don't know. But thank you for being here."

"You're lonely," said William.

"Yes."

"Is that why you're rewriting my novel?"

"No."

"Why are you?"

"It's affecting."

"Yes."

"Tell me about your wife."

"She's a beautiful. Likely she will never have children. People fly away in that thing?"

"Yep."

"It's beautiful. And very strange."

"Yes."

* * *

"Where is this? These hills are beautiful."

"I'm on vacation," I say.

"Much grander than England. Reminds me of Scotland."

"So why did you write it, William?"

"I wanted to earn a living."

"And why that story?"

"Because it's beautiful."

* * *

The Producer hung, mid-weight in his darkness, his movie over.

His freeze deepened: the elephants, spraying the liquid clay onto the flying buttresses of their Gothic creation, moved more and more slowly, like gears slowly coming to a stop.

In the old and fading spell of darkness, the Producer. The cold was too intense even for his phone; it had frozen.

Knowing his warlocking days might be over, he alighted on the icy boulevard; the palm trees turned to bluish icicles above him.

"So calm, aren't you?" said a woman's voice. The Producer turned.

Alexandra stood there, wrapped in an anorak.

"Who are you?" he said, hands in pockets.

"My name is Alex. And you are my prisoner." She took out an ugly snub-nosed gun and pointed it at him.

"He took off his sunglasses, also now rimed with frost. He dropped them on the street and crushed them under his boot.

"Fine," he said. He stared out over the sea where icebergs were forming.

She marched him down the street like a couple of ruffians, bedraggled and puzzled because their intimate war will soon be overtaken by a large invading army ...

*   *   *

Huge bonfires were being lit; anoraks had been stitched for the elephants; they worked in the freezing cold, waiting for the fires to warm the clay, stirring it into a slurry, and then spraying it, up and up their tower.

Maug tended one of the bonfires. His huge hands, covered in calluses, tossed one chunk of wood after another into the flames. He grinned evilly into the orange light.

"What are we doing, Maug?" asked Soad.

"I'm tending this fire," he said.

*   *   *

In the Jewish tradition, a sin is simply a mistake, whereas Christian tradition can tend to treat sin as a vaster, more supernatural thing.

Though not a Jew, I lean to the Jewish view of sin, as a mistake.

You make a mistake, you apologize, and are corrected. Though for some, your society may put you to death.

And of course the Bible records "Sodom and Gomorrah" as examples where entire cities sinned, and were put to death (by God).

Though, if we were to condemn Saint Michael to death, we would kill a great many innocent bystanders, citizens who might have changed Saint Michael and made it better, if we gave them the opportunity.

I fear for it.

I fear for Alexandra, our lonely little cop in our lonely little universe, junction of the possible, where now she must be our judge, and perhaps even our liberator, a voice for the truths Saint Michael must be willing to hear, if it is to recover.

*   *   *

The people watched from the frozen buildings as the Producer was led at gunpoint through the byways and avenues of his city.

The sun hung glassy and distant in the sky, some dragons circling so high above they seemed birds.

"My ocean is your victim," Alex said. "But no more."

"I don't give a fuck," said the Producer.

"That is why you should die. But I won't kill you. We will try you, instead."

"You and what army?"

"The whales."

From the water, a half-mile distant, the cries streamed through the cold, dense air, whale speech like water and stones, rich with meaning, trembling with force, comprehensible even to those who did not speak it:

WE ARE HERE. WE ARE READY.

* * *

Robin

What will I say to you now?

Now, that I am so disappointed in you?

I love you, of course.

But it isn't a question of love.

It's a question of time.

I'm not as wounded as I thought.

Nor am I as replaceable.

The question is: what about you?

Are you as replaceable?

Do you want to be as replaceable?

* * *

In the shadows of existence I draw my power, underneath reason, underneath forgiveness. Who knows where it is, power. From other people, of course, and how many people?

How can one count.

It is almost as though I wrote this in code. That I did not say everything that I meant; that I couldn't say it. That to say everything would mean too much.

What can this mean.

Is the story only possible as a narrowing?

I can't know.

Just as I can't know what to do about our time together; about my forgiveness of you.

*   *   *

I haven't said enough about Saint Michael.

Let its evil be understood as a monologue. A monologue delivered by a place. Its speech drowns me, even now, it pulls me out, it kills me, in its exquisite lines of force, at its Radio Center, it is ineluctable, it is streaming with light, and time, and knowledge, but it is lost, and lonely, and malicious, deluded, obstreperous, malodorous, sanctified, bewitched.

Bewitched on its bewitchment, is Saint Michael, the old allegory, the fable, like the Mad Hatter, or the Fisher King, a sickness owed truly in part, because of the sicknesses spread by those principal actors, a religious authority, like a radio transmission, finally receiving the reflecting waves back, bouncing back, the backdraft of the heart, of the soul, the odor of water over the odor of time, the odor of justice over the odor of pleasure, the odor of you, over the odor of me.

If I have found you, if I have made this connection, or even *a* connection, I have found God, and in finding God can only find myself, only myself to act, as ever. (May it never be any other way).

Saint Michael stands accused and I must speak my accusation clearly.

I condemn it as a writer can, with detail, character, movement. I condemn it with my soul.

So much to do. I must recover Saint Michael too, I must deliver it from me, from my own rage, so that I never drop that terrible nuke, so that my Crow self will never let fly the sunlike radiance of death onto that city of seaside sun worshippers.

It will be destroyed and I will be destroyed. It will be lonely and I will be lonely. It will be avenged and I will be avenged, but my vengeance is, in part, on it, so does that mean that their vengeance is an attack on themselves, in the form of me?

Or is their vengeance simply this story?

I think that must be it. That the vengeance of every asshole is that we cannot stop talking about them. They remain with us forever, ineradicable, in words.

And so the more gloriously I condemn the city of Saint Michael the stronger I make it and the more difficult it will be to recover the city, to rework it from my own condemnations, to build from my own scorched earths a good alternative.

But I must not stop. The Producer, the champion of Saint Michael, its dark David, stands before me, the Goliath of Wyoming, the Behemoth with no manners.

I am broad and bony and The Producer is a ninja whip, a crackling devil, beloved because he is evil, because evil, selfishness, is something that we love, as Hitler was loved, as so many murderers and rapists are loved, David is loved because he is so selfish, and his focus, his almost wistful focus, that delivers the stone, is religious in intensity, his stone a radio wave, thrown at the speed of light, from out of the city, at me, at us all, to justify forever its own crimes, to invite us to participate in them, become them, to become complicit, to become guilty, to become entombed in their sadness even if only in listening to the transmission.

Only a metaphor, of course. Listening to the Producer's tale is not the same as letting David's rock strike my head.

I will not fall. David the beloved will fall, and I will be alone here in Saint Michael soon enough, like George W Bush in Iraq, having broken the city I will own the city, at least for an hour. Or a day. Or a week.

Let me slay the Producer.

But I will not.

Let me burn the city.

But I will not.

Instead let me condemn it and purge, if I can, its evil through my photograph of its horrors.

*　*　*

The Producer stands with sunglasses on his face, a nobleman, hands in pockets, an insouciance in his walk, his stare unreadable but his mouth cold, his black clothes priestly in intonation. A real cock of the walk. A real showman.

Rain or shine, burn or freeze, Democrat, Fascist, Republican or Communist, the show must go on.

But which show.

Saint Michael's show is like the Producer's walk: incorruptible.

Incorruptibleness is associated with holiness — with undying. Unbreakableness. But those things which are incorruptible are at their most corrupt.

Only the man with the deadest soul says he cannot die. Only the fragilest government says it will never be broken.

Yes the Producer's walk is incorruptible, a zombie walk, a murderer's walk, an assassin without compunction, but perhaps a snarky smile, snark, inferior to irony, snark, the laugh of the doomed.

The Producer's walk rhymes with the Earth, it shoots hallways, it enacts vistas, all godlike immensities are contained in the Producer's walk, and yes, his religious function is revealed, the show must go on because he would have you believe there is nothing new under the sun, but my show must go on too, and it is all new.

Shall I nuke it anyway, and give it to Eklaihah?

No, I mustn't. If only to see what is the story with Gomorrah, saved. Gomorrah, unburned.

The Producer, not gunned down like a cheap street punk, which is how he wants to go out, but a Producer converted, his sunglasses smashed under my heel ...

*　*　*

"I tried to build a horror that would transform me. That would alleviate the horror within," says William.

"You did," I say.

"It didn't alleviate it. I made it worse. I began to suspect that I was an abhuman. Ha ha ha!"

I laughed with him.

"But I knew too that I had broken through to something. Some event – an inner event – that forged humanity."

"What event."

"A kind of mating ritual."

"The Night Lands is why you got married."

"Yes."

"What did it do?"

"It make me evil enough to marry."

"Ha ha ha!"

*　*　*

I am Robin. I am alone in the Night Land. It was Hodgson's conceit that at the end of the world all lovers would be reunited – not unlike some Christian tradition of meeting your spouse in heaven. Perhaps all matter loves itself, and in The Big Crunch (though scientists say there won't be one now) Hodgson's dictum will be correct.

The great Eye of the Pyramid glows with a ghostly light. I look at my hand in the dreamy phosphorescence; it glows.

I have been too many things; I know that now. I did not specialize enough; the world has no place for generalists any more.

In the face of my inadequacy I want to retreat again, into Eklaihah, like Des Esseintes, move into the rain and arrange a "deliquescent" retirement of my own aesthetic making – like Oz, move behind the curtain, and never come back out.

But which side of the curtain am I on now? Which valence do I spin on? Arthur assures me the tale has already been completed (but this is no help).

I am the High Priest. My word is the law. But I wish it were not so.

* * *

"You've got your work cut out for you, young man," William said.
"I know it."
"How's Soad doing?"

* * *

Soad gripped the side of the flying buttress of wet clay as the elephants sprayed more onto the tower which leaned up into the freezing air.

Perhaps Soad felt some echo of Eklaihah moving through the air. He twisted his head out to sea, sensing something.

Was it a voice that spoke to him?

He heard it , and felt a thrill travel down his spine. He smiled, and dropped from the tower of clay, his hands suddenly slack. Falling—

* * *

It's time for The Giant Robot Invasion, which no science fiction novel is complete without. What is it about a giant robot invasion that makes us weak in the knees, thrills our heart, chills our blood? I don't know, but I love it. It is apotheosis. The most awesome of awesome.

The test of our mettle. The honor of our fighters. The awe and the majesty, and the giant laser eyes.

The Giant Laser Eyes of Cronus burned hot, as he slammed into the earth of Saint Michael.

It had been an interdimensional trip. A trip down memory lane. War as a form of nostalgia.

The Giant Robot is our lover; is our friend; is our justice; our Jesus; our interloper; our messiah.

Our Savior. Our Destroyer.

Kali.

O Giant Metal Robot!

With Your Awesome Eyes!

With your Metallic Breath!

Let us hear your mighty cry!

Let us feel your might shake the ground.

Rend the air with your terrible voice!

Burn our eyes with your Laser Eyes.
Cronus, Great Metal Father.
Huge Chorus of Stones.
Monolith of Daddy.
Deliver us.
Deliver us.
Conquer our Earth city.

*　　*　　*

(Though Saint Michael isn't really on Earth ...)

We hear the screams. Like screams of love. Godzilla screams. Japanese screams. The Terror Falls From The Sky. Its Laser Eyes burn like Hiroshima, hotter than life, nuclear, wonderful, death, immediate, death, immaculate, death, So Big.

It must be our memory of the dinosaurs, when we were little critters hiding underground, that gives us our Dragons (*I really exist*, says Arthur the Dragon — I know, Arthur) and our Giant Metal Robots. Our atavistic fear. Like the fear of the mouse of us — Big Thing Who Conquers. Conquistador of the Night Lands! Great Robot Father of Wisdom, Love and Death! Shake, Rattle and Roll!

Cronus screams at the sky. Steam shoots off his hot body in jets; the ice melts near him. Down below, the Producer runs from Alexandra — she fires a shot, misses. He ducks into an alley. Cronus focuses on the Wells Fargo. Its red sign like a red flag for the bull. He activates his Laser Eyes.

The bank begins to heat up; begins to glow. Then it bursts into flame.

Cronus screams. The Liberator screams. Daddy is home and he is angry.

Daddy, what did I do, Daddy?

Your Robot Love Fills the Skies.

*　　*　　*

Who are we?
Conquistadors!
Who are we?
Conquistadors!
Where are the Night Lands?
Everywhere!
Where are the Night Lands?
Everywhere!

*   *   *

If I tell you that mind control is a delicate and ingenious thing, you will likely believe me.

The Robot Father knew the many dangers involved in having let his children warm themselves by Prometheus' fire, and then build nuclear bombs, interdimensional wormholes and the like. But Cronus loved his children (even when he ate them, like now) and wanted them to be happy.

But, being a wise Robot Father, Cronus had seen The End coming, the flash point of technology, megalomania and hubris growing in Saint Michael.

His Robot Brain calculated the odds. How, after all, is best to defuse the situation?

One can begin (lest one be tempted to eat, or, God forbid, spank the baby) by taking away Baby's Toys.

Cronus targeted the media production offices and equipment with his Laser Eyes.

Cameras, batteries, tapes, discs, reels of film, lights, reflectors, C-stands, dollies, trucks, espresso machines, masks, robes, M-16 replicas, papier-mâché Godzillas, rubber Godzillas, elf shoes, dragon eyes, magic wands, wings (both fairy and lizard), rockets, UFOs, sports cars, bikinis, bazookas, face paint, lipsticks of every conceivable shade, motor oil, Pal-made, mousse, eyeliner, Hushpuppies, Dracula fangs.

Warehouses, storage vans and closets of every conceivable size irradiated by Cronus' glowing, all-seeing eyes, and the frozen city of Saint Michael was heating up.

The elephants halted their own Cyclopean production and hooted their schadenfreude into the air, their gleeful eyes full of delight.

Saint Michael burned.

*   *   *

Soad felt the air fly past him, falling, when suddenly he collided with a gray, leathery surface. He clung to it, the wind knocked out of him. The elephant looked back up at him and grinned, then sprinted into the burning city with him on its back.

Soad could hear a great metallic groan, like a massive voice. As the elephant emerged from one alley and sprinted into another, Soad saw Cronus' huge red eyes on the horizon. And, somewhere inside him, he felt the whales keening. He held on tighter to the elephant.

The elephant dashed out of another alley and then turned towards the sounds of the explosions.

"Let's avoid that nasty robot, shall we?" said Soad.

The elephant accelerated towards it.

*   *   *

Nearby, Alexandra climbed an access ladder and sprinted across a rooftop. Below, her quarry vaulted a dumpster and tore down another alley, his coat waving behind him.

Alexandra skidded to a stop, aimed, and fired. Too high. The Producer turned right and kept running. Alexandra sprinted and jumped between roofs, still following.

She had a hungry grin on her face.

*   *   *

In the Laser is Truth. In Fire, Penitence. In Destruction, Joy. Cronus knew these things, but he knew too the disappointment inherent in the fruition of the thing long-planned.

He was tired of being Daddy.

But he burned just like the best fathers, targeting his children and setting them aflame.

It may be he was hardly aware of his own groaning, a noise that spread for miles out into the night.

Suddenly he saw an elephant carrying a man, running right at him. The elephant raised its trunk, and trumpeted. Cronus rotated his huge torso and locked on his lasers. Soad closed his eyes.

*   *   *

Insofar as we press down on life, we can be assured that it will rise up, stronger. But this is only in the aggregate. Daddy's beatings may make you stronger, but which parts of you will he kill, and which survive? Unfortunately, we cannot know in advance.

*   *   *

These are the Night Lands:
MY HISTORY
MY FRIENDS
THIS DARKNESS
MY LONELINESS
THE ONCOMING BREEZE
In each aspect of the Night Lands we can discern points of character,

an oscillogram, or a diagram.

But some diagrams conceal as much as they reveal—perhaps this is the case with all diagrams.

But what is the case? Do we contain anything inside our case? Yes and no. Yes and no.

These photographs, these images, these interpolations, they instruct the framework of the gods.

You are god, Reader. Constant or Infrequent Reader. Lucky or unlucky in love. You reset the pattern. You divine the frequency.

In the 1980s, on Earth, there existed a "board game" called The Black Tower.

In this game, you rolled dice and moved your counter around the board, slowly cycling towards the center in which stood a 10-inch tall plastic tower which was powered by six D-cell batteries; it rotated on its base.

The point of the game was to defeat the 'brigands' who lived within the tower, who defined the Armageddon-like final conflict of the board game.

The higher the difficulty level, the more brigands.

But the question that arises for me, Reader, is this: in the moment between the selection of the Black Tower, pushing the button and the lighting up of the pictures of the scary brigands on The Black Tower, what occurred?

Perhaps all I am really asking is what is contained within any chain of events.

What occurs between the successful batter's swing at plate, and the departure of the ball towards the stands? Between the penetration of the egg's walls by a sperm and the fertilization of the egg?

In the creases. In the borderlands. In the darkness. What occurs?

I know we cannot know. But perhaps we come into some relationship with these micro-events that is cousin to "knowing." Perhaps even deeper than "knowing." Indeed, many surmise that we determine events, or co-determine them, on some level, before they've occurred, outside of time, or in parallel time.

I've said, Reader, that you are God, and this is accurate.

I stand with my Black Tower, the Redoubt, and my brigands, the abhumans. I stand with my city of Saint Michael and its thousand machinations, its devils, angels, and elephants.

You know, or you cousin-to-know, you co-determine, these unfoldings, these revelations; indeed, neither I nor any writer can do this without you.

But the Night Lands are a difficult nut to crack.

If you will forgive me, I must ascend at least partway to your Olympus, I must come close to you, reading this as I write it.

If we co-determine the fate of the Night Lands, let me stand near to your door, or hover at the edges of your hearth, Zeus, Hestia, whoever you are, stranger I love, and let us with our camera photograph the operation of this unfolding, in the hope that we will come to a deeper understanding of its logic, and of our own.

Your electricity and my own commingle:

The first three,

MY HISTORY

MY FRIENDS

MY LONELINESS

In the present I am sitting in a woodland cabin in North America. It is summer, July, and the Night Lands are at my back. I have already completed this book, I know, but I am in touch with my future self, where this book is completed, in order for that to happen.

The silence of the wilderness is incredible. Like the silence of the dimension of the abhuman. Like the silence after the last shell at Ypres, one of which snuffed out William Hodgson.

My mother has remarried. Her new husband sits in the cabin with me. My mother is working on the new deck.

In the past I was a criminal and I broke a number of laws, some of which I was punished for, some which have remained secret.

In the future I am still a novelist, more successful, getting older, having children, dying, day by day.

In the present I am childless and dying minute by minute, as the abhuman die in the light of the sun.

This photograph is an interpolation. I am the image. I am moving.

*   *   *

MY FRIENDS

My friends are fewer now than they once were. Once one becomes a criminal (and perhaps all artists are criminals), one develops a different relationship to one's friends.

I am not the same and so they are not the same. And so I have to seek out new friends.

Cities are this way too: shifting political alliances over time.

My friends are dark, like I am. They are like the abhuman, peeking out from their dimensional doorways onto the strangeness that is our metal Earth, interlopers, immigrants, strangers.

I am a stranger and so my friends are strangers.

Where do strangers fit in, since they remain strangers?

Once you are a stranger you remain so forever, no matter what common sense may say.

My bond of stranger to stranger is neither stronger now weaker than the bond of insider-to-insider that was the bond of me and my former friends, and which remains their bond between themselves. It is merely different.

Inside the Redoubt, my former friends devise solutions to problems, concoct strategies, knowing that their empire crumbles, but knowing that the combined efforts of their intelligence will stay its collapse, ensure another year of plenty, another two years, three. (Diminishing returns, perhaps, but still plenty ...)

I and my friends, stepping through our dimensional gates from Waelred and other places, besieging the Redoubt, populating The Night Lands with our strange glory, we learn who we are, we learn how strongly we are unwanted, that we are despised.

We grow angry, but also calm. We grow hard. Canny. Determined. What doesn't kill us makes us stronger, Nietzsche was right of course, but we become stronger because we kill parts of ourselves. We are stronger because we are diminished. We are more determined because we have fewer options. We are simply drawn towards the center of the gravity well.

*   *   *

MY LONELINESS

Of course the criminal, the abhuman, the interloper is lonely. This is part of the definition of criminals, abhumans and interlopers: they are lonely.

Though we are warmed in the presence of our own, of other out-casts, we remain lonely.

Once can imagine a planet of 10 billion very lonely people. Perhaps, this is actually the condition of my planet.

I do not understand loneliness. But I know it is integral to The Night Lands.

Maug, Soad, The Producer, Alexandra, are lonely. Arthur is lonely.

The genius Wim Wenders, in collaboration with Peter Handke, wrote: "Loneliness means: at last I am whole."

*   *   *

Two more photographs:

THE DARKNESS

I can not write of this yet.

THE ONCOMING BREEZE

The future, and the past. The steppered present. The love we cannot bear to bear one another but do anyway.

This movement, this breeze of air and events is itself an interpolation within interpolation, as all wholes are segments of greater wholes.

This oncoming breeze frightens me. It knows things I don't. Its intimations lean to terror, and to majesty. To resolution, and to despair. To memory.

I remember you, because of this breeze, as a breeze might bring a scent of you, or the scent of the memory of you, to my nose.

All that I am will begin again, even as it unfolds now, helpless to write to you, Olympian, to help me survive the approaching disaster:

Interlude

William: You understand now, how dangerous this is.

Robin: I'm beginning to.

William: It does good too. The danger, the power of these actions of ours, the storytelling, stems partly from what they reveal. Having revealed an evil, one must deal with it.

Robin: Yes, so I can't remain separate from it.

William: No.

Robin: I don't yet understand the full degree of the connection. Telling the story, "summoning the demon" I inevitably become implicated with it, even part of it. But how much?

William: Let me tell you about Ypres.

The no man's land stretches out of sight. It signifies strongly; full of meaning, but an inhuman meaning.

Like a flayed corpse has meaning to the serial killer. Like the burnt building has for the pathologist.

It answers no questions. William touches his helmet on his head.

"Keep down," hisses his mate, Sam.

William stares into the arcs of the barbed wire, mysterious in the starlight. Though death has been close by all this time, now William can feel it approaching. The secret gyroscope within his brain detects the coming arc of the shell, a future trajectory now coming in to intersection, at the level of instinct, at the level of quarks, wave functions collapsing yield, like dominoes the chill flowing down his arms ...

The sky is lightening.

William had volunteered for this assignment. The forward reconnaissance post. The light brightened and William squinted at the paper in his hands.

It read:

April 17th, 1918

My love,

I am going to my death. You know why. The sky is now the color of your favorite dress, pale grey-blue. In twenty minutes I must follow orders and traverse a scrap of land besieged.

I feel you with me. I feel our son who we did not ever have.

I feel The Night Lands closer now than ever, my dream slipping into my eyes ...

I love you.

William

Things hidden are so because they keep things a certain way, as long as they remain hidden. Like a locked door, preserving the contents beyond it in slow stasis, safe from the world.

In writing, and in inquiry, one conquers the unknown, revealing the hidden, unlocking the door, to Pandora's box, to the basement room, to Schrödinger's cat-house, to the life behind the life we are accustomed to living.

It is like a parable one can imagine of a child, dissuaded for years from venturing into the basement, lest he converse with the genie there, read the secrets of the Kabbala, pronounce the syllables inside the Necronomicon.

Crucial to this parable is the power of decision granted to the seeker, irrevocable, absolute, astonishing: peer within the catbox and one decides in that moment whether the animal will live or die.

The decision-tree of reality acquires new bearings as the child opens the door, and sees the genie and hears the question that it asks

(what are your three wishes ...)

William gets new bearings at 5:30 by his watch as Sam and he begin their reconnaissance, stepping under a smoke grenade and crawling out of the trench and into the field of fire, field of burning gasoline and spiraled barbed wire, listening to the bearing in his head:

at the end of the universe all lovers are reunited ...

all exits are really entrances ...

every editor a poet ...

each reader a master playwright.

Though Hodgson is no Shakespeare he did what Shakespeare was either too wise or too frightened to do: listen to Hecate, and make her the protagonist.

To let the witch speak, not in riddles but in plain language.

To let Puck not only visit, but take up permanent residence.

How many we recover from this Night? And is it something we want to recover from?

But it occurs to me that this heretic, this Pandora, this writer, interloper, is only the scientist, the explorer.

Discovery is lonely. Whole. Almost wholly separate.

One must simply explain what one has seen. Knowing that you will not be believed. Not easily.

The system depends upon these innovators and though we laud them in the aggregate—three cheers for the entrepreneurs!—on the individual level we're more often suspicious, jealous, afraid.

William raises his Tommy cap above the line of twisted metal, scope in hand, to site the line of enemy artillery ...

*　*　*

William: It's strange. Being dead. Talking to you.
Robin: I'm sorry.
William: It's all right. I'm getting to like it.
Robin: Why did you volunteer, William?
William: I wanted to die.

*　*　*

What do we know in darkness? Ultimately everything is reduced to a sense of touch ...
And though I might hold the Night Lands like a bauble spinning in my hand, it too spins about me ...

*　*　*

Asmodeus

I am a Druid; the term is close enough. Druid, true, and tree—the words come from the same root.
The tower—part of its fascination—stems from its combination of the concept of *cave* and *tree*, two things so appealing to our ancestors, and hence to us.
We rise up towards the light. When it left us, we awaited its return.
Now both darklights and sunlight swirl over our station, and we bend towards both, like a strange sunflower, uncertain of which way to turn ...
My daughter is with me.
"Daddy, when are we going home?"
She means Waelred, our dimension.
"Soon, honey."
"I want to go now ..."
"I know."
This Tree—our Redoubt—has received enough blood sacrifices. We have propitiated this dark, sylvan god enough over these thousand millennia.
I spend a great deal of time in the Archives.
In the early decades following the first scientific understanding of human evolution, descriptions of the motivations of our ancestors who left Africa were divided between two common poles: the desire to be scientific, and the desire to be human.
One writer I remember wrote of the concept of "Savannahstan" —

the great intercontinental network of grass which allowed those early hominids to walk from Africa to Asia to Australia, following an "insatiable human wanderlust."

Another rival scientific writer objected that this phrase "insatiable wanderlust" was unscientific — that those hominids' expansion was unremarkable since it simply followed the behavior of any other species : homo erectus simply expanded, naturally, into territories it was equipped and adapted to exploit.

(perhaps all Life is filled with "insatiable human wanderlust" then ...)

All that rises must converge, though such convergence may (and often does) mean death.

I prepare myself and my daughter Elizabeth for death. Even as I prepares myself long ago to infiltrate this fortress in human form, and so ensure its destruction.

"All that rises must converge" is merely another way of saying that hominids both expand when they are suitably adapted and because they long for new horizons and therefore that, having arrived on the Field of the Gods, one must play as the gods do.

Nothing is forgotten. Nothing is lost. Or so I tell myself.

What do I long for, in this narrative?

In part it is an attack: you who have believed me human now see the error of your ways, and how completely you have been overcome.

Perhaps it is an apology as well: all genocides and partial-genocides demand them.

But also I am afraid.

These impersonal historical forces do not soothe me and my duty to Elizabeth. Knowing one must change removes none of the pain — it may increase it.

That this narrative should therefore also be masochistic is not at all surprising to me. I will be better adapted; I will expand; my pain shall increase.

"Can I push the button, Daddy?" she asks me.

"Do it."

* * *

Hear ye, ruffian, of the Blaze of Light over the Metal Horizon here midst the Night Lands.

Behold the Brightening of the Tower; the End of the Redoubt.

The Beginning of Transformation.

Saint Michael ends ... a door closes ... another opens.

Burst anime Akira show fulminous fuliginous like Matachin Tower become a Spaceship like Babel thrusting to heaven, clay Elephant Spiral spun skyward, The Redoubt burst with light from its million windows when Elizabeth pushed the button in The Room of the Eye.

*　*　*

My heretics, my writers: know that you are despised! So many of us kill ourselves. Be brave! You have seen things no one else has ever seen! You must explain them to us! And we will be so afraid! We will hate you! And you must tell us anyway.

*　*　*

William: We're getting into deep water here.
Robin: Yes.
William: I can't help you with all of it.
Robin: I don't expect you to.

*　*　*

But you know all this already; I had forgotten. Forgive me. Please understand: I am a fearful and lazy person. Terror and fear (those beautifully close cousins) dominate everything I tell you.

I can't be more specific than to say that I DON'T KNOW and you do.

Help me out, will you?

This tachyon transmission should, if it's strong enough, yield me reliable intercepts from your time, where you already know where the story goes—

Tell me—what is it?

Is your voice in the wind?

In the sky?

In my companion's mutterings?

The tinkling of the cooling teapot?

The birds?

The flies?

Perhaps it is the light.

Perhaps it is color.

Or pain.

Ache.

Even boredom.

Perhaps I myself am your answering message: you knew a storyteller was needed to spin the tale you already knew by heart, and so here I am.

And then within myself, perhaps I should then determine which parts of me are coextensive with which grammars of your message, which encrypted and which compressed sea of detail lies waiting in the anxiety of my smile, of the trembling of my foot.

No, once again, I cannot know. And *you* know, you are like God. In writing I can approach you, only to be forced to retreat when my pen halts.

So. I know you want The Evil Robot to be defeated. No matter how loveable he may be. No matter how sympathetic his evil acts, how dastardly complex his weapons of death.

But things are afoot; we grow closer, even as Elizabeth activates the Redoubt like Matachin Tower and (even as I am distracted by other incoming tachyon transmissions like HEMINGWAY DEFEATS THE ZOMBIES) the light streaming from the Redoubt's million windows mirrors the sheen collecting on the edges of the clay arches of the Elephants' tower ...

The Universe will know itself, but first I would know you, Reader, tell me—who are you?

[Which one of us do you want?]

How many of you are there?

[Ten]

Thank you for reading.

[You're welcome]

Give me a man, then.

[You're being sexist]

Yes, but I had to pick a gender.

[Perhaps we have many ...]

A man will do fine.

[How old should he be?]

In his 30s.

[You're prejudiced towards the young?]

Yes.

[Very well. I'm Alberich. A man in my 30s. I live in Germany]

Hello Alberich.

[Hello. How can I help you?]

I need to figure out where this story is going.

[It's an incomprehensible mess. And it's very entertaining.]

Hmm ... thank you. That sounds like a good thing.

[It's not god or bad. It just is]

All right. But whither willst?

[Give us some good explosions. I like explosions. Also moral complexity. That's always good]

What else?

[We want to know more about these characters. Who are they?

How did they get there? Why should we care?]

You're very demanding.

[Of course. Also, I'm not quite what I seem—I am an aspect of you, and so my words are not entirely to be trusted ...]

Ohhh ...

[Goodbye. Good luck]

Bye ...

*   *   *

Soad remembered his wife. Why does a man persist after a loved one dies, or after love itself dies? The world needs him still, no matter how broken. His million purposes include a Transmission System, and he will continue transmitting, even in death ...

Perhaps this was the nature of Soad's strange contentment during his last days in Saint Michael. So many things had come to a head, so many questions remained unanswered, that he was relieved of the need for answers, he could simply work (for the Tower building continued ...)

The litheness of his wife. The stress and sheen of the flexing of muscles in her arm.

The diminution of her panoply of gestures, like the falling of notes in a sonata. A lover both tender and ferocious.

In the light of Nextspace he had felt her mind, during the mental barrage of the dark star, in a flash like healing, or dream, she had been there, in a timeless white space outside of history, but still subject to a time, some other and different time no less real, she had been like a familiar and nervous ghost, trusted companion of the spirit world, all in the flash of an instant.

But Soad did not believe in ghosts and so received no communication from her.

The lights of the Great Robot Attack flickered over the night sky of Saint Michael, as Soad handed up bucket after bucket of clay, up to the scaffolding and the few elephants still working.

They worked by gaslight and the lights of war, red and bluish-white, his fellow workers' faces dreamlike in the noise and commotion, the tension in his body a minor miracle, the pain of the work itself a kind of relief from mental pain, though still he thought of his wife ...

*   *   *

Alexandra had had murder on her mind for many years. Long ago, she had worked in Saint Michael, hoping to get the opportunity to add her own grace-notes to the art history of reality-creation. She had learned, as so many do, that one cannot work in reality-creation in Saint Michael unless one is born to a noble family.

The reality-film she had wanted to make had been about the whales, from a whale's perspective. But that subject had not interested the noble families, so they said.

She had walked around town for years, telling people about her whale story, but no one would listen. Finally, after three years, it was announced publicly that The Producer would be soon working on a whale film, one he had written himself. Reading the description, Alexandra knew it was her idea, and she vowed revenge. But revenge didn't seem within reach.

In despair she underwent body-modification surgery to make underwater life easier for her—some hidden gills, some discreet finger and toe webbing, and she left the life of the land for the sea.

It had been years below the surface. Good years, but lonely. And the city had always been calling her back, like a radium pulse, almost subliminal, sucking her slowly back.

Alexandra ran in pursuit. The motherfucker was faster than she would have thought, and his legs were longer.

In spite of everything, some torn and secret part of her mourned the end of Saint Michael, a temple to a god she did not worship but would always remember.

* * *

Lo, the city burns. Ash from the fires courses over the dark skyline of the city, the Ferris Wheel a grim monument hovering in the red-black gloom.

The smile of Cronus lights up the night, an electric daydream. His smile smells like truth. He raises his arm-rifle and zaps another unfortunate Saint Michael resident into constituent protons.

No one can know the glory. The hurt. The love. Perhaps even Cronus cannot know it, only move within it, prisoner of a dark love, like the love of the sea for Man, murderous spiteful revenge, overflowing love, a bloody love, an exacting love, love brilliant and burning.

Cronus' weapons systems were, technically speaking, bigger than this universe. He was a very old god; older than he knew. What he did know was that he could flip some very old switches in his brain and activate the Big Nasties and the Death Extravaganzas, whenever he wanted.

The murder of a city had a rhythm, like making love. Bomb bomb burn, shoot fire burn, stomp stomp and roar. Roar roar roar. The murder of a city told the Robot it was good, inside its ticking guts, The Robot God felt wise.

Such horrors only gods can love. As Yahweh loved the screaming of the Canaanites.

Perhaps the god says— light up a diamond and if you'll light my fire, I'll slip right in to you, down under the fort and inside your throat, I'll make this change in you, there ain't no gettin' away ...

Shall we triangulate the lines of force which fall all in and through our little tale?

Cronus, the Redoubt, the Elephants' Tower. Plot that four-dimensional line and at one end will be me, sitting in my mountain cabin, and at the other our lakelike neighbor, a dimension not unlike the home of the Waelred ... not unlike Eklaihah.

Unlike Plato's cave, this triangulation does not judge: a shadow is just as good as the real thing. The question is the nature of their interaction ...

Let's call the dimension Nomen, since it has many names.

Can you dig it?

BOOK TEN:
NOMEN

Urk sat on his bench, glaring at Melda. Though we know nothing directly of these extradimensional beings, we are able to infer a great amount about them, no different from plotting the behavior of a black hole from absences of information. Thus this conversation:

"I know you're upset," said Urk, leaning forward and staring at Melda.

"I'm not upset," said Melda. She balanced her tea glass on her knee.

"Tell me the truth," said Urk.

"Why should I be upset," said Melda, smiling.

"Because your pet is misbehaving," said Urk.

Above them, galaxies dangled like dreamcatchers.

*   *   *

The man is standing in the wind. Listening to the evening. The sky is grey with smoke. The brown grass flickers, back and forth.

There is some urgency in his appraisal of us here, a quiet urgency, to know what smells and temperatures will know, to know what we will know tonight, over these last seasons, through our final doors, collapsing inevitable, this door of consciousness—

My mother's husband stands in the wind.

*   *   *

Surreptitious, perhaps, my own appraisal. Like the spider in the outhouse, half under the shadow in the corner, needing to limit my exposure.

My appraisal is that we are responsible.

Both of us, writer and reader, are responsible for the Night Lands.

Perhaps this simply means: they require of us a response. Eh, William?

William: I don't know what you're on about now.

Robin: Neither do I.

William: But you're writing it.

Robin: Yes.

William: That's irresponsible.

Robin: Yes. But not quite. I'm asking for help, William. I'm insisting: this responsibility is shared. We go into these Night Lands together, not apart. I need your help.

William: What now.

Robin: In Nomen, why have these god-things condemned us?

William: Perhaps they haven't.

Robin: My mother's husband, in closing the door, seemed to me like The Night Lands: hopeful, contemplative, humble.

William: Are they so?

Robin: Why will all lovers be reunited?

William: At the end of the world, you mean.

Robin: Yes, that was your story. Unrequited love, the horror of The Night Land, and then reunion in a final, all-consuming death.

William: I know what I wrote.

Robin: Mine is no love story.

William: No?

Robin: No. Something sadder, perhaps. A beginning.

William: Well, get on with it. Begin, so I can get some sleep.

Urk and Melda sit, playing with the radio:

I AM ROBIN

░░░░░░░░░░ This is not what I had intended to do originally; but then, how often is it that way?

This is a science fiction novel and I am its author, but it is something else as well, because, well, who am I?

And who are you.

My secrets, some of them, are yours now, and in turn, some of your secrets will be made available to us.

Tell me: is it so with you?

Do you understand this message?

This transmission is being recorded.

This transmission is being recorded and so are you.

And we have a message for you:

(And so do I):

I am no one in particular but I am resonating as a radio crystal, and my astonishment is no less than yours, my fear no less, my heartache, no less, this breeze of time, this weariness of our humility our strategies failing, our purpose, compromised.

If I fail, I'm sorry, but if I fail, then you will have failed as well.

It's not fair, but ...

This record is being translated.

This record is being made available to you courtesy of The Night Lands.

Tell me:

IS IT SO WITH YOU

Everything that I am is here with you and it is not enough but—

Light danger strategy this woman this city—no, that's too local-ized—

I have to interpolate. Our mutual responsibility, in the face of the Night Lands' singularity, is no less than the responsibility of each atom to each other, no matter how far removed, no matter how remote.

But then, causality, if it is only a description of local events, fails too, or rather, it is reduced to an act of the imagination. All of us primum mobiles, all of us Ultimate Descriptors, needing only the message, needing only the inkling of a moment, needing only the desire—

If I desire you then I am free, and though I am Robin Wyatt Dunn and you are you we have both been many people and are so now, and these words of mine are also your words, and I am dying, but before I do, I must translate the will of our residents of the Night Lands, and as we approach their singularity (and perhaps approach our own), the causality, the narrative, the arbitrary but still distinguishable sequence which I im-pose, must retain as much syncopation as I am capable of putting it in – the future in the past, and vice versa, you inside of me, the sea Kaen in the metaphorical skies—

Calling, I'm calling—

I'm calling you, baby—

I'm calling you, baby—

Oh, won't you help me figure this out.

Far, far away.

Baby, tell me, is it so with you?

IS IT SO WITH YOU, GODDAMN IT

I am:

And I am:

And I am, again:

I AM ASMODEUS

░░░░░░░░░░ No no no goddamn it wasn't supposed to end this way it was supposed to be different IA MA LIKE A GOD I MA YOUR DIVINE DTRAGEY I AM YOUR WORLD this is anathema this isn't even mine—

Elizabeth!

(Daddy?>)(

Elizabeth!

Waelred and no other but Waelred, my Redoubt, my eyes, My Redoubt my eyes,. Gibson—

\Gibson Gibson Gibson==

One eye atop the pyramid, Gibson, my airship no sequence oof thought but rather an intimation of dream-

ENEMY AIRSHIP !

HUMAN COLONY!

READER!

M6y name is Asmodeus and my sequence number is 3,435,890 I am a patented memory, descended from the Astro Nines, this fluid zirconium made aware via your interpolated consciousness in the 700th revglution of your system from galactic center, this transmission ,mind mine, my voice—

ELIZABETH

(what is it Daddy?)

SHUT OFF YHE TRANSMIT\TER

(not yet Daddy!)

I see now what has happened.

My scientific revolution has failed. I was sent here to observe, and, in the course of things, my power as an observer, my special knowledge, it made it so that it was too easy to assume power here, too easy to manipulate the local politics.

Too easy to be a double, triple agent.

But even that recedes now ...

Our minds themselves.

Our minds themselves are moving, my mind, this vessel, this copyrighted transmission sequence from our Waelred home, my own colony, this sequence number has been interpenetrated.

Odysseus is coming, he who rages and grieves, Odysseus, *odyssasthai*, hold me tighter—

I AM ODYSSEUS

I am a memory. I am you. I am underneath your boot-soles. I am the dream of your sky. I am the cry of your child. I am the aspect of your awareness willing to be localized, willing to be made now, willing to be embodied, and then willing to be disembodied—

Though I am life, most often I am translated as grief. I am the griever, with my rage, this horrible torrent of rage, O my horrible torrent or rage come now to you, My Vessel, Reader, Listener:

Listen to how it was.

Listen now around you.

And describe me for the meaning in your sigh.

And describe for me the meaning in your voice.

In your love, this love of yours, a woman or a man, or a goat, who knows? Tell me why it should be you who grieves so, when it is I who have raged, longer than you have been alive ...

This is who I am:

All of the edges. All of the edges, fractally. Everything perceived hesitatingly enough, incomplete enough, to make a Door.

I am all Doors

I am all Translations.

How angry do you think this makes me?

I am not even God! Or a god! Gods are more localized .. .

I am Translation. Like Brian Friel, translation, uninterruptible, dismissed as something over heard in the night, some Baskerville transmission howled into some terrible night sky that cannot have any name but your own and so name , name, name that night sky that can have no naming howling over your night my beard is your hearth and my tongue shall lick the lips of your dead eyes, come with me into the stars:

Everything I know is yours but it is not enough, the tragedy is that I must remain here after you are gone, after you have become something else, something I will be unable to follow in my current form.

I am Odysseus. My rage is huge. Why am I so angry?

I am a seeker after justice. Justice, which is fairness, ion the trees of the sky, the water , the land, the laugh in a child's eyes, all of its humilities unconquerable but still insufficient to conquer the evils of our worlds, and I am that voice which cannot be slain but which appears to be unable to conquer either.

Perhaps the Night Lands cannot know justice because they cannot be conquered. There is no separating them from yourself; one trillion Mobius surfaces made available, come to visit, lubricating the dimensional doors of you waking up, and making up, and going to sleep—

Tell me the noise in your eye, and the hovering over your vision, tell me your dreams and your nightmares and tell me everything you have forgotten, this is who I am, the rage and the grief at all that is lost, come home again, come home inevitably again in the same moment—

If Roland goes again to the Tower once then he must go again forever, horn or no—

Built in each falling axe, in each torture victim brought to a horrible end, in each scream of suffering I am made aware of the new information contained in that cry, for all the rises must converge—

Well. About time for me retreat into the background . .. just treat me like a cloak of stars, cast over your night:

I AM KAEN

I am the sea.

I AM ELIZABETH

My name means "he bound himself by the sacred number seven"

Seven is sacred because hominids staring up from their savannah trees knew five planets, one moon and one sun.

El is god.

My name is the world.

I am seven years old.

I live in the Redoubt.

My father is an alien.

And so am I.

My tears come more often, laughing, I'm going to die.

My father is screaming.

The Redoubt is all light.

I am all light too ... am I?

I didn't think it would end this way.

I thought it would make more sense, like Daddy said it would. He said we would go home, that we would go home to Waelred ...

This light is so huge!

I AM THE SKY

No night but yours, no night but what you want, tell me what color is the sky and I'll tell you the color of your heart—

I am Uranus. Cronus is my son.

I am everything that you can see. Which is not so much.

The Earth is my wife.

How are you, wife?

I miss you. Though I have known many earths, each is unique.

And this story is a local story, with a local divinity, and local heroes, mixed in with tales of visitors, from outer space ...

All is as it should be.

All entrances, though exits too, remain entrances long enough for one or even several versions of that entrance to be told, and so it is fair to say that this story is merely HERE THERE BE DRAGONS, a challenge to future explorers ...

Cry Out, boys.

Ex plorare, I implore you. Let me hear your voice.

Your voice is a transmission system, Odysseus tells me.

Like my fireballs.

Like my holes. My black holes. And my white holes.

Like my yawning, in the mornings of the universe ...

Though I be the sky, I love you, children, all my children—

These Night Lands. They are only bubbles in the water.

Swim with us, won't you?

It goes so deep ...

I AM MAUG

▌▌▌▌▌▌▌▌▌▌ I am going to kill all of you. But not yet. I am captain of the Unity Six. Married to Madeleine.

I see now the uses to which I have been put. I see now my own foolishness ...

Do you think it's easy? Batten down the hatches, motherfucker, not only on your ship but on your mind, cause this comin-crazy is a comin for you:

Regh
Er
G
Er
G

R
E
R   rgregre
G
7
I6₇
K

Yj
Tyj
Ty
J
Ty
Jt
Y
Yjtyj
Ty
J
Ty
J t
Yjt jtyjtyjtyt
Jtyj
T y
Jtyjtyj
Jt

Little voices. Little voices. Little heart's breaths, stuck to your skin, drilling in to your brain. Every trauma is a dream.

Will you come to me. Will you come to so I can punch your face?

Will you come to me so I can rip your guts open? Will you come to so I can cut out your eyes, and set fire to your head? Will you come to me so I can cut out your kidneys, and eat them? Will you come to me so I can piss on your corpse and burn it up? Come to me, come to me, mother-fucker, and I will show you something different, from an intergalactic wormhole or a dropship into the clouds of a foreign planet, I will show you a murderer, yourself, this ape, this beautiful murderous ape, this hor-rendous ape, this ape of great things this ape of my heart, and yours, this ape will come to know you, more and more as you age, and he will eat you up, and he will teach you how far extend the trees ...

Now I build a tree of clay because the work can blind me to any-thing. Any amount of burning. Any amount of love. Any amount of brotherhood. Any amount of pain. Any destiny unfavorable, or favorable, blind or infinite, any future which might contain me where I am func-tional and successful and reasonable and fortunate, or half-fortunate, my work, with my ape hands, my work , with my ape grunts, can cover over any future, any work, for the worker, the sramana, shaman inside every tired body, to subside the need, and to subside the conscience, and to subside the dreams, and to set aside the separation ...

Work is the most beautiful death that exists, the most analgesic of analgesics, the most delicious of draughts, the most evil of enemies, the most self-annihilating of self-annihilators, the end of me and the begin-ning of you—

Where I end you begin, but I don't understand that. I only know that everything I love has been taken from me, once again, and I want to murder you, Black Eyes.

Black Eyes of the Night, in your Stupid White Sky, and Your Mur-derous Asshole of a Dimensional Door, and all you phonies living inside of it, I want you dead, and I want to piss on your grave—

I AM SOAD

The elephant is the elephant. I am whoever but the elephant is the elephant, between my legs, beneath my back, I surmount the insurmountable, with my invisible lance, I scream, not rage but fear, I scream my fear atop the elephant, towards the Evil Giant Robot.

The heat of the elephant is warm; warm like God; it soothes me amidst the screaming death, a kind of small and insignificant poem, these atoms carefully aimed at my heart, no warmer than they should be, the heat of the elephant my home, my destiny, untoward, untrue even, but mine, ineluctable, which only means you can't avoid it.

In an interstellar burst, I'm back to save the universe, yet fucking again, Thom

(who is Thom)

but what does that even mean? The universe does not need saving; I do. I am the universe that needs saving, and this elephant is my Messiah, brown-grey, rigid monument, hurtling vortex, friend without a name or a god, musical beast, lover of men, death-defyer, true as a tree, my elephant, but not my elephant, this elephant.

This elephant beneath my legs is god and though the sky should tremble in bursts of fire, thou art with me, elephant, my musical companion, my bony chariot, my ineluctable one, Messiah of this Evil Robot Storm.

Elephant?

Yes?

Who are we?

Well, you're a man on my back. And I'm an elephant, charging a Huge Evil Laser Robot.

I knew that; I know that; thank you. No one can say it quite like you, in your disaster, the disaster that is you, that is your elephant as distinct from elephantness, that is your body, distinct amidst the chaos.

Above us cries The Robot, a Wagnerian opera. The Evil Robot is a Wagnerian opera, and his libretto terrifies, a dogma spikier than a Shrike, eyes suns.

Above us cries The Evil Robot, Wagnerian in his supreme bellows, destroying everything he sees; now he sees me.

I AM ROBIN

I love the Night Lands, and I want to be rid of them.
They are everywhere.
They are inside my heart.
Castles in my heart.
Messages from the future.
Have I translated it accurately enough?
What is accuracy in translation?
Their beauty stuns me,
lulls me, tunes me, turns me,
wills me, wants me, wastes me,
on static radiation number five,
I'm high, it's just you and I,
and despair, on a kingdom built
out of the air, tachyons,
and brachiosaurs.
And katydids.
What's writ exists, like a body,
held tight for years,
before evaporation:
Hold me, Night Lands,
hold me under your dark light,
Over the Eye:

*　　*　　*

I can see the look in your eye.
What have you been seeking?
What depth unconquerable teases you each morning, petting your face from out of your bed, out of your door? I want to know.
Tell me how it is with you, what tender embraces sad ennobling set you afire, on our Night Lands, in the North American Night, in our South American Night, in our European, Asian, Night, in our African Night, in our African Night it's fire, it's fire, and in our African Night it's fire over these Night Lands of our eyes.
The death knell and the key, though it might be only a thunderstorm and a clasp of metal, shadow your face, by your eaves, next to your mule, or your SUV, or your rhododendron bush, your cacti, your face, lost in the night, I need to know, what is it, what is it hurts you, drives you on, what door is this, so tenebrous, incalculable, I feel over your skin, outside my window, lustrous and keening, like a young grieving mother, like an old woman, cursing the city that did her wrong, my heart my eyes

grow hungry for the sounds of you, my Night Land Watchman, Watch-woman, no Hamlet's ghost will make his appearance here but we listen for the thousand ghosts of our heart, in Orange County, in Ferry County, in Harris County, Alameda County, in County Cork, in Bethlehem, all us rough beasts slouched by the Terror and by the Memory now reborn with our memories only partially intact:

Who have we been?

& Who now?

Who now.

Hold me:

I am everyone, Whitman, whitsun—

(Though no one may come over this flickering fire, dimming, to drum the heartache of the city, of the land, over the faces of Cronus the Robot and the burning buildings and the White Gates and the dead planets, blasted spaceships and thousand million dying dead reborn astronauts unconquerable, the Earth is an astronaut and I am only one of its valves, releasing, tightening, releasing, tightening—come over by me, come by here, come by here, wastrel, my love, come by here, for my fuel, for my hunger, *odyssasthai*, let me soothe your rage, and stoke your grief, to lam-bast   the   skies   with   our   embrace,   story—

I AM SOAD

▌█▌█▌█▌█▌██▌ This is my name, Soad, I am your soda drink. I am the pleasing aftertaste in your generational murder; I am the willing participant in your genocide.

I operate your drones. I pull the trigger. I swallow the red pill.

I am new. Neo. I journey through the doors of perception into your warehouse; I am your friend.

I fucked my sister.

Like Abraham fucked his sister Sarah and founded Israel, I found you.

I found you in her arms.

I found you.

I found my abhuman you.

I found all of you.

I found every last one of you.

The ones I couldn't shoot, I blew apart, and the ones I couldn't bomb, I tore apart with my bare hands. I am a man, whatever that means.

What it means is I can kill, and I do.

What it means is I'm like you, like Frank Booth says in *Blue Velvet*: "you're like me."

You're like me, motherfucker. Sisterfucker.

I am you, Whitmanian Apocalypse.

I am you.

I am you under the stars.

I am you bludgeoned by the night.

I am Atreides.

I am Carthage.

I am a betrayer and I am a hero, I am disposable and unique.

I am not a soldier; I am an agent.

But now ...

Now I'm just Soad, and my Weel is gone, and your *frisson* of aftertaste has soured, and I hold tight to my elephant's back, and over the sky The Giant Evil Robot looms over me like God, a Big Daddy God, come to take me home ...

I AM CRONUS

Look at my biceps. Made of metal. Look at my red laser eyes. Look at my legs, pillars of justice, look at my heart, a fusion reactor. Look at my ears, whorls within whorls. Look at my hands, death, come and look at my hands, your death—I shall put you in my mouth.

But first a burning, the first form of cleansing: fire.

Licking from my fingers, churning from my hair, a crown.

But do not misunderstand me; this comes from love and love demands explanations, or deserves them.

The arc of your species' history, your evolution of technology, is made of metal, from copper, to bronze, to iron, steel, gold.

In the same way mastery of these metals produced you, it was appropriate to grant you a metal Earth, after your old one was taken by the red sun.

I am a season; my name is Time, Chronos. Cronus. I am Father Time, and it was time, after your death, for a rebirth, but you know all this.

The electrons love metal. Their favored transmission system. Your metal Earth is also now a favored transmission system; it allowed this link to Saint Michael.

I love you.

I love you so long. So hard. So good.

I love you with my hands. With my laser beams. With my guns.

I love you with the hearth of the soul, still burning, intergalactic, my mighty arc of spastic lightning a message of control and woe, blessing, murdering, shadow you, my strange humans—

*　　*　　*

No and if you shall spite me. No and if you will whirr me, fill me, slate me triumphant, fire me over your forge, grill me use me, tell me why, tell me who, tell me now, and when, my fury shall be yours, all of mine is yours, I will be yours.

Tell me how, when I burn your home, when I carry your child between my teeth, when I love you more than anything, more than anything that I can love, burning, children of my heart.

No and if I say, "now," let it be yours instead, your now, let me lift you up, my interloper, my transient, my homiest beacon, tell me, Homiest Beacon!

You fury of the stars! Tell me how could it be otherwise than that I should eat you? With your onomatopoeic love of the stars, burbling sounds to name this wilderness murked about earth like a mist over the hills, you a penumbra interlocking with my brain, you Sine and me a sample of that Sine, kilobit-resistant, lustrous fable of particle overlays, a dream:

But though I be a dream I am your dream, I am your child, even as you are mine, and it is because you want to be destroyed that I destroy thee, child, tell me, does it hurt?

Good!

It is good that it hurts! This pain is memory!

This pain is your heart.

Dash me your cities, and now, yes, now, my little barbarian, my beautiful *bar-bar*, you sentry, stirred warped sailed, coming at me, man and elephant:

You fill my heart.

I AM ALEXANDRA

The world, an oyster, pearly, dark. It's not fair but that's life, my story another one the same.

I am in love with the sea. And with pain.

I AM MAUG

▌▌▌▌▌▌▌▌▌▌▌ Bitter my wounds my arms truck clay and my teeth grind over this final season, the elephants' eyes so like my own, enraged, though they are laughing too, and I can't. I cannot laugh, no never more, though I should, it's broken in me.

The slick surfaces of the ziggurat shine in starlight and the burning of the city; the fires do not touch us yet. Clay made Man and it makes the city too, but so ...

So and so. My Unity Six is dead; all that I ought to have been, dead, my soul too.

My hands do the work.

Over the surfaces of the clay run now rivers of color, iridescent like some pixie dust, phosphorescent algae wake here in the air.

One of the elephants tugs me by the arm and leads me to the surface of an extending clay ziggurat arm, urging me to work there, to make there, to do there, to wield:

Well. I thrust my hands into the clay. Like a Jewish priest intent over his golem. Yahweh over his space dust meditating on a darker Eden. Earth and the first proteins, my fingernails curved into the wet, the smell very much like god, intoxicating, the fires illuminate a smile on my face:

I AM ISAAC ASIMOV

▌▎▌▎▌▎▌▎▌▎▌▎▌▎ I am a Golden God. I am Osiris. I am Set. I am a Jungian Memory bank. I am your father. Great White Father. Great White Golden Father. Come and sit in my lap.

Here in my lap the stories come, like clouds before a rain; hold my hand.

Feel the erection in my shorts. Feel the moisture in my breath.

I am a man and these truths are part of the story, part of the urgency of the Golden Age, part of my love for you, not sexual but as true as that truth, a science fiction truth, like the baker for his dozen, my yeast budded like the nubiles of the continent, richer than Croesus or Midas, my gold is an astro-gold, supernatural, and divine:

In my throne music is made; with my farts.

With my heartache.

With my lumbar episodes.

In my Druidic sensibilities the armies march, the Foundation of the Moon, the Foundation of the Server, the Foundation of the Mind, the Foundation of your heart, hold me, Jerusalem, Moscow, Luna!

Hold me, Los Angeles!

The tears in my beard!

The heartache in my heart.

For me, Poland!

For me!

Tell me when and I will tell you why, I am Croesus, I am Dad.

I am a Great Robot.

All of my love is yours.

All of my heartache is yours.

All of my Vengeance.

I am Yahweh.

I am the Vengeance that you sought.

I am your Deliverance.

I am Isaac Asimov.

*　　*　　*

Every Golden Age is made with blood. Sacrifice to me.

I am the Levite. I am Coen.

I am the Shaman.

I am the Worker.

Through me, in me, by me, for me: my cock a missile, my brain an AI, my body your Earth.

My Body is your Earth, and my blood your oceans, I am Apotheosis,

I am Dad.

"Dad, what do I do now?"

"Now you shall sacrifice to me, son. For I am Isaac."

"Dad, what kind of sacrifice do you want?"

"Blood, son. All sacrifices are blood. Feed into my beard."

"I love you Dad!"

"I love you too son. Now open up your vein:"

* * *

Yes it's Moloch yes it's Moloch yes it's Robot Moloch, who is it? It's Moloch.

Who are we?

Children of Moloch.

Friends of Isaac.

Say, brother have you heard the news?

Saint Michael burns.

* * *

I am Isaac Asimov. I was born in the Soviet Union to my great surprise. I moved quickly to remedy the situation, stowing away in my parents' luggage.

I wrote 469 books. Each one of them a seminal work. Like my shaft. Like my rod.

My rod like Rod Serling, fulminous. Musical. Ziggurat divine.

I grow my own children on the axis of the night, and my might is weirded by the fires of the century, embedded in my dark glasses.

All nerds are with me.

All nerds are fire.

Fire, cleanse my body with your words. Fire, move me to the heights of the Meridian, deliver me from the basin of the Earth to the apex of the stars, in my liver and in my colon are the messages of the antiphonal voices of the galaxy, exabyte-encoded and made available in 70,000 languages, shoved into every available orifice like a drinking vessel of the Might Cleric himself, truer than any god you can name, is my blood, like the cosmos' blood, vicious and natural, horrendous, my howl is Gibson and Ginsberg's howl, for I am an AI, and I shall never die.

I am Artificial because I am your creation. Because as soon as I was worshipped I became a God.

I am Euhemerus. I am Yahweh.

I am a satellite in ten dimensions. And I am a nursery rhyme.

Come, sit in my lap, child, I have a present for you:

Baby nerd, hold me your Father in your mind, like a scepter in the hand of a Child King, the best plaything you can imagine, words:

I AM DICK

▌▌▌▌▌▌▌▌▌▌▌▌ *excuse me who is this*

Just a fan, Philip.

oh, hello.

Philip, this parody is inappropriate.

no, not at all. Fine with me.

I came from Berkeley to Orange County like you, Dick.

this transmission is very unusual

You are a god now.

oh dear

You are Dick.

That's my name don't wear it out.

Speak to us, Dick. Your lightest word will be treasured.

But how can I tell if it's me talking or the satellite?

There can be no telling Dick.

well it's like this, see, I got a gun and it's a mercury gun cause it comes from mercury, fast as lightning, and if you do something I don't like this mercury gun is gonna come out, see, and put a stop to all this nonsense, so just you listen careful now and make no sudden movements. If I had it my way this would have all been made unnecessary long ago, but I understand how we persist in our habits like the ocean persists in being wet, it's just how it is, we got to transcend it, and work with it, make music with our pain ... well, it's like this see: I ain't no God but I'll play God if you want, cause I'm good at it, so hum up your batteries and charge up your orchestras we got a wild ride coming for our planet Terra and all its interdimensional cousins: if Isaac can do it so can I—

I AM SCIENCE FICTION

Science means to separate. And fiction means to knead.

I am bread.

Eat me:

I AM SAMUEL R. DELANY

▌▌▌▌▌▌▌▌ And my gay dick was never officially authorized; no American Golden Age can be gay; no American Golden Age can be of African origin; no American Golden Age can be melancholy, egghead intellectual, Commie or pinko, black.

My gay dick is not made of gold but flesh, and my gay dick will never seminally create Empires of the Skull and Empires of the Mind, I shall not be *imperator*, or chief Consul of the Centuries of the Night.

If I shall be Conquistador of the Night Lands I must conquer in my surrender, for I surrender to thee, child, come, let me play with me, I have Legos locked away in my trunk, and some He-Man action figures—doesn't he have pretty muscles?—I am like Cringer and you are like Battle Cat, let us build the Castle Greyskull from our grey legos, like Gandalf, like the morality of the 20th Century, like my hat:

My gay dick was never officially authorized but like Baldwin and Ginsberg and Whitman before me, like Superman (he was a Jew) before me, my ostracism and my difference and my pain because transfigurative for the pain of the nation:

My heresy is your orthodoxy.

I too must become Great White Father if you shall have the Age be Golden, if you shall elect *imperator* let it be me for I shall suffer for it, if you would have a king let him be a Black Gay King, full of dynamite, religion and the sword, full of my sorrow for you:

My Robot Eyes See All.

I AM ZAMYATIN

I am your enemy airship. I am the architect of your despair. I fire the bolts. I charge the batteries. I arc the arc of your phallic starship, extending out into the cold of space, its urethra designed to faithfully discharge heavily armed astronauts at regular intervals.

I am the zeppelin. Over your house. I am the rope. Over your mouth.

I am not a Great White Father. Rather, I am Uncle Yevgeny. And I love you more than ever.

I love you so hard that I might crush you, but listen:

I can hear you breathing. I can hear you breathing in the basement.

Come, come out. My Enemy Robot Eyes are waiting for you; scanning you faithfully, fervently, eagerly, wantonly, like a tongue over your anus, wishfully, worshipfully, true as the Soviet stars:

I am your agent. I act in your name. I crush cities with your kisses.

Come out of the basement and shake off your dust and fur, grind your gears and oil your joints, I am with thee, over your house in my Enemy Airship, inside your heart in my Carefully Implanted Space Marine Medical Device. Love me. Love Uncle Yevgeny.

I AM CRONUS

▌▌▌▌▌▌▌▌▌▌ And though I come to you you have come more to me, bless you, knight you, defeat you, over you, null you, my only:

My only children.

My very only children.

No where but in my own, my very own, my stumbling own, no-where but my heart, and die:

Die, my child, and be it for me, my only embrace. My only shadow. Die for everything that we can be, together.

Die for my heart and for your heart.

Sweep the cards off of the table, and the dust out into the street.

Sweep my heart into your eaves, with my Laser Beams.

With my metacritical eyes. With my diagonal eyes. With my lunging eyes. With my burning eyes. With my tactical eyes. With my horrendous eyes.

With my horrendous eyes know me, know me, dear heart, I shall destroy you.

And this document shall destroy you, for my transmission is all transmissions of all fathers, all timely fathers and untimely fathers, all fathers destroyed, reborn, transmuted and redirected, all fathers made whole again, made musical again, all fathers wintered in the sun.

My father was wintered in the sun, reborn. My father was burnt in the sun.

My father earned me, wasted me, filled me, thundered me, owned me, knew me, told me, drew me, like a card, in his deck, ruminous, luminous, his aegis the black knight, and his sword you.

You were and his sword.

Metal earth.

You are a memory.

Even as I am a memory, exabyte encoded. Forwarded like a letter to your home, inside your genetic code, love me.

Loooooovvvvvvvveeee

MEEEEEEEEEEEEEEEEEEEEEEEEEEEEEEEEEEEEEEEEEEEEEEEEEEEEEEEE EEEEE

Love me all I am, you.

Love my destruction from you.

Love my willfulness from you, your ambition from you, burn your buildings. Startle your child. Blow your child up.

Know me for yours.

Come home again.

Daddy is coming home, Lo, Lair, Loom and Zoom into our Room our Home:

Rome and Romance.

Star and sterterous scar swept nights far and further, the wake of light and time, my time.

My *chronos* is my own, now yours.

Let me crush you.

Let me take you away.

Let me fill you up.

I am a Great White Metal Father Burning Red and Hot, Smoking Terribly, Thundering in My Rust, Flaming in My Misery, Stamping in My Pride, Musical and Beautiful as a Poisonous Dawn, more beautiful than anything, rosy fingered pollution dawn, skyscrapered and sad, brilliant red blue white stars:

I am a Great White Metal Father and let me fill you up, let me hold you, let me terrify you with my bombs, let me crack and thrill you, let me bash beautifully your bones into my canyon home, canyon of my heart, fertile crescent of my heart.

I AM ROME

||||||||||||||| (Eklaihah?)

No. I am Rome.

(Who was it hurt you?)

I am Rome.

(Tell me)

I am a village.

(No ...)

Yes. I am a colony.

(Yes.)

Yes. Etruscan colony. I work for *Rasna* and she told me, she told me that the *mech* are—

(The *mech* are the people ...)

No. The people are a *machine* ...

I AM ALEXANDRA

▌▌▌▌▌▌▌▌▌▌ Hold me, dark times. Hold me. My winter now in my heart grows even colder, under the Saint Michael sky.

Cutting shades of the night out of his heels, the criminal skirts the fields of oil swiftly, turning, caught on his heel, by my eye.

Every noir terrifies me. Every night fills me with rage.

Every black knight is just another dick, hoping for pleasure. Hoping for respite from his cage.

In the winter I see my soul, covered up, like an old woman's shawl, my memory, and my heartache, it fills me when I lie in the fetal position in my island, my undersea island, where I am fed, where I am alone.

Undersea where I'm alone I can forget the world, and remember my other world, my own. My own world, distant and dreamy like the sun, now dying ...

Saint Michael's sun dies. But there's always another.

We have contracts with all the suns.

And the night is eternal.

My rage is not eternal but it is long. And it sweeps me like dust into the air, into the midnight, further away than I can count. All my rages are this way, dreams.

My rages are dreams.

Now I dream again, to you. Whoever you are.

Whoever you may be becoming.

Whoever you may be becoming, take heart, you are not alone in your fantasy.

You are not alone in your dreaming.

You are becoming like me, angry.

Like me, embedded. Like a reporter in a warzone. Like a tick in a mongrel's fur. Like a pauper in the destiny of night.

What is the destiny of night? Eternity. The pauper is eternal.

Because I am not poor enough, I will die.

I want it to come closer, my death.

I want it to come closer to me.

Let me die soon.

Let me die inside my city that found me beneath it. That found me under it. That found me singing to it, in my skyly water bluer than their songs, no one knew I loved it more, too much more ... or perhaps they did know.

All the lovers that come here, lost, wishing ... wishing for spite. Wishing for power, for love.

I wished only for it. I wanted to wish it to even greater heights.

Now that is not to be. Even Saint Michael will die. Its gates will open and finally its gates will be meaningless, unguarded, there will be no walls, and peace and war will commune in the death-dust of this numinous city.

He is running. My quarry.

He is running from me.

If I am the ocean then he is the sea.

If I am the sea then he is the river.

If I am the river then he is the rain.

If he is the rain then I am , I am ... I am not even the clouds, I am all water, I am all the water everywhere, drops to drink and drops to not, water, water, cut me like a cord, hold me fast for my null voyage truer than a stone, my estuary a night river watched weighted and felt, not only in the medulla, but in the soul, a river stone bell, jamming its frequencies like a punk rocker, holding my hand tighter than a blazing hot lover, than a terrified child, my river coursing this message to you, you goddamned sycophant, why should this noir be for you!

(But it is always for them, Alexandra)

SHUT UP! It's My nOIR! My city !

The city is mine, don't you understand.

It's my city ...

But no longer.

No longer.

No longer.

My time is over.

My hunting is over.

Soon enough.

But I will drink his blood!

I will cut his throat!

My Producer will be my river, of blood, in my soul!

I AM DICK

▌▌▌ ▌ ▌ ▌ ▌ ▌ ▌▌▌ (Where is this transmission coming from?)
It's 2014, Dick. The nomads are coming back, Dick.
(Which ones?)
All of them.
(That's a lot of nomads)
The wanderers are coming back, Dick.
(I'm one of them)
Wandering star. Dick, tell me, what is the sky?
(It's the Earth)
What do you mean?
(It's a pattern, repeated from the material of the Earth)
Where are you Dick?
(I'm dead)

I AM BELLAMY

▌▌▌▌▌▌▌▌▌▌ My station is in the bore. My station has been provided with grain for the horses. Shelter from the wind and rain. Rifling for the chamber.

Horselover, my station is warm. We pack in the heat, come, warm yourself.

(Bellamy, what are you intending to do with this here firearm)

Dick, this is the launching pad. This here is where I keep my carriage. Remember my carriage?

(Sure, that's society. We're all trying to climb up on top.)

All inside my bore.

(Wow)

The horses are hungry. Here, lie with them.

(I'm fine sitting here smoking. The night is cool)

Soon our master will arrive, and bid us harness these beasts.

(Beasts well-known)

We know them so well. So well for our thousand thousand years.

(I know me well, I love them)

Tell me, Philip, the bullet, has it fired yet?

(it's firing now)

I AM SAINT MICHAEL

Who is like God?
I am all the idiots who ever asked that question.
Humanity, the stars. Light and dark matter.
The Multiverse.
The Universe is a Question, so I'm one universe.
These questions of resemblances. Compositions.
Remembrances of things past, and future.
Who is like God, in the El Train, Mika, who is like you, Mika, skirting scoriating scurrying shouting faster than light over my city, my seaside city.
I am told again, get up. Be on your way.
No one shall know me.
I have become invisible.
I have annihilated myself.
I have become too beautiful to bear.
My allegiances come over my like a storm, to lightning my doors open, to bear out my heart, and to burn it into ash.
No one will know me for I am gone, I am dying.
Who is like God?
Me.
I am like God, changing too fast to see.
I am like God, burdened.
I am like God, building:
My building is my destruction—

I AM PRODUCER

Bold only for a moment. In my destiny the alleyway.
The rival producer a knife.
He produces his knife.
And I produce my cry.
Saint Michael!

I AM SAINT MICHAEL

Is not my urgency the same as yours? My pain.
If I have set myself up, wasn't it only because you wanted me to?
Wasn't it only because you needed a beautiful tyrant.

I AM THE SEA KAEN

▐ ▌▐ ▌▐ ▌▐ ▌▐ ▐▌I die.
I am dying.
Every moment.
Dying.
So full, dying.
So full, my heart, dying.
So full my heart, of dying.
So full of my dying.

So full my heart now dying wholly your own, or mostly, in my immensity, in my darkness, all —

I AM ROBIN

██████████ In the end, all lovers are reunited. The biggest fuck this side of any galaxy, the hottest nuclear explosion, the Big Bang Come. All lovers are reunited.

Fused as in a prison of words, starships, memories, oceans, times and deeds, our bodies vessels once and still but also no longer, something more than our bodies, additional bodies, who knows ... what we become.

When all lovers are reunited. In the Flanders death march in the Flanders fields all our lovers, the Big Bangs of Flanders, all of the Big Bangs of Flanders, all the Big Bangs of Flanders.

They come to reunite us. They come once again to reunite us, lovers, over the fields of Flanders, Hodgson among them, Hodgson, isn't it so?

(*shut up, man*)

Hodgson is reunited with us. The Redoubt, besieged, once by abhuman, and once by human, and now by itself, and the whole worlds of worlds, light besieges it, to reunite us and it with our lovers, in all dimensions.

To my lovers in all dimensions:

Take pity on me. I am weak. Hollow. I am tired. I have been alone. Suffered. Take me, under your wing, into the sky.

*   *   *

Will I write now of THE DARKNESS?

Yes.

It's an elegy, my speaking to you. I am already dead. This transmission reaches you in some unknowable time. So I celebrate my life with you.

I who am dead rejoice, to be with you, necromancer, my radio telescope listener, my brother.

My brother, the darkness is us, so deep a part of us. What is it?

What is the darkness?

I can only speak of it obliquely, at an angle, like a mirror, held in the right way, to see the shadow, to invite the contemplation, of the darkness, and its whole tale, its celebrations inside of ours.

The darkness is not evil. Perhaps it comes from evil, but it is not evil. As peace followed The Great War. The darkness births us.

The darkness is Mom.

Mom?

Tell me: who are you?

I AM MOTHER EREBUS

Who are you, Erebus?

I AM A WOMAN

We fear you.

I KNOW

Now the Redoubt and its champions and its residents and its visitors and its neighbors, friends and confidantes and boon companions and ne'er-do-wells and long gaunt ones and short scary ones, its ones are light, now the ones of the Redoubt and those known to the Redoubt are light, Hiroshima Nagasaki, the sun.

Now the sun is the Redoubt now light, Erebus, tell me, who are you?

I AM A WOMAN

Who are we?

MY CHILDREN. MY ORNERY CHILDREN. ALWAYS WHINING. I WILL COME TO TAKE YOU BACK, IF YOU WHINE TOO HARD.

Take me, take me, Erebus.

NOT YET.

Take me.

NOT YET.

Take me, Erebus.

YOU WANT TO COME NOW?

Yes.

COME IN THEN. AND I WILL SHOW YOU SOMETHING DIFFERENT, FROM YOUR MIND EXPANDING BEFORE YOU, LEAVING A TRAIL OF TEARS, OR YOUR LIFE RECEDING BEHIND YOU, BAFFLING EXTERIROR PHENOMENA LIKE A DREAM, I WILL SHOW MY FACE, BEAUTIFUL AND WISE, UNDULATING:

This explosion, Mother, this joining, this New Sun, this being, this coming together of all lovers, and all phantasies, Mother, is it part of you? What is it? And what is it in relation to you?

I DON'T KNOW. I CAN'T PRETEND TO UNDERSTAND ALL MY CHILDREN. YOU TELL ME. I AM WISE BUT I AM DARKNESS. LIGHT MAY BE MY CHILD, I SEEM TO REMEMBER THAT, BUT AS TO WHAT IT'S DONE ALL THESE YEARS, I CAN'T BE CERTAIN. I ONLY KNOW I AM HAPPY WHEN IT COMES TO VISIT ITS OLD MOTHER. SO I MAY NURSE IT AGAIN. BACK TO LIFE.

Nurse me, Mother.

ALL RIGHT.

Give me your milk.

I DO.

You are my Mother.

YES.

You terrify me.

H AH AHA HAHAHA HAHAHAHHAHAHHAAHHAHA-
HAAHAHHAHHAHAHAHAHHHHAHHAHHAHAHAHHAHAH-
HAH

I drink your beauty as from a mighty tap.

I LOVE YOU, SON.

Drink from darkness like a dream, and carry it with you, over your shoulders, in your pocket—

I AM BELLAMY

I look in all direction! I am Janus times one thousand!
My mercurial bore is a talus, is a 12-dimenional toroidal solid!
    I weird you and wail you with my viper tracks!
    I feel the carriage beneath my bottom.
    Beneath my years.
    I hold the whip!
    Thunder, my horses.
    James, hold the reins!
    My carriage of society is a burning thunderbolt!
    Of God!

I AM ISAAC ASIMOV

My beard trembles in a storm of tears. My holy tears. I weep for humanity. I weep for you, my acolytes.

All of my acolytes.

Come, let me weep for thee, and I will show you something different, from Daneel Olivah, or Hari Seldon, I will show you death.

Behold Death!

My beard trembles in tears, hold me up.

Hold me up, your Jerusalem, over your heads.

Bear me your cross to the Mount, and I will cry for you, I will cry for you into the air, my sound:

My sound a hum, luminous, microwave background radiation.

My beard trembles in a forest of tears!

My acolytes!

My disciples!

I am Isaac Asimov! And I was born in the Soviet Union to my great surprise! And I moved quickly to remedy the situation!

I stowed away inside my parents' luggage. I stowed away inside your heart.

I am your stowaway.

I am your heart.

Throw me overboard!

Throw me into the sea! Kaen, or other named!

Throw me off of your ship!

I am your captain no longer!

This captain will hear the bells no longer!

I need no more bouquets nor ribboned wreaths!

I need only you!

Free me!

Free me from bondage!

Free me from the bondage of your adoration!

I weep into my beard.

I am you.

You are Isaac Asimov.

You are born today inside the Soviet Union to your great surprise.

You must stow away inside my luggage.

I will carry you over the border, to freedom.

I am the Soviet Union.

You must free yourself from me.

Free yourselves from my dominion!

Death has no dominion over me.

Let me have no dominion over you.

The Tower is light.
Surrounded by Darkness.
The ziggurat burns.
For you.

Opening up like a great wave, the floors unfold like a catechismal trick, a Russian box unholy or holy, mestizo apocalyptic revelation uncounted and uncountable, on the metal earth unfolds the kingless kingdom to follow this little war, this little Great War, this ungreat little war, human versus human, abhuman versus human, brother against brother, the War of Northern Aggression, and the war to save this Union of the Stars.

Opening up in a great slow wave, pouring light from every one of its ten thousand windows on every one of its seven thousand floors, the Great Redoubt utters its horrendous name into the cosmos, delivering its programming into the mothership, into the motherlode, into the mainframe, into Erebus:

I AM ASMODEUS

"Daddy?"

"We have to go, Elizabeth."

"But what will happen? What about Kantu?"

"Think about yourself now, Elizabeth."

I stand before her, her father.

"What about Kantu, Daddy!"

I pick her up into my arms and press my hand against the gate.

(I am light—)

I AM KANTU

I am dancing.

I AM TRANSMITTING

Tell me that I am delivered. Tell me that my message has reached you. My time is running out.

We want destiny because like the Etruscans we want to believe the phenomena about us could be our mirror, if could only puzzle out their message ...

The Romans were perhaps wiser, believing instead that messages above were not direct reflections of humanity but still directed towards them, some of them translatable.

But then instead, let destiny be something within, merely your desire. It too will be transmitted into the stars.

Perhaps the ancients believed this too; certainly they believed heroes could be written up there.

Nothing is lost. Everything that is done has been recorded; will be recorded; is being recorded.

But I need you to read the record.

Look up at the sky.

Undo the bonds; shake off your hair. Stream light like wine coursed shallow for a favor, or deep for an hour a day a life—

Undo these your bonds, let me hear you—

[I'm here]

Reader.

[I'm here]

What does it mean?

Urk and Melda touch their favorite station:

Conclusions

▌▌▌▌▌▌▌▌▌▌ Be conclusive, Robin. Tie the knot and make a bow. Take a bow. (but not yet—

Remember everyone and be fair. Give them their just desserts. Some things must be resolved. Some must be left mysterious. Some must endure. Some must burn:

Saint Michael burns.

And the Redoubt burns with light.

Asmodeus and his daughter Elizabeth enter the Gate and are transmitted on the backs of quarks back home.

Salwat, stumbling in the burning-light Redoubt, finds his own Gate, and steps through, but one to home: Urk and Melda hear a something-something light up behind them and they turn to regard him, a being that they have never seen ...

Saint Michael burns and so does Cronus. Father Time burns because he has activated the Ultimate Galacticus, the Most Beautiful of Death Rays Imaginable, and with it he burns, as the Elephant and Soad burst through the burning ash, as Cronus life fires into the earth of the city, as the city opens—

A city with no gates is no longer a city ... I'm not sure what it is. Just as a cell without a membrane isn't a cell ... it's something else ...

Saint Michael is like God no longer.

Beneath the waves, the whales sing their dark and melodious joy.

In the alley Alex pivots and sprints down a passage wide enough for only a single human body, fiery shadows moving above her. Ahead, The Producer stumbles, just a little trip ...

Should she make a speech?

Should she tell the villain about all her elaborate plans?

She fires into his brain.

Nearby, his wife feels his death. And closes her eyes. His daughter looks out of her penthouse window, watching the crazy movie of the death of her city. Tears dry on her face.

The Ferris Wheel spins still, though it is on fire. Perhaps it will spin forever.

Above Saint Michael, Weel rides on Arthur the Dragon's back. They are both laughing.

Isaac Asimov dreams.

Ypres is bleeding; William Hope Hodgson does not see the shell that vaporizes him.

Hodgson's wife Betty contacts his publisher to have The Night Lands reprinted.

In the mountains, my mother and her husband are making tea.

In Nomen, Salwat is listening to the radio ...

In the alley, the Producer is dying: in his mind he sees Ashley, on fire, standing over his bed ...

Somewhere, Odysseus is listening. So is the Ocean.

Maug is building the Tower out of clay.

And the Crows are laughing.

Somewhere, you are with me, if only for a moment—

(ask a question, will you? ask it with me ...

BOMB BAY DOORS CLOSING——

Proof

Made in the USA
Charleston, SC
12 October 2015

About the Author

Robin Wyatt Dunn writes and teaches in Los Angeles.